A

FAIR

CORPSE

A FAIR CORPSE

AN ART OF MURDER MYSTERY

HELEN A. HARRISON

To Roy, always

1939 New York World's Fair

Major attractions and exhibits

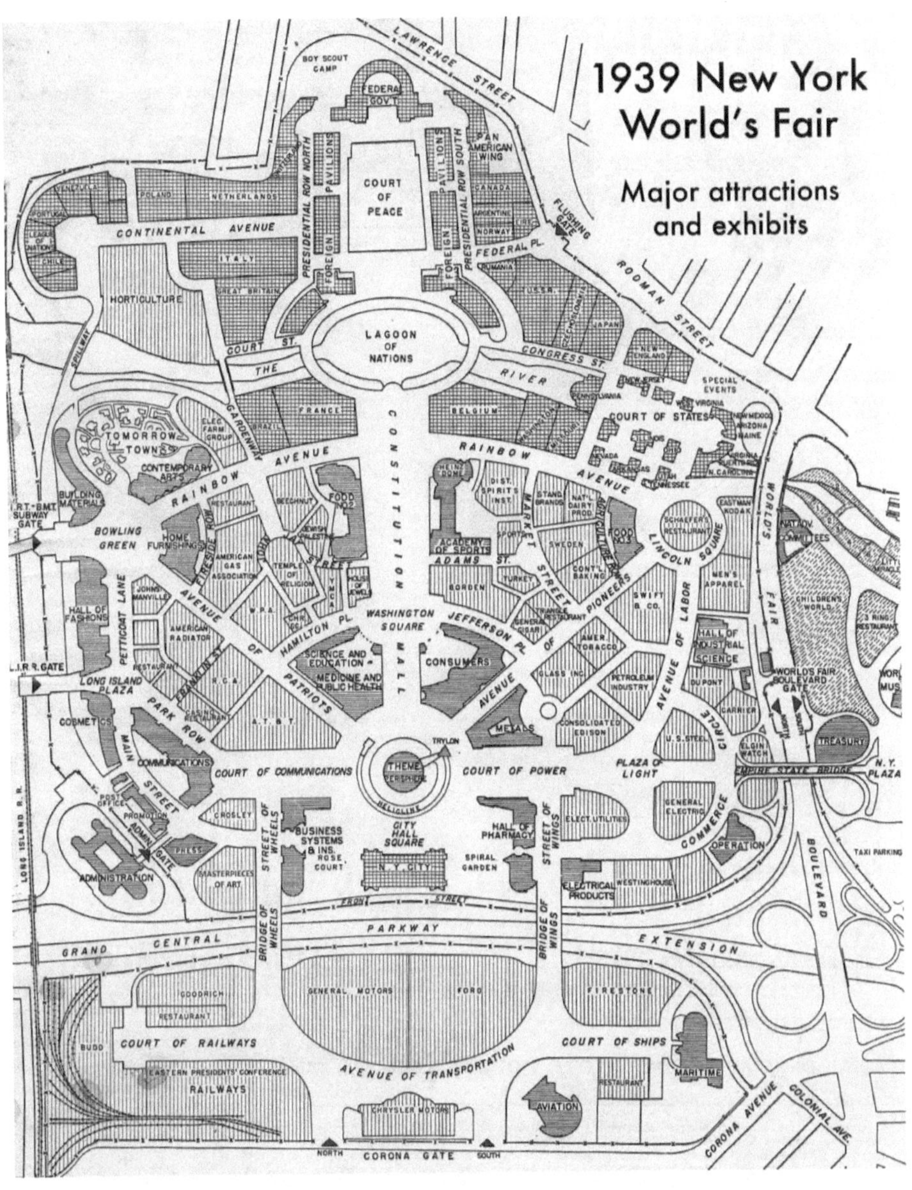

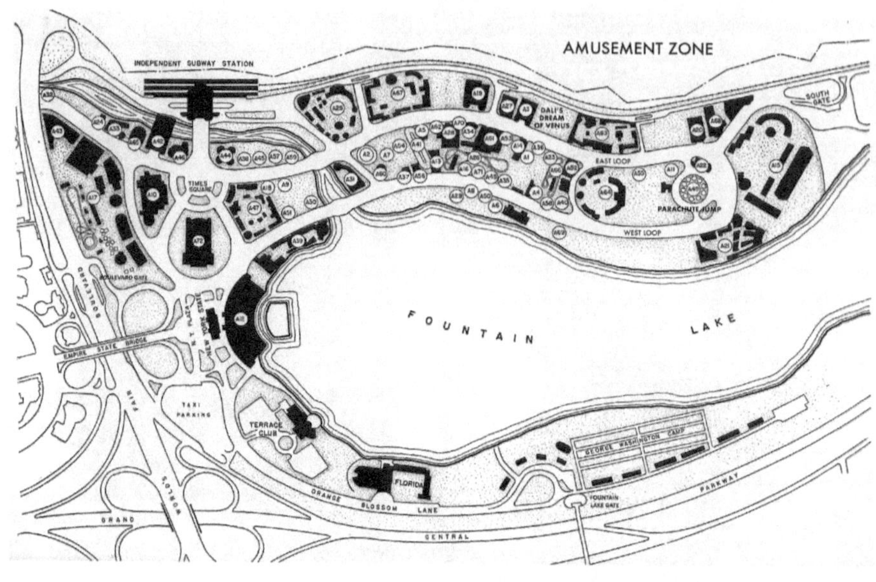

KEY TO AMUSEMENT MAP

1 —Adm. Byrd's Penguin Island
2 —Aerial Joy Ride
3 —Amazon Warriors
4 —Archery and Hunting Lodge
5 —Arctic Girl's Ice Temple
6 —Artist Village
7 —Auto Dodgem
8-9—Automatic Photography
10—Ballantine's Three Ring Inn
11—Bel Geddes' Show
12—Billy Rose's Aquacade
13—Brass Rail Restaurant
14—Caruso Restaurant
15—Cavalcade of Centaurs
16—Centipede
17—Children's World
18—Chime Ball
19—Creation
20—Crystal Palace
21—Cuban Village
22—Doughnut Corp. of America
23—Drive-a-Drome
24—Enchanted Forest
25—Frank Buck's Jungleland
26—Giant Roller Coaster
27—Giant's Causeway
28—Gangbusters
29—Hawaiian Village
30—Headless Girl
31—Heineken's on the Zuider Zee
32—Host House (Borough of Queens)
33—Infant Incubator
34—Jitterbug
35—Laff in the Dark
36—Laff Land
37—Live Monsters
38—Living Magazine Covers
39—Merrie England
40—Meteor
41—Midget Auto Race
42—Morris Gest's Little Miracle Town
43—National Advisory Committee
44—National Cash Register
45—Nature's Mistakes
46—New York Zoological Society
47—Old New York
48—Over the Top
49—Parachute Jump
50—Penny Arcade
51—Pretzel Shop
52—Savoy Ballroom
53—Seminole Village
54—Serpentine
55-6—Shooting Gallery
57—Silver Streak
58—Skee Ball
59—Sky Ride
60—Snapper
61—Strange as It Seems
62—Stratoship
63—Sun Valley and Winter Wonderland
64—Sun Worshippers
65—Theatre of Time and Space
66—The Bobsled
67—Village
68—Victoria Falls
69—Sons of the American Revolution Building
70—We Humans
71—Whip
72—World's Fair Hall of Music

March 30, 1939

He parked his car in front of the Marine Transportation Building and looked up at the enormous façade on which his mural—five vignettes of stylized vessels sailing across the 120-foot-wide wall—was taking shape. Their abstracted forms seemed to float on imaginary waters, and dynamic linear patterns made them appear to be in motion. The artist breathed a deep sigh of approval.

His escape from persecution in Nazi Germany, where his paintings had been vilified as degenerate modernism, and return to his native New York City had been a perilous journey with no promise of a happy ending. But it had worked out better than he had dared to hope. Two commissions for murals at the New York World's Fair were providing financial support for him and his family, and his dealer had assured him that exposure of his work at such a prominent venue was bound to stimulate interest from critics, curators, and collectors.

He got out of his car and joined the crew of mural painters who were assembling for the day's campaign. They greeted him warmly with handshakes and backslaps, and marched with him to the tall ladder that led to the ledge on which the scaffold was erected. A stretch of good weather was allowing them to make excellent progress. The exposition was scheduled to open in one month, and the entire site was humming with activity day and night.

When lunch break was called, he decided to keep working, taking advantage of the sunlight and energized by the race to the finish. He told the foreman he wasn't hungry, but would take a rest if he felt tired. At age sixty-seven, he was decades older than the rest of the crew, who admired his stamina as well as the beautiful imagery he had created.

Working on alone, he felt movement on the scaffold. Someone he didn't recognize had climbed up and approached him. Apologizing for the interruption, the stranger told him he was wanted in the Administration Building. He cleaned his brush, unhooked his safety harness, and walked to the ladder as the stranger followed. Turning to step on the ladder, the artist felt a blow to his chest. He lost his balance, fell backward, and plunged to his death twenty feet below.

Chapter One

It was marvelous. Awe-inspiring. Gazing up at its towering pylon and immense globe, its intricate steel framework now nearly covered in white tymstone-coated gypsum board, Officer Brian F. X. Fitzgerald of the New York City Police Department felt the thrill of optimism. As he stood in the courtyard outside the New York City Building, the Theme Center structures overwhelmed him, making him feel small and uplifted at the same time. He pondered the paradox, and concluded that was the point. Each of us is only a little speck in this big world, he mused, but working together we can accomplish great things. Just look around.

A future of peace and prosperity was taking shape a stone's throw from his Long Island City home, in the most unlikely place he could have imagined. Until a few years ago, it had been the Corona Dump, a smoldering, reeking blight on the Queens County landscape, where for decades the Brooklyn Ash Removal Company had deposited the refuse from the neighboring borough's coal-burning furnaces. A wasteland with a stagnant open sewer ironically called the Flushing River, as if it ever flushed out the filth. As a kid, riding across it on the IRT/BMT elevated train to visit his uncle Ryan and aunt Agnes, he and the family would speculate about what—and who—might be buried under the ash-heaps.

No one but a crazy visionary could ever have pictured this devastated terrain as a manicured park filled with handsome modern buildings and monumental statuary. But, incredibly, that vision was becoming reality, and he was standing in the middle of it.

* * *

"Why don't you do it, Daddy?"

That was the question posed to Joseph F. Shadgen, a civil engineer, in July 1934 by his daughter Jacqueline. She had asked him whether he knew of any plans to celebrate the 150th anniversary of George Washington's inauguration as the new nation's first president, on April 30, 1789, in New York City. His answer was no, and her response got him thinking. How about a World's Fair, like the successful one then underway in Chicago? It would create lots of jobs, and reclaim the Corona Dump. As a resident of Jackson Heights, a neighborhood close enough to it that he was personally familiar with its stench, Shadgen considered it the ideal site for the project he envisioned.

"Tell you what, Jackie," he told his daughter, "I'll work up a proposal and see if I can get enough support from the money men to make it happen."

A presentation to the city's business and financial leaders found a welcome reception, and Shadgen's concept gained traction. But the Fair's overall focus was uncertain. There were plenty of opinions, ranging from a traditional trade fair in a single large pavilion like London's Crystal Palace, or a grouping of unified buildings based on Chicago's 1893 White City model, to something completely different: a Fair of the Future. Ultimately, the futurists prevailed.

At a lavish dinner at the New York Civic Club in December 1935, the distinguished social commentator and urban theorist Lewis Mumford laid out the vision.

"The story we have to tell," he explained, "is the story of this planned environment, this planned industry, this planned civilization." His scope was nothing short of global: "If we allow ourselves to think for the world at large, we may lay the foundation for a pattern of life which would have an enormous impact in times to come."

The appeal of a model of social, cultural, and economic progress based on planning for maximum public benefit was seductive. The press was all over it, avidly reporting on the planning process as the details were worked out.

Absent from the deliberations was Joseph F. Shadgen, who was left in the dust of the stampede toward what had been dubbed the World of Tomorrow. There was no room for him in any of the busy administrative and operational divisions, which were borrowing some of his early concepts without acknowledgment. His consolation prize was a job in the Drafting Department, where he was essentially sidelined, sharpening pencils, coloring maps, and staring at the walls all day, according to his own account.

As an engineer, he would have relished a seat on the Board of Design, in charge of developing a unified architectural and decorative program, but the offer never came. Instead, that slot went to Richmond H. Shreve, an engineer whose firm had constructed the Empire State Building, where the Fair Corporation's offices were located. That certainly weighed in his favor, as did the fact that the world's tallest building had been completed early and under budget. The Fair planners were praying for a similar outcome for their enterprise.

Chapter Two

Only recently promoted from probationary status, Officer Fitzgerald, known to his friends and fellow cops as Fitz, had lobbied for the assignment. Actually, he didn't have to work too hard at it. The more senior officers weren't all that keen on patrolling the site of what was to become the 1939 New York World's Fair. Guard duty, they called it, not like proper police work. Really fit only for the lazy, those looking for a change of pace, and rookies like Fitz with no status on the streets, who had to be spoon-fed by the veterans. Prowling the vast 1,216-acre construction site would be good practice for pounding the beat, and it would keep him out of sight and out of mind.

The scion of a long line of New York City cops, eldest son of Captain Timothy C. Fitzgerald of the 59th Precinct in Long Island City, Fitz never questioned his career path. His mother had tried to steer him in a safer direction, like the priesthood, but he was not about to take the celibacy vow. Nor was he interested in teaching or any of the manual trades. He idolized his father, whose ginger hair and green eyes he had inherited, and wanted nothing more than to follow in his footsteps.

He did not, however, want to be under the old man's thumb, so when he graduated from the Police Academy in 1937, he asked for posting to the 110th Precinct in Elmhurst, close to home but not on his dad's patch. For the past two years, the surrounding neighborhood had been watching with growing excitement as the Corona eyesore was rapidly being transformed, in the words of Park Commissioner Robert Moses, "from dump to glory."

The vast and complex reclamation project brought much-needed jobs to an area still deeply in the grip of the Great Depression. The goal was to have the grounds ready for construction of the Fair's pavilions to begin within a year, and indeed, the first structure, the Administration Building, was completed and occupied by November 1937.

Fitz had only just joined the 110th Precinct then, but as a native of nearby Long Island City, he had been watching the fairgrounds develop since the beginning. Now, from the top window in the station house tower, he could follow the progress as, one after another, the buildings began to go up. Most were slated to be torn down after the Fair closed, but the New York City Building was to be a permanent sports facility in the public park Moses was planning for the site. It was completed in mid 1938, adjacent to the Fair's Theme Center, the Trylon and Perisphere.

With other low-ranking officers and those seeking a break from regular duty, in January 1939 Fitz was assigned to World's Fair patrol. The detail, rotating on eight-hour shifts, reported to a bare-bones outpost in the City Building. Staffed by a civilian clerk rather than a desk sergeant, it consisted of little more than a recess in the lobby, with benches, a counter, and a telephone linked to the main precinct and call stations peppered around the fairgrounds.

As far as Fitz was concerned, its major amenities were central heating and indoor plumbing. Late January proved to be an exceptionally cold period, with temperatures dipping into the single digits. He and his fellow patrolmen took every opportunity to check in during their rounds of the frigid, windswept site, still awaiting the topsoil and plantings that would cover the dusty cinders and fill in the muddy potholes.

There wasn't really a lot for them to do. Most of the buildings were only partly finished, and with the deadline looming, work was progressing furiously, day and night. Banks of arc lights kept the site fully illuminated after dark. The foremen of individual construction crews were responsible for their own outfits' safety and security, but the grounds as a whole, which were City property leased to the Fair, were the police's territory. Much of their time was spent monitoring the steady flow of workers and suppliers in and out of the entrance gates and ensuring that no unauthorized people or vehicles were coming through. They did regular rounds of the fences to make sure there were no gaps where neighborhood kids could sneak onto the dangerous property, and broke up the occasional squabble among workmen. Each of them covered a manageable area within the main grounds, taking prescribed routes just as they would on the city streets.

Their least favorite duty was escorting the visiting dignitaries who were regularly ferried in by the Fair's president, Grover Aloysius Whalen, who never tired of extolling its wonders, as if he were personally responsible for them. In a sense, he was, since it was his job to recruit the exhibitors. Whalen, a former Commissioner of Police, was a stickler for formalities. Even though he'd been out of that office for nearly ten years, he insisted the cops salute him when he and his entourage appeared on the grounds. This did not sit well with the uniformed force, nor did they appreciate being required to show up on demand whenever Whalen wanted to impress his audience by turning out a contingent of New York's Finest, but they got used to it.

On the positive side, the Fair had laid on a fleet of four Salsbury Motor Glide scooters, allowing patrolmen to reach remote parts of the grounds more quickly and efficiently than on foot. Once or twice a day, one of them would hop on a scooter, ride south across the Empire State Bridge that spanned Horace Harding Boulevard, and take a turn around the Amusement Zone, where all sorts of carnival-style entertainments were under construction. Scooter detail was much more fun than walking around the grounds, not to mention trailing along on the Whalen tours, and they took it in turns.

The occasional scooter ride was not enough to relieve the general tedium for most of his colleagues on Fair duty, but Fitz couldn't get enough of the place. The sheer scale of it excited him. The architecture was incredible, and the ingenuity behind the overarching concept made him feel part of something revolutionary. There were new things happening every day. A street would be paved overnight. A statue would suddenly appear in a plaza. A wall that had been nothing but steel girders a couple of weeks before would sport a colorful mural. A fountain would spring to life in a reflecting pool that had been an empty hole only a few days ago. He never went home to Crescent Street without an account of some novelty, to the point where his mother took to greeting him with, "Hello, Brian. What miracle did you witness today?"

Chapter Three

When Fitz told his father that he was thinking of requesting assignment to the fairgrounds, Timothy was less than enthusiastic.

"You'll be bored, son," he cautioned. "And you'll be isolated from the rest of the precinct, where you should be making friends with your fellow officers and the staff, and brown-nosing the brass. You can do yourself a lot more good in the house than out in the wilds of Corona."

Having inherited the family stubborn streak, Fitz was not to be dissuaded. "I'm already in pretty good with the other cops. Sure, they rib me about you watching over me, but I tell them, if only that were true! It's all in fun—they know favoritism doesn't get you the job of cleaning up the squad room. And I've been there a year, so they're used to me, and I think they like me. At least most of them do."

"Anyone in particular giving you trouble?"

Fitz was sorry he'd let that slip. Detective Clarence O'Toole had taken an instant dislike to him, but he wasn't about to share a grievance, in case his father did decide to intervene. With an enviable record of investigative success, O'Toole, who only just made the NYPD's five-foot-eight height requirement, was wiry and pugnacious, a living caricature of the scrappy Irishman. His relentless pursuit of even the most baffling cases and his aggressive interrogation tactics had inspired his nickname, Hammer, playing on both his surname and his personality. He relished the title, boasting that, when it came to detective work, he was the right tool for the job and always nailed his man.

O'Toole's animus puzzled Fitz at first. It wasn't like he'd been out of line, disrespectful, or was guilty of any other infraction. He was well aware of the pecking order. After one especially blatant snub, he'd asked a couple of his buddies if they knew why the detective seemed to have it in for him, but they couldn't explain it. The only reason he could think of was that he was Captain Fitzgerald's son. It must be something in the two men's history, and the only way to find out would be to ask one of them. If he asked his father, he'd be giving it away, and if he asked O'Toole, he'd likely alienate him further. Better to let it lie and try to steer as clear of O'Toole as possible. Best not to let Hammer nail him.

Since Fitz was much less likely to encounter O'Toole on the fairgrounds than in the 110th Precinct station house, the remote posting was especially attractive. Still, the primary motive was his fascination with the Fair, as both a breathtaking reclamation project and a tangible demonstration of how planning could shape society. The result would be a harmonious, integrated ensemble that exploited modern design concepts and innovative exhibition techniques, at least in the main area.

The Amusement Zone was a free-for-all, with Coney Island-style rides and attractions designed to amaze, thrill, and titillate. The official policy called for tasteful content, like Billy Rose's Aquacade water pageant and specially tailored versions of Broadway shows in the Hall of Music. Nothing indecent or offensive, but not every concessionaire would follow the rules. Young ladies flaunting their charms would be billed as Living Magazine Covers, "a sparkling show of feminine pulchritude softened by trick lighting." In the Crystal Gazing Palace, described as "a polyscopic paradise for peeping Toms," a topless Crystal Lassie dancing in a mirrored room was to be reflected sixty times; with a semi-nude mannequin on the façade, the marquee proclaimed, "Inside She's Real." At the Congress of World's Beauties, "a tribute to the body beautiful," so-called sun worshipers were going to lounge around in nothing but skimpy panties.

***

Needless to say, no one was taking a sunbath in frosty February. Almost all the amusement concessions were still under construction. The most remarkable was the nearly complete Parachute Jump, a 250-foot steel structure that was quickly dubbed the Eiffel Tower of Flushing.

Adapted from a military training device, it had twelve parachutes, each with a double seat to accommodate daring couples who would be hauled up to the top and then released to float gently to earth, their landing cushioned by shock absorbers. Cruising past it on the Motor Glide, Fitz admired its lacy structure of metal girders topped by an umbrella-shaped array of drop stations. He resolved to take his girlfriend, Mary Dolan, on the ride as soon as it opened.

Returning to the City Building via the East Loop, Fitz was startled when a young woman, wearing only a bathing suit, ran out of a pavilion under construction and almost collided with him. He jammed on the brakes just in time to avoid hitting her and skidded to a stop.

She rushed at him, grabbed his arm, and nearly pulled him off the scooter. "Help me, please," she shouted. "Hurry, it's Mr. Dolly! He's drowning!"

It was all he could do to get the kickstand down before she dragged him between a pair of giant female legs, past a box office shaped like a grotesque fish head, and into the Dream of Venus, a Surrealist fantasia designed by the movement's master showman, Salvador Dalí, according to his self-invented paranoiac-critical method. The façade boasted bare-breasted mermaid sculptures cradled in the niches of a reef-like structure adorned with jutting shapes that looked like branching coral and reproductions of paintings by Leonardo and Botticelli. With a mixture of puzzlement and curiosity, Fitz had watched it take shape. Based on the bizarre exterior, more than a little bit sexually suggestive, his imagination was working overtime on what the interior might hold.

All it held at the moment was a huge fish tank, thirty feet wide and nearly ten feet tall, in which a fully clothed man was flailing wildly, bobbing and splashing with gusto. His efforts to reach the top were hampered by his full-length black cape, which floated and swirled around him.

"¡Ayúdeme! Aidez moi! No sé nadir!" he cried, followed by curses in

Spanish and French every time his head broke water.

Next to the tank were steps leading to a platform that served as a staging area. On it were a couple of young women in swimsuits and bathrobes, huddled together in apparent shock. Fitz quickly scaled the steps and made his way toward Dalí, who spotted him and thrust an arm upward, which only made him countersink. Fitz could see why the girls were hanging back. They wouldn't have the strength to haul him out, and if he pulled them in, they might drown, too.

Fitz lay flat on the platform and extended his left arm into the tank. Dalí clutched at it and got a firm grip on the sleeve of his uniform. Fitz pulled back and steered him toward the edge. Dalí stopped kicking and focused on raising his head clear of the water, coughing and sputtering as he groped for the rim with his free hand. Fitz reached down and unfastened the waterlogged cape, which sank and lightened Dalí's weight considerably.

"Hold on with both hands," said Fitz, not sure if he understood English, but Dalí nodded and did as he was told. Now that he could breathe and see that a strong young police officer had taken charge, he relaxed and let Fitz grab him under the arms and haul him onto the platform, where he landed like a beached sea bass.

As Dalí pulled himself together, the woman, now wrapped in a robe, who had flagged Fitz down, told him her name was Harriet and explained the situation.

"We were rehearsing the underwater act, where we swim in the tank in front of the spectators, with a bunch of weird props in a sort of living room, what Mr. Dolly calls his dream house. There's all kinds of crazy furniture, a telephone shaped like a lobster, even a piano with a naked mannequin lying on it. The idea is for us to pretend to live in the place, like mermaids would do if they had a house in the ocean."

"Was that his idea?" asked Fitz, pointing to the sodden figure spitting up water and failing to raise himself to a dignified position. He had heard of Dalí, whose picture had been on the cover of *Time* magazine three years earlier, when he had a widely publicized show in Manhattan. In town for the occasion, he cut a flamboyant figure walking his pet ocelot on Fifth Avenue in his flowing cape, black cashmere with a scarlet lining that flashed in the breeze like a warning signal. His World's Fair fun-house and his recent contract to design window displays for Bonwit Teller department store had earned him a reputation among his fellow Surrealists as a commercial sellout. The movement's founder, André Breton, coined the anagram Avida Dollars to express his contempt for Dalí's desire to cash in on Surrealism's more theatrical aspects.

"Oh, yeah," Harriet nodded. "He dreamed up the whole nutty thing. The Living Liquid Ladies, that's what we're supposed to be. Hey, a job's a job, especially these days."

"I guess that explains why you're here," said Fitz, "but how did he wind up in the water?"

"He said he was here to check on the progress, see how the installation was going, make sure we were doing it the way he wanted. But there's a choreographer who's in charge of the underwater ballet, and set dressers from the theater who handle the props, so he really didn't need to be here."

She leaned in. "You wanna know what I think? He wanted to cop a feel. He ain't that old, but he's a letch. Said he needed to check our suits to make sure they show enough of what the public'll pay to see, if you follow me." She winked.

"Well, the girls, me included, ain't all that ready to get, you know, costume adjustments from him, especially Lucy, the blonde over there, and she pushed him away. Between you and me, he'd been drinking and wasn't all that steady on his pins, so when she pushed, he kinda stumbled and lost his balance and ended up in the tank. He can't swim, and that stupid cape was all over him, so he couldn't make it to the little ladder, down at the other end, that we use to get in and out."

"I need to file an incident report," Fitz told her, "so I'll ask you and the other girls to come down and find someplace where I can take your statements."

"There's a few chairs in the lobby area," said Harriet, pointing out toward the entrance. "What about him?" she added, looking down at the waterlogged artist, who was making an effort to sit up.

Fitz knelt down and gave him a hand. "How are you feeling, Mr. Dolly?

Should I call an ambulance? Do you understand what I'm asking?"

Disoriented and unfocused, Dalí nodded. "Si, si, I understand. I have good English, in my head if not on my tongue. I am, what is the word, okay, but I am cold. Is there a manta, a wrap?"

Lucy, who was feeling a bit guilty, came forward with a large bath towel from a pile at the far end of the platform. "Here, Mr. Dolly, put this around you," she coaxed. "I bet one of the men can find you some dry clothes."

"Where are the men?" asked Fitz. "How come there was no one here to get him out of the tank?"

"The crew went to lunch over at the canteen in the New York State Building, where they'll be doing the water show," Lucy explained. "I'm gonna audition for that," she added, looking sideways, with unspoken disapproval, at Dalí. "He said he'd watch the place while they were gone. They're supposed to bring us some sandwiches, should be back any time now."

Harriet snickered. "He shoulda kept his eyes on the equipment and his hands in his pockets. He could hardly wait for them to leave so he could make his moves."

Dalí began to protest, but Fitz cut him off. "Let's get you down off the platform and over to someplace where you can warm up. Think you can stand? Here, let me help you." He locked forearms with the artist, who was a couple of inches shorter and slender, and got him to his feet with little trouble. As he steadied him, Fitz felt a hip flask in his pocket, confirming Harriet's suspicions.

With Fitz supporting him, Dalí slowly descended the steps and made his way to the lobby. As he groped for a chair with one hand, the other reached for the flask. He sat, uncorked it, and took a long swallow, followed by a deep sigh. "At least I shall be warm inside," he quipped.

When everyone was seated, Fitz took out his notebook. All three women—the third was named Carol—were more uncomfortable than Dalí, whose color had returned as he continued to self-medicate. After he got their particulars, Fitz put their minds to rest.

"I'm going to report this as an accident, no one at fault," he said. He turned to the artist. "The way I see it, you went up on the platform to take a look at the setup from above, leaned too far over, and lost your balance. That sound right to you?"

The implication was not lost on Dalí. If Lucy was blamed, she could lose her job, and maybe Billy Rose wouldn't hire her for the Aquacade. And he'd have to admit why she pushed him. If he tried to contradict her account, the other Living Liquid Ladies would back her up. He shrugged and nodded. "Si, it is right," he said, meaning it was the right story to tell, not that it was true.

* * *

Over dinner that night, Fitz amused the family with the tale of the soggy Surrealist.

"He looked like a load of laundry, swirling around in a big washtub. The only way you could tell there was a man in there was that he was yelling his head off—when he could get it above water—in two languages, neither of them English."

His little brother Andy wanted to hear more about what Dalí was doing with the bathing beauties. "What kind of costume adjustments, Bri? Was he pullin' their straps down so you could see, you know…?"

Fitz chuckled. "Use your overactive imagination! Anyway, it happened before I got there, and the girls didn't do into detail. Harriet said he was just trying to feel them up, but who knows where it would've gone if he hadn't taken a dive? Or rather, if Lucy hadn't given him a shove."

Sitting next to him, sister Alice piped up. "Good for Lucy for defending her dignity. I bet the letch didn't know how strong lady swimmers are, or he wouldn't have tried anything funny."

"I'll remember that next summer when I take Mary to Astoria Pool," said Fitz. "She can swim rings around me, and she's got a mean right jab."

Their mother, Bridget, wanted to know more about the scandalous pavilion. "Does it really have statues of naked mermaids on the front? And from what you say, the swimsuits are going to be pretty revealing. I wonder if Mr. Whalen knows about that. In the papers, it says he's quite strict about not allowing naughty exhibits like girlie shows. All the amusements are supposed to be wholesome entertainment."

"Sounds pretty dull," said their father. "Give me a good old-fashioned sideshow, complete with fire eaters, sword swallowers, and plenty of dancing girls in skimpy costumes doin' the hoochie-coochie." He got up from the table and demonstrated.

"Timothy Connor Fitzgerald, you sit down this minute and stop embarrassing yourself in front of the children," scolded Bridget with mock outrage.

"Who are you calling children?" Fitz wanted to know. "I just turned twenty-two, and Andy isn't far behind me. Allie is practically decrepit." He gave his sister a look of pity. "What are you now, twenty-four? We should call the old folks' home and reserve her a room."

Alice turned and punched his arm playfully. "Careful, baby brother. I've got a pretty mean right jab myself."

Chapter Four

Grover Whalen was in a good mood, though there was still plenty of promotion to do, frequent publicity stunts to arrange, and many problems to iron out. With less than three months to go until opening day, construction was proceeding nicely. From his office in the Administration Building on site, he could observe progress on a daily basis. He looked out the window and liked what he saw.

His intercom buzzed, and his secretary informed him that Mr. Shadgen was on the phone. His mood turned from sunny to sour. *Why is that goddamned has-been making a pest of himself? The matter was settled.*

"Tell Mr. Shadgen I'm not available, and that if he wishes to communicate with me, he should do so in writing." He closed the intercom connection.

After ten months of exile in the Drafting Department, Shadgen had been fired, allegedly for incompetence. Furious, he promptly sued the Fair for wrongful termination, asking a million dollars. They offered a $45,000 settlement—paltry compared to his demand, but the equivalent of six years' pay. To their surprise, Shadgen accepted, chalking it up as a moral victory and vowing never to visit the exposition he had inspired.

Now, for whatever reason, he was back and wanting Whalen's ear. Certainly not hoping to get his old job reinstated, and unlikely to be looking to bury the hatchet—unless it was in Whalen's skull. That thought gave him pause. *Could Shadgen be regretting taking the settlement, maybe wanting revenge? He said he'd never come here, but what if he changes his mind? He might be dangerous, who can say?*

Whalen picked up the phone and asked to be connected to Joseph Consolla, the commanding officer at the 110th Precinct.

"Captain Consolla, this is Grover Whalen. Good to speak to you. I hope you and the family are well. Glad to hear it. I wonder if you'll do me a favor." He never launched straight into demands, always couching them as personal kindnesses or polite requests, but his clout usually made pulling rank unnecessary. Consolla knew he'd once been Police Commissioner and was close to Mayor LaGuardia and the rest of New York's top brass.

"Of course, Mr. Whalen. What do you need?"

"I just had a call from a man I fired from the World's Fair a couple of years ago. Shadgen is his name. There were unusual circumstances, maybe you read about it in the papers. It was all over and done with last November. I expected never to hear from him again, but now he's trying to get in touch. I didn't take the call, and I'm worried that he might try to come to the office and make trouble. I wouldn't want my staff to have to deal with him." As if he were more concerned for them than for his own safety.

"If I send over Shadgen's photograph and description, will you circulate it to the men you have posted on the fairgrounds and order them not to admit him? He may still have his World's Fair Corporation identity card, which would allow him access."

"Consider it done, Mr. Whalen. As soon as you can get me the information, I'll see that every officer on Fair duty has it and will be on the lookout. You can be sure this guy Shadgen won't get past them."

Whalen spread on a little butter. "Your men are doing an outstanding job of patrolling the grounds, and they're always pleased to serve as my escorts when I show my guests around. I'll be sure to commend your precinct to my dear friend, Commissioner Valentine."

At the other end of the line, Consolla was beaming. "That's very kind of you, sir. You can always count on the One Ten to deliver the goods."

"You'll have the material you need before the end of the day," Whalen assured him. "I leave the matter in your capable hands."

Chapter Five

"For Christ's sake, Grover, can't you keep that son of a bitch in line?" Harvey D. Gibson, president of Manufacturers Trust Company and chairman of the Fair's Finance Committee, was not having a good day. The stress had begun to show. He was responsible for selling the bonds and lining up the bankers, corporations, and other investors who were paying the enormous sums that had to be laid out before the Fair could earn one penny of revenue from admissions and concessions. His call to Whalen's office was sparked by the latest in a string of exasperating problems that had plagued the construction project almost from the outset.

What was supposed to have been a well-oiled, efficient engine racing toward the finish line had too often been derailed by labor strikes, cost overruns, and bad weather, not to mention disputes with exhibitors over what they considered exorbitant charges by contractors. Since the Fair was a closed shop, the trade unions controlled all aspects of construction and installation, including wages, hours, and working conditions. If an employee of one of the pavilions hooked up a generator to test equipment, or even ran a wire from a union-installed outlet, the electrical workers would walk out.

Today's crisis came courtesy of George E. Browne, president of the United Scenic Artists of America, Local 829, who was demanding that any muralist who touched a paintbrush to a Fair building's wall be a union member. A former business agent of the stagehands' union Local 2 in Chicago, Browne was a battle-hardened, no-nonsense negotiator. He had learned that several of the artists occupying the scaffolds that festooned the nearly completed pavilions were members of the National Society of Mural

Painters, a professional organization not affiliated with Local 829. Either they would have to pay their dues and get union cards, or the hundreds of his members who were fabricating the exhibits, displays, and dioramas would down their tools.

Whalen listened with sympathy and concern as Gibson fulminated. "I spoke to Geoffrey Norman, head of the mural painters' society, and he's adamant that they won't join. He says the union is for commercial artists who paint scenery—he made it sound like a curse word—and not suitable, as he put it, for fine artists. We can't afford that kind of snobbery, especially at this late date."

"No good arguing with Browne," said Whalen. "I've tried it, and I failed. He came to me complaining about the crew that's fabricating the so-called City of Light in the Consolidated Edison Building. It's a fantastic thing, Harvey, a huge scale model of New York that goes through a twenty-four-hour cycle, showing how electricity powers the metropolis. They're billing it as the world's largest diorama. I don't know if that's true, but it's certainly striking. Anyway, Browne said he found out that some of the men Con Ed hired weren't union members. I settled it by persuading Con Ed to sign them up and pay their initiation fee. Maybe Norman would accept a similar offer, if the Fair will foot the bill."

Groaning inwardly at the prospect of yet another unexpected expense he'd have to find a way to cover, Gibson saw a glimmer of hope.

"Would you propose it to him, Grover? You know I'm no good at dealing with these temperamental types." Comfortable in the boardroom, at gentlemen's clubs, and on the golf course, Gibson was profoundly ill at ease handling people outside his sphere of influence. Whalen, on the other hand, was renowned for a genial manner that was equally effective with visiting heads of state and the local press, even the office cleaning service. He knew how to pitch it.

"You have to admit that Browne's point of view, shall we call it, is not unreasonable," said Whalen. "The Fair Corporation agreed to a hundred percent union labor, and even if these muralists call themselves fine artists, they are workers doing a job and getting paid for it, either by us or by the exhibitors. There are over thirty of them on our payroll alone."

* * *

Right from the start, the provision of murals and sculpture had been central to the overall architectural program. Art was to be so well integrated into the Fair itself that there was no plan for a stand-alone art exhibition. It was only after complaints from New York's cultural leaders that the Fair authorized separate buildings for historical and modern art.

Contemporary Art was appropriately located in the Community Interests Zone, in a prime position adjacent to the IRT/BMT elevated railway entrance gate. The exhibition's director, Holger Cahill, was head of the Works Progress Administration's Federal Art Project, which had put thousands of artists on the government payroll since August 1935 as part of the New Deal's vast national employment scheme during the Depression. Many of the muralists and sculptors now working for the Fair were WPA alumni.

A privately-funded Masterpieces of Art pavilion was erected on a vacant plot provided free by the Fair Corporation. The architects had hired the distinguished German-American artist Lyonel Feininger to paint murals for the central courtyard's outside walls, surrounding a reflecting pool. Loans from the city's foremost museums were promised, and their directors had secured works from collections around the country and abroad, including the Louvre in Paris, the Rijksmuseum in Amsterdam, London's National Gallery, and as far afield as the Melbourne Art Museum in Australia.

Feininger was one of the muralists who had caught Browne's attention. Luckily, he'd been away from the art pavilion job when the Local 829 inspector came by, so he slipped through. But it was a different story at the Marine Transportation Building, where the Fair had commissioned him to create a huge mural for the façade.

Although he had lived in Europe, primarily in Germany, since he was a teenager, Feininger was born in New York City. As a child, he'd been fascinated by the steamships and sailing vessels he saw in the harbor, and he often painted maritime subjects. This was a great opportunity to create nautical imagery on a monumental scale. Beside the entrance shaped like two giant ocean liner prows, "Sea Traffic," a 25-foot-tall frieze of stylized vessels, was designed to cover 120 running feet of exterior wall.

A large team of union painters was hard at work scaling up Feininger's sketches when the artist arrived, climbed onto the scaffold, and began to pitch in.

"Who the fuck are you?" asked the crew's foreman, Fred Olsen, when he saw a stranger on the job.

"I am Lyonel Feininger, the artist," he replied. "This is my design."

"Oh," said Olsen. "Glad to know you, Mr. Feininger. Let's see your card."

Feininger took out his driver's license. "This will verify my identity."

"No, no, not your I.D. Your union card."

Feininger looked confused. "I do not belong to a labor union. I am an employee of the World's Fair, and as such, I have a right to work on my own mural."

"'Fraid not," said Olsen. His tone was stern. "Fair's a closed shop. Only union members get to paint the murals, including yours. Either get a card or get off the scaffold. Now."

When Feininger refused to leave the job, the police were called, and Fitz was dispatched to the scene.

The building was in the Transportation Zone, across the Bridge of Wings from the City Building. Fitz hopped on a scooter and was there in under five minutes. He managed to coax Feininger down off the scaffold by persuading him that he was in danger without proper safety gear, which would be provided when the dispute was settled. Once he was on the ground, winded from his climb and a bit shaky, under his bluster and consternation, Fitz could detect relief that the law had come between him and the burly, equally obstinate, foreman.

"He ain't allowed on the job if he ain't a union man," said Olsen.

"I, Lyonel Feininger, am the artist who created this composition. Surely I have the right to supervise my own work, even to participate in its execution if I so choose."

Olsen was adamant. "Don't matter if he did design the mural, he can't paint on it without a card."

Feininger's many years teaching at the Bauhaus had instilled an ethic based on personal craftsmanship and direct involvement in all aspects of the creative process. Notwithstanding his age and the obvious physical challenges of painting such an enormous wall, he was not about to divorce himself entirely from the project.

"You must understand," he explained, "in Germany, the Nazis denounced my work as degenerate abstraction. I must ensure that my design is not tampered with to make it more palatable to those unreceptive to such innovations."

He needn't have worried on that score. Such innovations were the order of the day in the World of Tomorrow. Modernist architects and avant-garde industrial designers were responsible for many of the pavilions and interior displays, both Fair-sponsored and private.

Fitz decided to put a little distance between the artist and the foreman. He turned to Olsen. "I'll ask management to settle the matter," he told him. And to Feininger, he said, "How did you get here? Do you have a car?"

"Yes," he replied. "It is parked over there." He pointed to a group of vehicles in the forecourt. His rather formal manner of speaking betrayed his long absence from the city of his birth.

Fitz nodded. "Good. I'll take you over to the Administration Building so we can get Mr. Whalen's advice. I'm sure he'll see your side of things. But I wouldn't want to ask you to hitch a ride on my scooter. It's only a one-man seat." He smiled. "If I want to take my girl for a spin, she'll have to sit on my lap. Strictly against regulations, but the chief isn't around much."

His banter lightened the mood. Olsen backed off, Feininger visibly relaxed, and Fitz asked him politely to follow the scooter across the parkway.

* * *

Riding along the Avenue of Transportation, Fitz slowed down to take in the stunning shapes of the huge Ford and General Motors Buildings. Although his patrols were supposed to be confined to the grounds, he often sneaked inside these architectural wonders to catch a glimpse of the installations in progress. Armies of fabricators and technicians swarmed over the displays, putting the finishing touches on what amounted to giant three-dimensional billboards advertising the car makers' wares. Even Fitz, who traveled everywhere by subway or bus and couldn't have imagined himself owning a car, felt a craving to test drive one of the latest models.

As they turned right and crossed the Bridge of Wheels, Feininger pulled up beside the scooter and signaled Fitz to stop. "I want to show you something," he called out, and stepped out of his car.

"What is it, Mr. Feininger?" Fitz asked as he dismounted.

The artist directed him to the Masterpieces of Art Building on the left. He exchanged a few words with the guard and took Fitz through the entrance and into the courtyard.

"Here you will see what I am capable of when I am allowed to have control over my work," he said. "Of course, I had assistants, but they were under my supervision from start to finish."

As they walked around the courtyard and Fitz admired the subtly rendered, simplified shapes of buildings and mountains, Feininger explained his imagery.

"I was honored to be invited to decorate this pavilion. I chose to depict landscapes based on my personal memories of Europe, such as Pomeranian seaside towns and Thuringian villages, because it will contain European art of past centuries, lent by the great museums here and abroad, which are preserving it for the bright future this Fair envisions. I think it is splendid that these institutions have been so generous, reminding people that throughout the ages, in spite of wars, revolutions, and other catastrophes, art has survived and flourished."

He paused and turned to speak to Fitz directly. "You must understand that, while I was born in America, I have spent almost all of my mature life in Germany, where—as you can tell from my surname—my family originated. I did not return here out of homesickness, but due to the threat of Nazi persecution. Their regime is a pestilence, infecting the culture that gave rise to some of the world's greatest artists. If art is to prosper in the future to which this Fair is dedicated, they must be stopped."

He gestured toward the murals. "You may wonder why these scenes around us seem to be dissolving, the edges of the buildings blurred, the hills fragmented, the arches incomplete. I myself am not sure why. It may be an expression of how memory works, never allowing us to recall our experiences fully or clearly. Or, God forbid, it may be my premonition of what will happen to those quaint towns and peaceful villages if the Nazis prevail."

"Well," said Fitz, "they are shaking things up overseas. Even here at the Fair. The Czechoslovak pavilion had to find American sponsors after Hitler took over the country. The Czech government cancelled its lease. The papers say Hitler believes the country's really part of Germany, so he was uniting it with the homeland, and that was all he wanted."

Feininger shook his head. "You must not swallow his propaganda. Der Fürer's real aim was to take control of the region's industries so he could build up his military arsenal. Why do you think he has no German pavilion at this exposition? He cannot afford to spend money on such frivolity when he needs to pay for tanks and planes and guns to conquer all of Europe!"

"You think there's going to be another war?"

"I know it."

"But it's Europe's fight, not ours. We wouldn't get dragged in like last time."

Feininger put a hand on Fitz's shoulder. "For your sake, and that of all the young men of your generation, I hope you are right."

Chapter Six

Posted at the Administration Gate one morning in early March, Fitz was checking the I.D.s of those arriving for work. Following orders from Consolla, he was keeping an eye out for Shadgen when he was startled by an ambulance siren. He waved aside the waiting cars to allow the ambulance through.

"Where you headed?" he asked the driver.

"Dispatcher said Communications," he replied.

"That's it straight ahead," said Fitz, pointing to a streamlined structure distinguished by two bright red 160-foot pylons. "You have to drive around to get to it. Turn left here, then right at the junction, and it'll be directly in front of you. Then turn right and first left. Entrance is between those towers."

The driver thanked him and headed off.

"Wonder who's hurt bad enough to need an ambulance," said Fitz to the booth attendant. "I thought they were pretty much done with major work in Communications." There had been a steady stream of injuries all around the grounds during construction, more than the usual quota, though to be expected given the furious pace of work. But like most Fair-sponsored buildings, this one was almost ready to open.

It wasn't long before the ambulance returned to the gate, on its way back to Flushing Hospital. Fitz asked the driver, "Is it serious?"

"Nah, just a broken arm. Could be serious for him, though. He's the artist who's painting the mural in the main hall, and if it's his painting arm, he'll be out of commission."

"What happened?"

"Looks like he fell off the scaffold. Not from high up, or it woulda been his neck that got broke. He was in a sleeping bag. Seems he was on the lowest level, about seven feet up. Must've rolled off in his sleep. Morning shift found him out cold on the floor. Guess maybe he hit his head, too. Better get him to the doc." On went the siren and off went the ambulance.

"How do you like that?" said Fitz to the gate man. "Strictly against the rules to sleep in the buildings overnight. A daytime nap is one thing—nobody would object to a little break—but spending the night asleep on a scaffold is asking for trouble."

* * *

When his relief arrived, Fitz headed over to Communications to learn more about the accident.

Above the entrance, the building boasted one of the Fair's most eye-catching exterior murals, "Means of Communication," a giant allegory by the academician Eugene Savage, whose undulating figures rendered in brilliant colors represented various aspects of the subject. Anchored by an Indian making smoke signals, against a background of musical notes in a lightning-bolt motif surrounded by books and newspapers, the mythological imagery featured the winged horse, Pegasus; Terpsichore, the goddess of poetry, dance, and song; and three muses swooping toward Atlas supporting the Earth. That mural was finished, but apparently another one inside was still in progress.

The guard opened up for him. In the main hall, only work lights showed the way to the huge wall on which the artist had been painting. Forty-four feet tall and 136 feet long, the mural used graphic white lines on a solid black background—a stark contrast to Savage's colorful mural on the façade—to depict a more down-to-earth version of communication history, from a human runner and a carrier pigeon to the latest developments in electronic transmission.

Only the lower parts were finished. The rest of the design was still in preparation, with chalked outlines showing what would be pictured. Through the lattice of scaffolding, Fitz could make out a schematic printing press, a telegraph key, a microphone, a film strip, even a television camera, though he didn't know what that was. Hands symbolized sign language, and an ear received radio signals. A nice touch was an airmail letter addressed to "N.Y. World's Fair 1939."

At the far end of the scaffold, a few feet below the mural's bottom edge, was evidence of the artist's occupation: a portable radio, sandwich wrappings, and an empty pint of Four Roses. Not far above the platform was his signature, Stuart Davis. The name meant nothing to Fitz, whose sole exposure to contemporary art before the Fair had been a school field trip to the newly-opened Whitney Museum of American Art when he was fourteen. Not that he remembered any of the works from the founder's personal collection, including paintings by Davis, on display in the renovated townhouses on West Eighth Street in Greenwich Village. What he did remember was the glamorous Mrs. Whitney herself greeting the students in the lobby and leading them up the twin curving staircases to the galleries.

* * *

Wondering whether he should collect what Davis had left on the scaffold, Fitz heard a door close and saw a man in overalls enter the hall. He moved closer to a work light so the fellow could see that he was a uniformed policeman.

"Hi, Officer," said the man. "I guess you're here about the accident. I'm Jeffries, in charge of maintenance. How can I help?"

They shook hands, and Fitz told him, "I'm just checking the scene in case I need to make an incident report. I met the ambulance at the gate and directed it to the building. Were you here when they came?"

Jeffries nodded. "Yeah, I showed 'em where he was. Didn't want to move him, so I just left him here on the floor." He pointed to a spot below Davis's belongings. "He was in a sleeping bag, but partly out of it. It could have caught on the scaffold when he fell. I thought he might be dead, so I checked his pulse, and it was steady. But he was unconscious, so I decided to call the medics. Turns out he has a broken arm, maybe a concussion, too."

"What do you think happened?"

"I think he just rolled over the edge in his sleep. The bag wouldn't be much of a cushion, so he musta been pretty uncomfortable on those hard planks. And I guess he was under the influence. Ain't no bourbon left in that bottle."

"Not foul play, you think? Not like anyone pushed him over?"

"The night watchman saw him asleep around six a.m., snoring his head off. There was no one else around. Except for this wall, the focal exhibit is finished, so there's only the mural painters working in this area, and they don't work nights. The commercial displays are through there." He gestured toward large doors leading to the general exhibition area.

"Aren't workers forbidden to sleep on the job? And why was he even here when the mural painters have the nights off?"

"He wasn't what you'd call regular crew," Jeffries told him. "He was supposed to be supervising the scenic artists who do the actual painting. But he wanted to work on it, too, and it turns out he's a union member, United American Artists. He told me it started out in 1934 as the Artists Union, agitating for government support, and really started to take off when the WPA came along. Last year, it became a CIO affiliate and changed its name to the UAA, so they had to accept it."

"So you're saying he'd have access to the place at all hours. Even if the rest of the crew weren't around?"

"Sure. Everyone's racing toward opening day, and if he wants to keep working all night, nobody's gonna stop him, since he's doing it on his own time. Muralists commissioned by the Fair are paid a flat fee for their designs, so he don't get overtime pay. They don't even have to show up at all, just hand over their sketches to the union guys."

"Don't they belong to the UAA?" asked Fitz.

"You gotta understand," explained Jeffries, "there's two different kinds of muralists. There's the old-guard academics, like that Savage guy whose painting's on the wall out front. Him and the others like him belong to a professional society. They think unions are for laborers, not good enough for real artists, and as far as they're concerned, the UAA is just a bunch of

Bolshies. Savage was plenty sore when he was told he couldn't touch the wall, but he wouldn't lower himself to join a union.

"Now, guys like Davis, who learned the trade on the WPA, they think of themselves more like workers, 'cause Uncle Sam pays 'em a weekly wage. They paint murals for public buildings like schools and libraries. Davis told me he did one last year for a housing project in Brooklyn. Put art where regular folks can enjoy it, not in a museum where you have to pay to get in or a rich collector's living room where you can't get in at all. That's their motto. He said he had to quit the WPA to take the Fair commission, but it was such a plum gig he couldn't pass it up. And he can probably go back on the payroll once he's finished here."

Fitz was sympathetic. "Millions of people will see this mural, so I get how it follows his philosophy. I hope he's not hurt too bad. It would be a shame if he couldn't finish it himself. I don't know much about art—really nothing, to tell the truth—but seeing it all over the Fair makes me realize how it livens up the surroundings. If this really is what the World of Tomorrow will look like, I'll be glad to be living in it."

Chapter Seven

"So that's the second artist to take a tumble," said Fitz as he wrapped up his account of Stuart Davis' mishap. "Both of 'em after hitting the bottle as well."

"Serves 'em right," said his father, a teetotaler who had taken the pledge after his alcoholic mother drank herself to death. A bit judgmental, perhaps, but his first-hand experience had left him with a deep sadness and a promise to himself that he wouldn't visit such pain on his own family. Among the many things Fitz admired about Tim was his commitment to his principles. Once he settled on a belief, he held onto it. To some people—especially his wife—that made him stubborn, which he freely admitted.

"Well," said Bridget, "I hope they learned their lessons. Thank the Lord their accidents weren't fatal." She crossed herself.

Alice and Andy were both out, so Fitz and his parents were having a quiet evening at home, Tim and Bridget on the couch, and Fitz in the armchair opposite them.

"Speaking of artists," said Tim, "I can't help thinking about what that fellow Feininger told you. About how dangerous Hitler is, and that he's getting ready to take Germany to war again. I agree with him. It's coming, and soon. You remember that Nazi rally at Madison Square Garden a couple of weeks ago? The German-American Bund, they call themselves, wrapping themselves in the Stars and Stripes, pretending to be patriots. LaGuardia ordered every available cop to cover it. I sent a squad from Five Nine."

"Some guys from One Ten went, too," said Fitz, "But not me. I'm still a rookie, and they wanted experienced officers in case things got nasty."

Tim took a swig of his ginger ale and continued. "They were ready for a riot, but it didn't happen. I was surprised how many Nazi sympathizers turned up. I heard it was twenty thousand. The protestors outside the Garden outnumbered them five to one, but they were pretty well behaved. Lots of cursing and shoving, and a couple of fist fights, nothing serious, only about a dozen arrests. But inside, a guy attacked the leader, fellow called Kuhn, and the Nazi guards were on top of him pretty quick. The cops pulled him away before they could hurt him too badly.

"Now, I wasn't there, so I didn't hear him myself, but the boys who were there told me Kuhn was ranting and raving against the Jews. He said they're taking over, and people should rise up and fight for a country run by white Gentiles. He even said the President and the Mayor are Jewish, which they aren't. With a name like Fiorello LaGuardia, you'd think Hizonner would be a Catholic, but he goes to the Episcopal church. That's his choice. Okay, his mother's Jewish, so technically that makes him one, too, so what? And the President—Kuhn called him Rosenfelt—also worships Episcopal, though he comes from a long line of Dutch Protestants, but I don't hold that against him."

"Are people taking this Kuhn and his followers seriously?" asked Bridget. "I can't imagine many New Yorkers agreeing with him."

Tim set her straight. "Honey, the group's headquarters is right here, in Yorkville on the Upper East Side. A lot of Germans live in that neighborhood, but the Bund's not preaching to the choir. The patriotic pitch is a smoke screen to hide their real purpose, which is to stir up American sympathy for Hitler's policies, so we won't want to fight against him when the war does come. Last time, the isolationists kept us out of it for three years. We wouldn't have gone in at all if the German U-boats hadn't started sinking our commercial shipping."

Tim turned to his son. "You were born just a few months before we declared war on Germany. Millions of men and women went overseas, and lots of them didn't come back. Then, after it ended, we had the terrible influenza epidemic, and many more people died. Your mother and I were afraid it would take you kids. Andy wasn't even a year old. Thank God all of us came through."

Bridget reached out and took her husband's hand. "What I thank God for is that you weren't called up. If the war had lasted any longer, I don't know what would have happened. But with me at home raising two small kids, with Andy on the way, you were low on the draft list. Being on the police force was in your favor, too, even if it didn't completely exempt you."

Tim squeezed her hand and grinned. "Son," he said to Fitz, "Maybe you and Mary should tie the knot now. Then get her pregnant with twins. There's your insurance policy in case we get dragged in again."

* * *

As the Fitzgerald and Dolan families left St. Patrick Roman Catholic Church after Sunday morning Mass on March 26, Fitz and Mary excused themselves and headed to the nearby diner in Queens Plaza for breakfast on their own. They had been a couple since their senior year in high school. Everyone had assumed they'd marry as soon as they graduated, but unlike many of their classmates, who were already hitched and raising the next generation, they were still just sweethearts.

Their friends often wondered what was holding them back. Fitz always dodged the question, joking that they were more like brother and sister than boyfriend and girlfriend, but the truth was that Mary wouldn't agree to marry a young man whose heart was set on joining the police force. Despite her feelings, she told him, she wouldn't have a cop for a husband. Her father, a detective in the 59th Precinct, had been killed in a raid on a bootlegging operation during Prohibition, when she was just thirteen.

One of sixteen New York City cops to die in the line of duty in 1930, Detective James Patrick Dolan left a devastated widow and three heartbroken children. Their mother retreated into herself and never really emerged, leaving it to Mary, the eldest, to raise her two younger brothers. That she finished high school was a minor miracle, since she not only took care of the boys but also worked part-time at the local five and ten to supplement her mother's meager widow's pension. Still, she was determined to make something of herself, earned a commercial degree, and managed to land a clerical job in the administrative office. She liked to say she never actually graduated from Long Island City High School; she just moved up a grade.

As they sat together over pancakes and coffee, Fitz gave her a World's Fair progress report. The late-March weather had turned unusually warm, and there'd been no rain for more than a week, so work was moving ahead full blast.

"It's only about a month to go," he told her, "and things are looking great. The buildings are pretty much done, and they're already planting the trees, supposed to be ten thousand of them, all different kinds that Moses wants for the post-Fair park. Course, the gardens aren't in yet, but they're gonna be spectacular. The Dutch are sending a million tulip bulbs, and there'll be lots of other flowers, all coordinated to match the color schemes in the different zones."

"Gosh, Bri, the way you describe it, I can hardly wait to see it. But I guess I'll have to wait a little longer."

That gave Fitz an idea. "Say, Mary, how about I take you over there now? It's a beautiful day, I'm off duty, and I can show you around. There's already plenty to see."

She was reluctant. "I'm not dressed for a long walk. The fairgrounds are huge, aren't they?"

"That's not a problem. We have a little fleet of motor scooters. We can see the sights on wheels."

"Really? That sounds like fun! Oh, but I have to tell Mom where I'm going so she won't worry. And I wouldn't mind changing my shoes, just in case we do want to do some walking. Let's drop by my house first."

"Deal," said Fitz as he paid the check.

Chapter Eight

A fifteen-minute ride on the el took them to the IRT/BMT gate, where Fitz displayed his shield and was waved through. "Giving my girl the V.I.P. tour," he told the attendant, who nodded in approval. "She's a lot prettier than that the swells Grover brings around," he observed. Mary giggled, and Fitz explained the onerous escort duty to her.

He asked the attendant, "Anyone seen that Shadgen guy Grover's on the lookout for?"

"Not at this gate, and none of the others, as far as I know. I got his picture taped to the wall in here, so if he does show up, he won't be getting past me or anyone else manning this booth."

"We'll see you on the way out," Fitz told him. "Couple of hours, I guess, or until Mary's tired of me dragging her around. The way I get all het up about the Fair, she'll probably be bored stiff in no time. We're headed over to the City Building to pick up a scooter, so at least she won't be dragged around on foot."

As they walked arm in arm through the Communications Zone, Fitz pointed out the building where Stuart Davis' accident occurred. "Wanna go in and take a look? The mural's really interesting."

"Sure, I'd love to see it. I'm not too crazy about this one," she said, looking up at the building's façade. "I thought the idea was to imagine the future, but smoke signals aren't even modern, much less forward-looking. And how does ancient mythology fit in? Or am I being too literal? It is lively and colorful, I'll give it that. And I like the musical zig-zag. I can't imagine a future without music."

* * *

Music was what greeted them as they entered the main hall. Accompanied by WNEW-AM's Sunday morning jazz program on the portable radio, several men were at work on the mural. It was easy to identify Davis, painting vigorously with his right arm. His left arm was in a sling.

The couple watched as he applied strokes of brilliant white paint to the linear composition, which had been sketched out in chalk on the flat black background, like a giant blackboard. When he turned to load his brush, Fitz waved and got his attention.

"I hope we're not disturbing you, Mr. Davis," he called out. His voice echoed in the cavernous hall. "I'm glad to see you back at work."

"Time for a break," said Davis, laying down the brush, wiping his hand on a paint rag, and unhooking his safety harness. He walked to the end of the platform and, using his one good arm to swing himself around, got onto the ladder and descended.

Fitz introduced himself and Mary and explained his interest. "I was on duty when the ambulance picked you up. They told me you'd broken your arm, but I see it hasn't put you out of commission. It would've been a shame if you hadn't been able to finish the painting."

"Goddamn right. Excuse me," he said, turning to Mary, who assured him she wasn't offended. He tapped his bandaged arm. "It's actually a dislocated shoulder. Hit my head, too, but it was a mild concussion. They only kept me in for a couple of days. The medic said I probably rolled off the platform in my sleep, but I very much doubt it."

"What do you mean?" asked Fitz.

"I sleep like the dead. Never move a muscle all night. My wife says it's uncanny how still I am."

"Couldn't you have been uncomfortable enough on those hard planks that you'd get restless?"

"Sonny, I've slept on more floors than you've ever walked on. Not that I don't prefer my own soft bed, but my sleeping bag is plenty comfortable on the planks. There's no chance I'd roll off all by myself."

Fitz was skeptical. "I asked the maintenance man, Jeffries, whether he thought there might have been foul play, like maybe someone pushed you off. It's a routine question when there's an apparent accident like that with no witnesses, but he dismissed the idea, said there was no one around."

Davis pointed to a couple of benches near the entrance. "Let's sit over there, and I'll give you my take on it," he said. "I hope you don't mind, Miss Dolan, but I'd like to get Officer Fitzgerald's opinion."

"Certainly not, Mr. Davis," she replied. "I'm curious to know what makes you think it wasn't an accident. And please, it's Fitz when he's off duty, and I'm Mary."

"And I'm Stuart. Glad to know you both."

* * *

They turned one of the benches to face the mural and sat.

"As you can see," said Davis, "this is a huge project, nearly six thousand square feet of wall to cover. I only got the job in January, so I had to work fast. Fortunately, they accepted my proposal without changes. It's a vast topic with plenty of potential imagery, but I had to boil it down to the most significant. I want it to be stimulating and memorable. The linear style gives it more visual punch. I worked up the design and made the cartoon in my studio."

Fitz interrupted him. "Wait, you're a cartoonist? What's that got to do with the mural?" He imagined a drawing board with comic strip panels like in the Sunday funnies.

"No, not a newspaper cartoon. That's what we call the full-scale working drawing for a mural," Davis explained. "It's done in sections on big sheets of paper. Holes are punched in the lines, then the sheets are taped to the wall so the design can be transferred by a technique called pouncing. Usually it's done with a bag of charcoal dust, but since this wall is black, we used powdered white chalk. You hit the lines with the bag, and the powder goes through the holes to the wall. Take down the paper, and you have the schematic design."

"Gosh," said Mary, "that sounds like a lot of work before you even get to do the actual painting."

"It sure was, Mary. And don't forget, I couldn't even start to paint until they'd built the wall and the scaffold. The scenic artists' crew did the prep work, then I came in to supervise the pouncing and work on the painting. My original idea was to use phosphorescent paint that would glow when the room is darkened for the animated display, but it was too expensive, so I had to use ordinary white. It's only one color, which simplifies things." He cocked his head toward the mural. "These fellows know their stuff, but it's my baby, and I need to be sure it's handled the way I want."

"I heard the same thing from Mr. Feininger, the artist who's doing the Marine Transportation mural," said Fitz. "He wasn't a union member, so Mr. Whalen had to get him enrolled. I think the Fair paid his dues."

Davis leaned in. "Now you're getting to the point, Fitz. The crew is in the union they got Lyonel into, but I'm in a different union. One of the men told his boss, a tough guy named Browne, that I wasn't a member of the United Scenic Artists of America, and Browne lodged a complaint. There was arbitration, and Browne had to recognize the United American Artists, Congress of Industrial Organizations Local 60—of which I happen to be a very active member—as valid within the closed-shop rules. That did not make him happy. His argument was that, as a commissioned artist, if I work on the painting, I'm displacing a wage earner. He was even more irate when he found out I was working at night. If one of his members did that, he'd get overtime pay, but I don't. And he had no legitimate way to stop me."

"Are you saying he tried an illegitimate way? Like staging an accident?"

Davis leaned back. "That's exactly what I'm saying. I think he got one of his henchmen to push me off the scaffold. My guess is that the night watchman tipped Browne off, and he sent someone over to handle it. Just a warning, though it could've been worse. Might've broken my neck. Those boys play rough."

"Unfortunately, you can't prove it, unless there was a witness. If the watchman was in on it, he's not going to come forward."

"Of course he was in on it. He'd have to open the door for the goon."

Fitz shook his head. "I'm sorry, Mr. Davis—Stuart, that is. Without any evidence, there's nothing the police can do. As you say, you're lucky your injuries weren't any worse, and you've been able to return to work. Even if your thinking is correct, I doubt Browne will try anything more. Another accident would really look suspicious."

"Speaking of returning to work," said Davis as he stood, "it's time for me to do just that. You're right, Fitz, I can't press charges. I just wanted to get it off my chest. I'm as pro-labor as they come, so I can understand why Browne would be sore, but it burns me that he'd attack a fellow union man for exercising his rights. And I'll be damned if I'll be scared off. This job means a lot to me, and I'm going to see it through."

****

"Do you believe him? asked Mary as she and Fitz continued on their way to the City Building.

"If it's true that he never moves in his sleep, I'd have to say yes. But there's the matter of the empty whiskey bottle, which he didn't mention. Does he drink that much every night before bed, which puts him out like a stiff, or was he using it to dull the discomfort that was making him restless? With that much under his belt, he may not even remember."

As the couple entered the building, the desk clerk greeted Fitz, who introduced Mary. "She's my best girl, and I'd like to treat her to a scooter ride around the grounds. Okay if I sign out a Motor Glide?"

The clerk, whose name was Nancy, reassured him. "I won't note that you're not on duty. If anyone asks where the scooter is, I'll tell them you were called to rescue a damsel in distress. You've already got a track record in that department."

"I heard all about the Living Liquid Ladies escapade," said Mary. "I hope we can take a look at that place. I don't think his mother believed him when he described it, so I want to check that he didn't exaggerate."

"You couldn't exaggerate that one, dearie," said Nancy. "It's called the Dream of Venus, but it looks more like a nightmare to me. And the artist is just as crazy as his exhibit."

Meanwhile, Fitz had rolled out a scooter and headed to the door. "Come on, Mary, I'll show it to you. You'll have to sit on my lap, but you've had plenty of practice. Better button up your jacket, it's likely to be breezy."

Once outside, Fitz hit the ignition, and off they went. They passed through the Production and Distribution Zone, where industrial giants like Westinghouse, General Electric, DuPont and United States Steel would be showing off their latest innovations—acrylic plastic, nylon, home air conditioning, fluorescent lighting and all manner of labor-saving appliances—in displays designed to amaze and inspire. The message was that the World of Tomorrow could not be built without these technological marvels.

They crossed the bridge into the Amusement Zone and rode around the main loop. "From what you told me, I think your dad would enjoy himself here," Mary observed as they cruised past the Living Magazine Covers, Congress of World's Beauties, and Crystal Lassies before arriving at the Dream of Venus. She hopped off the scooter and gave it the once-over. "Boy, were you not kidding! Let's go in. I want to meet the Living Liquid Ladies and get the details, girl to girl."

Unfortunately, the building was locked, and their knocking didn't bring anyone to open up. "They must take Sundays off," said Fitz. "Guess we'll have to wait until the Fair opens, then we'll go in together. And up on the Parachute Jump, too." He pointed to the giant steel tower that anchored the loop road.

Mary's blue eyes widened, and she gasped in horror. "Oh, no, not me, no thank you! I don't even like standing on a ladder. You'll never get me up that high."

"Where's your sense of adventure? It'll be exciting."

"No, it won't, 'cause I won't be doing it."

* * *

"Are you warm enough?" Fitz asked as they cruised back into the main fairgrounds and turned north toward the Food Zone. Mary said yes, but he drew her a bit closer as she perched awkwardly on his knees. The breeze rustled her ash-blonde curls, and they tickled his nose.

She was a little thing, only five-foot-two and about a hundred pounds dripping wet. He'd have no trouble carrying her across the threshold, if only she'd have him. He was in love with her, and knew his feelings were returned, but he also knew that as long as he was a police officer, she wouldn't marry him. Her father's death had left too deep a wound, one that not even love could heal.

In moments like this, of casual intimacy and shared pleasure, he used to hope she might change her mind. But it was wishful thinking, and he'd given up asking her. So he'd settled for loving companionship, complicated by sexual frustration such as only a devout Catholic girl can induce. After they went together to see *Swing Time*, in which Ginger Rogers and Fred Astaire sing "A Fine Romance" to each other, they joked that it was their theme song.

When Fitz told the clerk that Mary was his best girl, he implied she wasn't his only girl. Having been on the hook for so long, he naturally considered alternatives. For that matter, so did she. They had broken up a few times, only to patch things up again. A young teller at the local bank had taken a shine to Mary, but after a couple of dates, she found him dull. One of the Long Island City High School teachers tried to get more than friendly with her, but failed. Fitz had had a fling with a fellow Police Academy cadet, training for the Women's Bureau, but it quickly fizzled out. An embarrassing blind date with a fellow cop's sister made him give up on that route to romance. Somehow, no one ever measured up. They had spoiled themselves for others.

Chapter Nine

When Fitz left the City Building to take the morning shift on Monday, he was met at the door by a tall, dark-haired man wearing a parka over paint-stained overalls.

"Good morning, Officer," he said. "Maybe you can help me. I want to report something suspicious over at the WPA Building."

"Was there a break-in?" asked Fitz.

"No, it's outside. I think it's sabotage."

Fitz took out his notebook. "Please let me have your name and occupation."

"I'm Philip Guston. I'm painting the mural on the front of the building. If you'll come with me, I'll show you the problem."

As they walked the short distance along the Avenue of Patriots in the Community Interest Zone, Guston told Fitz about the Federal Art Project.

"Since the WPA started in thirty-five, millions of unemployed people have been put back to work, mostly in construction jobs. You can see for yourself how many improvements they've made—parks, roads, bridges, housing—all for public benefit. But it benefits the workers, too, not just with money to live on but with the dignity of an honest wage for honest labor."

He lit a cigarette and offered one to Fitz, who declined. "For artists, it's been a godsend. Most of us didn't have regular jobs even before the Depression. There's no market for our work. The collectors only want blue-chip stuff, old masters or European moderns. They don't take us young Americans seriously. Before the WPA came along, I had to go to Mexico to paint a mural and only got room and board. Since then, I've gotten a weekly paycheck for painting two of them. This one's number three."

They had reached the WPA Building. On the entrance façade, his partly completed mural, "Maintaining America's Skills," was taking shape behind a scaffold. The monumental figure of a bricklayer anchored the twenty-five-foot-tall composition, which also featured a surveyor, a pneumatic drill operator, and a female scientist with a microscope, grouped in a montage of overlapping images. Their simplified forms interacted with one another in an artificially flattened space that emphasized their monumentality.

The aim, Guston explained, was to show that productive labor was supported by the federal work-relief program. The whole building would be devoted to displays illustrating various aspects of it and would offer demonstrations, lectures, and concerts by WPA artists, writers, dancers and musicians.

"There are four artists working on interior murals," said Guston, "but they're painting them on canvas panels, then they'll mount them like wallpaper. They're working in a rented scenery studio in Brooklyn, where I did my cartoon. That's what the preparatory design is called."

"I know what that is," said Fitz. "Stuart Davis explained it to me. I stopped in to see how he was making out after the accident, and he gave me the gist."

"He's one of the top WPA muralists. He really knows how to fill a wall. I heard what happened to him. How's he doing?"

"He's back at work, nursing a dislocated left shoulder. Fortunately, he's right-handed."

Guston stubbed out his cigarette. "I thought he was covering up his own carelessness when he accused someone of pushing him off, but now I'm not so sure."

"What makes you say that?"

"I'll show you."

They walked toward the entrance, an open colonnade leading to a courtyard, over which a canopy served as a platform on which the scaffold sat. To reach it from the ground, a twenty-foot ladder had been lashed to one end.

Guston pointed to the top of the ladder. "See where it's tied to the scaffold?" Fitz nodded. "Someone has loosened the rope. It's just looped around the standard. If you jerked the ladder or were unsteady as you climbed, it could come down and take you with it."

"You're sure the rope couldn't have loosened up on its own? Someone had to untie it?"

"I check it myself every night when I leave. I don't like working at night under the arc lights, can't get the color balance right. There's a lot of pressure to finish, so I come in as soon as it's light enough, usually before my assistants arrive. It was lucky I spotted it before someone got hurt, or worse. I told the men to stay off until I reported it."

"Do you have a scenic artists crew, like Mr. Davis?"

"No, we're all on the WPA payroll. The scenic guys grumbled plenty about us taking their jobs, but the building is a WPA project, and anyway, we're all members of the United American Artists union, so they have no grounds to gripe. Which doesn't mean they accept us. What I think is that they're expressing their displeasure in a more roundabout way."

"That's a pretty serious accusation, Mr. Guston. Are you asking for an investigation? In which case, I'll have to call in the detective branch." This was not Fitz's favored approach, since it would mean referring the complaint to O'Toole.

Guston relieved him of that duty. "That's why I went to report it, but I'm having second thoughts. Workers are coming and going all night. It's out in the open, so anyone could have done it. Even if someone saw him, none of the other men would rat on him. Shit, they probably put him up to it. Anyway, I'm glad I told you about it. Just in case it happens again, or something like it."

* * *

It was a short walk from the WPA Building to the Long Island Rail Road gate, so Fitz decided to find out whether any unauthorized people, Shadgen in particular, had tried to gain admission. Coming from his home in Jackson Heights, he'd be expected to try the IRT/BMT el entrance, but he might figure he'd have an easier time at the rail station. In any case, the two gates were close together, so Fitz would check them both.

It seemed more likely to him that Browne was behind what now looked like two cases of sabotaging UAA muralists, but Shadgen couldn't be ruled out. He could have changed his appearance, faked an I.D., and come in with the night shift. But why go after artists? If his beef was with Whalen and the Fair Corporation for dumping him, there were more likely targets, like the Administration Building, where his enemies hung out, or the Theme Center, where some of his ideas had been used without credit.

Fitz never passed the Theme Center—the Fair's only pure white structure—without being captivated by its magnificence. Its soaring spire directed his thoughts toward the future in a tangible way, pointing upward to the heavens, encouraging him to imagine the possibilities ahead, even as its giant globe represented the here and now, the planet we all inhabit. That anyone could dream up something like that, much less actually build it, was amazing. Now it was finished, and already offering previews for the press and the backers who had financed it. Fitz had been in a couple of times, on duty as an escort for Whalen's guests, and was just as enthusiastic about what was inside.

The earliest proposal, in simplified classical style, with two blocky towers rising 250 feet above a circular auditorium, had been scrapped as too traditional. Something visionary was called for, so the architects, Wallace Harrison and André Fouilhoux, put their team to work. They produced more than a thousand preliminary sketches, each one more fanciful than the next, with several inspired by Soviet Constructivism.

"We considered a tower fifteen hundred feet high," Harrison told the architecture magazine *Pencil Points* in April 1937, when the final design was unveiled. "We conceived of towers on top of balls and balls on top of towers. Other ideas included a large glass tower with a spiral track running up to the top, a hoop on top of a sphere with a car swooping around the hoop, various forms of theaters, great rising platforms, twin towers joined at the top, and even a great eagle holding a sphere on its back."

Such conceptual flights of fancy were interesting exercises, but the Theme Center was not merely symbolic. It also had to serve the practical purpose of housing the Fair's defining exhibit, which would distill the essence of the thematic zones to express the overarching message of enlightened planning as the basis of a prosperous and peaceful future. Attenuated towers, swooping cars, and globe-toting eagles weren't going to do the job.

The final design comprised three basic geometric elements—a triangular tower joined to a ball circled by a spiral ramp—which were both evocative and functional. Novel words derived from the Greek were coined to describe them: Trylon, a three-sided pylon; Perisphere, a redundancy that meant a round globe; and Helicline, for the ramp that curved gracefully from the Perisphere's exit, fifty feet up, around a reflecting pool to the ground. Fountains in the pool concealed the pilings that supported the Perisphere, making it appear to float above the water.

Inside the Perisphere, accessed by the world's longest escalator, visitors entered a rotunda twice the size of Radio City Music Hall and stepped onto two moving platforms that circled "Democracity," a scale model of a future metropolis called Centerton and five surrounding satellite towns, accompanied by stirring narration and uplifting music. This utopian vision unfolded in a mere six minutes, after which the spectators, suitably awed, departed via the Helicline, which offered breathtaking views of the entire exposition.

If Shadgen is hell-bent on revenge, thought Fitz, *this would be his obvious target. A couple of buckets of paint spilled onto the Democracity diorama from one of the platforms would make an almighty mess. The escalator could be disabled by a short circuit. A monkey wrench in the complicated control system could bring the whole production to a halt. With so many workers around at all hours, it wouldn't be too hard for him to slip in and do his dirty work.*

It would be a lot harder to go after Whalen in his office, where he'd have to bypass secretaries and assistants before he could get to the boss. A more likely approach would be to confront him on the street, maybe coming out of his home in Dobbs Ferry, a charming village in Westchester County, where he'd be far more vulnerable. That was way outside Fitz's jurisdiction, but he was sure he would have heard if anything like that had happened.

Chapter Ten

"Hey, Fitz, ain't you the expert on artists' mishaps?" The question came from his fellow officer, Sean Smith, who had just returned from scooter patrol in the Transportation Zone as Fitz was leaving the City Building to make the rounds.

"I guess you could say so, Smitty," Fitz replied. His accounts of the incidents were well known. "I've looked into three of them so far. Don't tell me there's been another one."

"That is what I'm tellin' you. Guy painting a wall in the Aviation Building just took a tumble down a staircase. Think maybe he broke a leg. Ambulance is on the way."

"Mind if I take the Motor Glide? I'd like to see what's up over there."

Smith handed over the scooter. "I'll tell Nancy you got it," he said as Fitz headed off.

Like the nearby Marine Transportation Building, with its twin ocean liner prows, Aviation's architecture reflected its theme. The building was shaped like a large, modern airport terminal. Inside were various types of aircraft, from a Piper J-3 Cub to a huge military transport plane, with its propellers rotating, suspended inside a half-dome on which clouds were projected to make the aircraft appear to be in flight.

Pulling up in the Aviation Building's courtyard, Fitz saw that the ambulance was already there. Inside, he found the hapless artist lying on a gurney and groaning in pain as the medic applied a splint to his right calf. He was so tall that his feet hung over one end of the gurney, and his shock of thick black hair draped over the other. His heavy moustache twitched with every application of pressure to his leg.

Hovering over him, stroking his forehead and trying to calm him with murmured words of comfort, was a woman wearing a paint-smeared apron over slacks and a sweatshirt. As Fitz approached, she looked up, and he was struck by her beauty. Her dark brown hair was tucked under a beret from which a few random curls escaped, decorating a heart-shaped face with sultry grey-green eyes, tantalizing lips, and a slightly cleft chin. She wore no makeup, and clearly needed none. A paint smudge on one cheekbone added a beguiling exclamation point to her flawless skin.

Momentarily at a loss for words, Fitz took out his notebook, fumbling with it as his tongue untied.

"Excuse me, miss. Can you tell me what happened here?"

"I told the other officer," she said. Her husky voice sent a sensual signal that he tried but failed to ignore, though clearly she had no interest in him. She was focused on the man in distress, who clutched her left hand and pleaded, "Stay with me," as the medics wheeled him out.

"Sorry, miss," said the attendant, "but you can't come to the hospital with him unless you're next of kin. Are you his wife?" He removed her hand from the artist's grip, glanced at it, and saw no wedding ring.

She noticed, and reluctantly told him the truth. "No, I'm his assistant on the mural job."

"Then I'm afraid you'll have to stay behind. Do you know who we should notify?"

"His father, I guess, but I don't know how to reach him. He was living in Rhode Island, last I knew."

"Well then, if not his father, Mr. Gorky will have to tell us who'll be responsible for him. He'll be on crutches for a while, so someone will need to come get him and take him home."

"You mean he won't be able to go back to work?"

The attendant shook his head. "No way he can climb onto that scaffold until the bone is fully healed. Could be a couple of months, maybe more, depending on how bad the break is. An X-ray will tell. Meanwhile, he should keep his weight off it as much as possible."

A mixture of distress and resignation crossed her lovely face. "What rotten luck. He had just stepped off the scaffold onto the stairs below when the step gave way. The tread must not have been fixed in place, though I've been up and down those stairs for the past couple of weeks and never noticed anything loose."

This gave Fitz the opening he needed. "You were here when it happened?"

"Yes," she replied. "I was on the top level, blocking out the solid colors. Then Arshile will fill in the motifs." She stopped herself. "Oh, no, he can't, not now. What are we going to do?"

* * *

"I need to back up a little," said Fitz. "First, let's find a place for you to sit, and you can give me the details." There were some folding chairs piled in a corner, so he set up a couple and opened his notebook again.

"I know you already spoke to Officer Smith. He's the one who told me about the accident. He knew I'd been involved in other incidents like this, so he thought I'd be interested."

She gave him a curious look. "What do you mean, like this?"

"I'll explain, but first, please tell me your name."

"Corinne West."

"And who is Arshile?"

"Arshile Gorky." She spelled it for him. "I met him when I was at the Art Students League, and we became close friends." How close was left unstated, but from her behavior, Fitz guessed their relationship was intimate. "He's originally from Armenia. He came to this country as a teenager. He had some success before the Depression hit, but when the bottom fell out, he got a WPA job and was able to make a living. For a couple of years, he worked on a large series of murals at Newark Airport. He spent a lot of time studying aviation subjects, and on the strength of that experience, he got this commission. It's a major advance for him, not just artistically. On the WPA, he got a weekly wage, only about twenty-five dollars, to paint ten large panels, which took him months. But the Fair is paying him a thousand dollars for just a few weeks' work on a single panel. For someone who's just scraped by all his life, it's a huge windfall."

She swept her hand toward the mural, titled "Man's Conquest of the Air." Much of the basic work was done, but several areas had just been sketched in, awaiting Gorky's finishing touches. The upper section was a forty-foot frieze of stylized flying machines and abstract shapes derived from aircraft components. In the lower section, framed by the staircase, the rotors, propeller, and landing gear of a Kellett Autogiro butted up against a row of windows that suggested the wings of a biplane, cleverly incorporating an architectural feature to create hybrid aircraft imagery.

"You told the medic that you're Mr. Gorky's assistant," said Fitz. "Do you think he'd authorize you to finish the mural for him?"

"I guess he'll have to. All his color studies are here. Even if he can't actually do any painting, he can supervise me. And there are a couple of WPA artists who could help. Maybe Bill de Kooning will be available. He and Arshile are like brothers."

"He'll need to be a United American Artists member," cautioned Fitz. "I assume you and Mr. Gorky are, or they wouldn't have let you work in here."

"Oh, yes. Our cards were checked. Most of the WPA artists are members. Arshile used to be quite active when it was the Artists Union. I'm not on the Project, but I signed up, too, so I could work with him."

"I'm told that the other painters' union doesn't recognize the UAA, or at least doesn't like sharing these jobs with its members. Which brings me to your 'like this' question. I hadn't forgotten."

Fitz told her about Stuart Davis' fall from the scaffold and Philip Guston's report of tampering with his ladder. "They both believe it was deliberate. Mr. Davis thinks he was pushed off in his sleep, and Mr. Guston thinks it was sabotage. That's why I'm curious about the circumstances here. Please show me where Mr. Gorky fell."

They walked over to the staircase, which led to exhibits on the lower level. The scaffold rested on two sidewalls, on which railings had yet to be installed. The stairs had been cordoned off during work on the mural. Underneath the scaffold, the top tread was cracked in half.

"In a way, it was his own fault," said West. "He should have walked to the end of the scaffold and stepped onto the sidewall, but he has a habit of jumping down from the bottom level. It's not very high, and as you saw, he's very tall, so he'll just swing his feet over and hop down. This time, when he hit the step, it just caved in. He must have had his weight on his right side, 'cause that's the leg he landed on."

Fitz crouched and examined the damage. Then he stepped over the broken tread, went down the staircase, and looked at it from below. It was a freestanding structure, so the underside was exposed. Satisfied, he came back up to continue questioning West.

"You said you were on the level above him, so you didn't see him land?"

"No, but I heard the crash, and him shout a curse word. Then he cried out in pain, and I came down as quickly as I could. His foot was right through the step, and he'd fallen on his side. I pulled the broken piece away and managed to get his leg out, then I ran outside and saw the policeman on his scooter and flagged him down. He's the one who called the ambulance."

"You had no trouble getting the broken piece loose?"

West turned her gorgeous eyes on Fitz as she considered his question, and he felt himself flush slightly. *Wow,* he thought, *what a knockout. This Gorky character is one lucky dog.*

"I didn't think about it at the time, I just went into action, but now that you ask, it's surprising how easy it was. It sort of came away, I hardly had to pull to lift it."

Fitz held up the broken tread. "This is pretty heavy-duty. It would have to be, to handle all the visitors running up and down it. How could it crack under one man's weight, even if he did jump on it? And how could you pull it loose so easily? It must have been tampered with." He flipped it over. "Look at the break. The top is splintered, but underneath the break is clean, like someone sawed it part way through. And there are no nails or screws in the end where it was attached to the sidewall, but there are holes for them. They've been removed."

Her eyes widened as she stared at the board in his hand. "You're telling me that someone deliberately tried to injure Arshile? Why on earth would anyone do that?"

"To get him off the job, and fill his place with a member of the rival union. I'll bet you dollars to donuts they'll be sending someone around to sub for him."

West was indignant. "You mean a total stranger, who never worked with him before? Who knows nothing about his aesthetic? No! They can't do that!"

"I'm afraid they probably can. Their members have most of the Fair mural contracts, and I'm sure they can make the case for one of their men to take over."

"But what if they were responsible for this?" She pointed to the broken tread. "That would be a crime, wouldn't it? You must find out who did it. Whoever it was should go to jail."

For that to happen, Fitz would need to refer the matter to O'Toole, an action he was reluctant to take for purely personal reasons. On the other hand, his sympathies were with the winsome Miss West. He believed what he'd found justified an investigation, and that was Hammer's purview.

"Keep everyone away from this area while I get a detective over here to investigate," he told her. "You won't be able to do any more work on the mural today. Maybe not for a few days. Let's see what the detective comes up with."

"I understand," she said, looking both disappointed and determined to get to the bottom of what she felt was a deliberate assault on her lover. If the job had to be interrupted, so be it. Meanwhile, she assured Fitz that she would fight to get a qualified artist to help her complete the work, instead of turning it over to an anonymous, no-nothing scenic painter.

Once again, Fitz felt himself drawn to those magnetic eyes, brimming with righteous indignation and resolution. She held his gaze and announced, "I'll get in touch with Bill. He'll know what to do."

Chapter Eleven

When the call came in to request his presence at the Aviation Building to investigate a possible case of sabotage, Clarence "Hammer" O'Toole admitted to himself that he was curious to see what was going on at the former garbage dump. He'd observed the progress from a distance, but hadn't actually set foot on the fairgrounds. In law enforcement terms, it might as well have been Siberia, where they sent the no-goodniks as punishment. But the Fair itself was shaping up, and with only a few weeks left before opening day, it would be interesting to check it out.

He ordered a patrol car to take him to the Corona Gate South. Aviation was right next to it. With its sleek styling and huge half-dome, the building was certainly impressive, as were the nearby Ford, General Motors, Firestone and Marine Transportation pavilions. If he could wrap up this case quickly, maybe he'd do a little exploring before returning to One Ten.

Officers Fitzgerald and Smith were waiting with West by the staircase. Fitz had asked Smith to make the call, since he was first on the scene, but since Fitz had found the evidence, he knew he'd couldn't avoid being there. One glance from O'Toole told him his presence was not welcome. Nor was the detective pleased to find a woman in attendance.

O'Toole was not dazzled by her charms. To him, she was just another witness, one he'd describe as a "looker," which automatically made her unreliable. "Can't trust 'em to tell you the time of day," was his opinion. "Good-looking dames think you'll fall for any line they hand you. With me, they got another think coming."

Ignoring both Fitz and West, he turned to Smith. "What have you got for me?"

Smith knew he had it in for Fitz, and also was aware of his attitude toward female witnesses, so he was prepared to take the lead. He explained the circumstances and showed O'Toole the broken tread.

"What makes you think this was done on purpose?" he asked Smith.

West spoke up. "The stairs are off limits to everyone but the mural painters. We go up and down them all the time, and never noticed any weakness. Mr. Gorky sometimes jumped down onto that step from the scaffold, and it was solid until this morning. Officer Fitzgerald saw the partial cut on the underside, and the missing nails. He said that couldn't be an accident."

O'Toole gave Fitz a hard look. "So now you're a detective, are you?"

"Oh, no, sir. It just seemed suspicious to me, that's all. I'm sure you'll get to the bottom of it." He wanted to mention the two other suspicious incidents, but thought better of it.

"Damn right I will. If there's anything to get to the bottom of." Reluctantly, he turned to West. "Who do you think is responsible?"

Failing to pick up on O'Toole's sarcasm, she complicated matters by crediting Fitz. "Officer Fitzgerald thinks it's someone from a rival union who wants the job."

"Oh, does he? Maybe he's a detective after all. Maybe I should just hand over my shield and let him solve the case."

West realized her faux pas, and Fitz silently berated himself for not warning her about O'Toole's antipathy. Smith knew the score, but she had no idea he was on the detective's shit list. So he decided to try some damage control. He was damned if he'd be obsequious, but deferential would be appropriate.

"I explained to Miss West that there's bad blood between Mr. Gorky's union and the one the scenic artists belong to. I only know this because two other artists have told me there might be some funny business going on with them, a couple of accidents that maybe weren't accidents, but they didn't want to press charges, so the matters were dropped. But when Miss West said she wanted an investigation, I asked Officer Smith to refer it to you. You're the one with the authority and experience to handle it."

O'Toole's ice melted almost imperceptibly, but enough to allow him to move on. "Who's in charge of this building?" he asked Smith, who said he'd find out. West pointed him to an office near the entrance and told him to ask for the head of maintenance, who let them in every morning. But there was also a night shift, and if it was sabotage, that's most likely when it was done, so the night man would need to be questioned. It was beginning to look like O'Toole wouldn't be getting off early after all, and that prospect did not improve his disposition.

* * *

After O'Toole finished questioning West—which Fitz had to admit was done with thorough professionalism, if not sympathy—she asked if she could call the hospital to find out how Gorky was doing. Fitz offered to take her to use the phone in the City Building.

"I'm afraid you'll have to sit on my lap," he told her. "The scooter only has one seat. But it's a short ride, just across the bridge, so you won't be uncomfortable for too long."

She smiled and chuckled, which he found unsettling. "I'm sure your lap is used to having girls sit on it," she quipped. Her seductive voice unsettled him even more, especially as he was looking forward to putting an arm around her as they rode. Even under her work clothes, her shapely body was evident. *Jeez,* he said to himself, *I'm no better than that letch, Dolly. Only now it's the other way around. She's practically encouraging me, and she's the older one. I bet she's at least thirty. Not that I have anything against older women. Christ, what am I thinking? Calm down, Brian, and act like a pro. If O'Toole can handle himself correctly, so can you.*

She retrieved her coat and purse from a row of lockers reserved for the work crew and Fitz helped her onto the Motor Glide, where she settled on his knees. She was not as light as Mary, but his arm easily circled her slender waist. They reached the City Building too soon to suit him, but she was eager to make the call and hopped off the scooter as soon as he pulled up to the door. Again, he concluded she wasn't toying with him. It was just her innate charm that came out naturally, without intending to tease. Gorky was the man on her mind, and all she wanted now was to get an update on his condition.

Nancy, the desk clerk, was immediately sympathetic, and offered to call the hospital for her. She said they'd be more likely to talk to a police representative, so West waited while Nancy dialed. She identified herself and was put through to the Emergency Department. She was told that Mr. Gorky had a broken ankle that had been put in a plaster cast. He was resting comfortably and would be discharged in the morning, unless there were complications.

"Like what?" whispered West, who was listening on an extension, hand over the mouthpiece.

"Possibly a blood clot, or a fever," said the doctor. "The skin is broken, so we need to watch for infection. Someone should come to collect him in a car or a taxi, since he'll have a lot of trouble walking until he gets used to the crutches. He said his girlfriend, Corinne, who was with him when he fell, would find someone to help him. But she has no phone, so we can't call her."

"Please tell them I'm with you and want to speak to him," said West. Nancy asked if that would be possible, but was told no, there was no outside phone in the ward.

West took her hand off the mouthpiece. "This is Corinne. May I visit him? I can take the el and be there in fifteen or twenty minutes. Then we can figure out what to do." Permission to visit was granted.

Fitz had been standing by, and offered to run her over to the subway gate on the scooter. She accepted his offer gratefully.

"I can't thank you enough for all you've done," she said as they headed out. "I don't think anyone would have believed my story if you hadn't backed me up, and it was you who spotted the tampering." When she hopped on his lap, he had to restrain an impulse to embrace her. Instead, he cleared his throat and advised, "Turn around and hold onto the handlebars. You'll be more comfortable that way. This ride is a little bit longer, but I'll have you there in no time." All business, no nonsense.

Chapter Twelve

"It's beginning to look like someone has it in for the UAA muralists," said Fitz. "I just can't believe that all three so-called accidents aren't related. I'd like to get to the bottom of it. It's going to be hard to pin it on Browne or one of his henchmen, but who else would have a motive?"

Tim put down his coffee cup, shook a Lucky Strike from a pack on the table, and lit up. He and his son had lingered over breakfast after the rest of the family were done and out.

"You know that's not your responsibility, Brian. It's a matter for the detectives now. One detective in particular. Hammer O'Toole, am I right?"

Fitz nodded. "Yeah, it's him handling the Gorky case. The other two didn't press charges, since they had no one specific to accuse. Come to it, neither does Miss West, but she's convinced that someone from the other union is to blame, and since she's more than just the guy's assistant, she has all the more reason to want justice done. And the evidence of tampering is pretty convincing, even to O'Toole."

"Don't sell him short," said Tim. "He and I don't get along, but he's a damned good detective. Just a bit too unorthodox for my taste."

Fitz sensed an opening to explore the animosity between his father and Hammer, so he decided to probe. "How do you mean, unorthodox?"

"We were in the same Police Academy class. Even then, he was a cocky little mick, had a mouth on him and wasn't afraid to use it if he disagreed with you, or even the instructors. It was just that his mind was always working, looking for the overlooked and sometimes finding mistakes or ways to improve on established procedures. That did not endear him to the brass, even when he was right, but he was an outstanding cadet in all other respects, so they tended to make allowances. Some of them even had a grudging respect for his tenacity, even if they didn't appreciate his lip.

"After graduation, we were both assigned to Five Nine, where he was just as outspoken and not well-liked in the house or on the street. The rest of us were kind of relieved when he put in for detective, since we figured it would be a good channel for his belligerence. And goddamn, it was. He was like a crusader on every case, but sometimes he carried it too far. I just didn't like his tactics."

Tim appeared ready to let the matter drop, but Fitz pressed on. "Was it something in particular, Dad?"

"Look, you have to work with the guy, so you need to form your own opinion. I don't want to prejudice you."

Fitz leveled with him. "I do have an opinion. I believe he has it in for me, but I don't know why. Do you?"

His cigarette finished, Tim stared at his empty coffee cup, poured himself a refill from the percolator, and continued.

"About a year after he made detective, I arrested a young streetwalker for solicitation. Not a local girl, from up in Spanish Harlem, working out of her neighborhood. I thought she was Puerto Rican, but turns out she was Mexican, spoke very little English. When I was booking her, O'Toole happened to be there and demanded to question her. He'd been working with the vice squad, investigating a prostitution ring based in Hunters Point, and hadn't yet identified the pimp, so he was hoping she'd give him up.

"She was already terrified when he took her into the interrogation room. I asked to be present, but he refused. He did have a police woman standing by, but he wouldn't let me in, even though she was my collar. So I stood outside, and I could hear him right through the door. He started shouting at her, maybe not realizing she didn't understand most of what he was saying, telling her he was gonna lock her up and throw away the key. Solicitation is only a misdemeanor, though she could've faced some jail time, but he made it seem like a life sentence.

"No matter how hard he pushed, she wouldn't name her pimp or give him anything on the Hunters Point ring. I think she was freelancing, so she didn't know anything about it. Then he told her if she didn't start talking, he'd have her deported. She understood that word for sure, and broke down sobbing and begging him not to send her back to Mexico.

"I was getting ready to intervene, whether he liked it or not, when he cut it short and told the police woman to lock her in an isolation cell to think it over. That's where they found her dead the next morning. She had used her stockings to hang herself from the bars. She was eighteen."

They both sat in silence for a few minutes, Tim coping with the memory of that traumatic experience and Fitz taking in the gravity of his father's revelation. But there was more.

"To my mind, O'Toole was responsible. The way he went after her was terrible to hear. He literally scared her to death. The chief was ready to mark it as regrettable and close the book on it, but I filed a complaint. The female officer very reluctantly backed me up. He was disciplined and transferred to One Ten, so it's no wonder that when my son landed on his doorstep, his deep resentment of me would be visited on you."

* * *

Walking down the Avenue of Patriots, on his way from the el station to report for duty, Fitz saw an ambulance parked in front of the Medicine and Public Health Building. *Now what?* he thought, and decided to investigate.

Inside the Hall of Medical Science, a group was gathered around a man lying under a wall above the corridor that led to the displays. A ten-by-sixteen-foot area had been marked out for the installation of a mural, for which scaffolding had been built. The ladder leading up to the platform had fallen to the floor and apparently taken the man with it. A large can of industrial adhesive lay on the ground nearby.

In addition to the ambulance crew and maintenance staff, there was a uniformed officer in attendance, his friend Smitty. He spotted Fitz and waved him over.

"Here's another artist mishap for you," said Smith. "Seems the guy was climbing the ladder when it fell over and pitched him down. He was carrying that can of glue, which may have caused him to lose his balance. Medic says he has broken bones, probably internal injuries, maybe a skull fracture. Might not make it."

"Anybody see or hear him fall?" asked Fitz.

"According to the guard, who let him in early, he was on his own in here. He said he wanted to check the wall, make sure it was smooth and ready for the canvas. That's the scenic artists' job, but this guy didn't trust them to do it to his satisfaction."

"So who is this guy?" Fitz looked down at the unconscious man, wearing painter's overalls, with dark hair and a luxuriant moustache on a head that was being cushioned by the ambulance attendant in preparation for moving him to the gurney.

"Building manager over there says his name's Ilya Bolotowsky. He's one of six painters working on murals for this area, but he's the only one ready to install. They paint 'em someplace else, then bring 'em in and paste 'em up."

"Yeah. That Guston fella told me it's like putting up wallpaper, only a lot more complicated, since they're so big and heavy." He glanced up at the canvas, which was rolled on a tube and resting on the scaffold platform. "This one doesn't look all that big, but more than one man could handle. Where's the rest of the crew?"

"There's supposed to be two assistants, due in any time now. Guess they won't be working today, with the artist out of the picture."

Fitz gave him a sidelong glance that said he didn't appreciate the pun. "Come on, let's take a look at that scaffold."

They walked over to the structure and called to the manager, who introduced himself as Lou Phillips, to join them.

"What do you think happened here?" asked Fitz.

"I think Bolotowsky was going up the ladder with the glue in one hand, so he's using only one hand to climb. Must have got most of the way up. Maybe he leaned to the side carrying the glue, shifted the ladder, and over he went."

"Isn't it pretty rare for a ladder to collapse like this?" Smith asked him.

"Sure, it's rare," Phillips replied, "but our equipment has gotten pretty heavy use in lots of other buildings. After each job, it's taken apart and sent where it's needed next. Could be rusty, especially at the joints, if the parts were left outside for a while. There is some rust on it, but that's not what caused it to fail. Take a look here." He pointed to two slightly rusty areas on the bottom crossbar. "On a small portable scaffold like this, the ladder is attached to the cross bracing with top and bottom clamps. Those marks show where the bottom ones fit. All four clamps are missing."

"Who put this thing together?"

"The maintenance crew, under my supervision. No parts were missing when we received them. I'm sure the clamps were installed."

"In other words," said Smith, "you're saying someone removed them."

Phillips nodded. "I sure am."

"So it went up yesterday, and it was okay when your crew finished it," said Fitz, who was taking notes. "That means any tampering had to happen overnight, right?"

"That's how I figure it."

"In which case, the night watchman had to let in whoever did it, unless he did it himself."

Phillips offered an alternative. "Not necessarily. Sometimes a man will work overtime to finish up a job or get things ready for the morning. He can let himself out, and the door locks behind him. Someone could have clocked out at the usual time but stayed in, so there'd be no record of him working late. No way to tell when he left."

Fitz checked his notes. "You told us the scenic artists are preparing the walls. Could one of them have stayed behind?"

Before Phillips could answer, Fitz heard a familiar voice coming toward him. Stuart Davis had rushed over from the nearby Communications Building.

"I heard Ilya had an accident. Is he all right, Fitz?" he asked, then corrected himself, "I mean Officer Fitzgerald," since his friend was in uniform.

"That's okay, Stuart, I'm Fitz to you," he said, "but I'm afraid Ilya is not all right. The ladder collapsed, and he fell off. He's very badly injured."

Davis walked over to where the unconscious artist was being loaded onto a gurney. "Jesus fucking Christ," he said under his breath. He raised his voice. "This time, they've gone too far. That bastard Browne and his thugs will pay for this!"

Smith asked to be filled in on that accusation, so they stepped aside and let the attendants roll the gurney out as Davis explained himself. He verified that Bolotowsky, like the five other artists painting murals for the building, were WPA employees and United American Artists members, therefore anathema to Browne. Since he was convinced the rival union boss was responsible for his own purported accident, as well as tampering with Guston's ladder and causing Gorky's broken ankle, he naturally blamed him for Bolotowsky's fall.

"So you think all four incidents were aimed at either scaring off or disabling UAA members so they'd be replaced by men from Local 829?" asked Smith.

"Who else had a reason to want us off the jobs?" said Davis. "This was no accident. Maybe they only meant to disable Ilya, but suppose he doesn't survive? I demand an investigation." Not only was it a potential fatality, but apparently caused by sabotage, like the Gorky case. The two were probably linked, so this was another one for Detective O'Toole.

Fitz was dreading more involvement with Hammer, but there was no way to avoid it. Again, he asked Smith to call it in, if only to delay the inevitable. At least he now knew the reason for the detective's hostility.

Chapter Thirteen

It had been a long taxi ride from Flushing Hospital to 36 Union Square, made longer by Gorky's incessant complaints about the discomfort of the cast on his leg, the awkwardness of his crutches, and his impatience to get back to work on the Aviation mural. Operating as a team, Corinne West and Willem de Kooning had managed to get him upstairs to his studio, where a pot of coffee and a plan of action were put on the front burner.

"My vork on the Hall of Pharmacy is almost done, so I should be able to get over there next veek," said de Kooning, a Dutch transplant who had yet to master the letter w in English. His mural, on a curving ninety-foot exterior wall of the Fair-sponsored building, pictured a chemist, surrounded by stylized raw ingredients and tools of his trade, formulating life-saving drugs, together with a generic family symbolizing the beneficiaries of his work. Since de Kooning was already on the Fair's payroll, he reckoned it would be no problem to move over to Aviation for the short time it would take to finish Gorky's mural.

"You are a savior, Bill," said Gorky, clearly relieved that his comrade would be available to help West complete the painting. The two men were as mismatched a pair as one could imagine. Nearly a head shorter than Gorky, de Kooning was blond and blue-eyed, in stark contrast to his friend's jet black hair and deep brown eyes. They had been close since the early thirties, when Gorky, who was making a meager living as an art teacher, encouraged his fellow immigrant to explore modernism. De Kooning was then a Sunday painter who supported himself with commercial decorating jobs, but with Gorky's guidance, he became more and more determined to pursue his own work. The chance to do just that came in 1935, when the WPA Federal Art Project began, and they both signed up immediately.

The head of the Project's mural division had recommended de Kooning for the Fair commission. One of the first muralists hired, he'd snagged a major outdoor wall, adjacent to the Theme Center and the New York City Building. It would be seen by millions of fairgoers even if they never set foot inside the Hall of Pharmacy, where they could visit the "Drug Store of Tomorrow," order a malted milk at the streamlined "Soda Fountain of the Future," and ogle the oversized products on the world's largest medicine cabinet's mirrored shelves.

"Have you had any trouble from the scenic artists?" asked West. "There's a big crew on the Pharmacy job, isn't there? Are you the only UAA painter?"

"Ja, they vere a bit surly at first, so I figured I'd join their union, too. I vas a decorator myself for years, so I know the ropes." Using American idioms always made him feel more at home in his adopted country, and he slipped them in whenever possible.

Gorky nodded. "That was a smart move, Bill. No wonder your mural has gone so smoothly. So Browne will have no cause to complain when you take over on mine. And I doubt he'd risk threatening Corinne with you in charge. Still, we must check that everything is correct before we go back to work."

She picked up on his choice of pronoun. "You said 'we.' Are you saying you'll be going to the job, even if you can't actually paint? We can't afford cabs every day, so you'll have to go by subway. Do you think you can manage?"

Navigating the stairs to the Union Square station and changing trains at Grand Central, not to mention the long walk from the Fair gate to the Aviation Building, would be challenging on crutches, especially for someone as tall as Gorky, but he insisted he would see the project through. "Just let me know when you are ready to start, Bill, and I will get there."

De Kooning and West both said okay, but averted their eyes. Gorky looked from one to the other, and realized he had offended them. They evidently thought he didn't trust them to finish the mural as he wanted it done, and he hastened to reassure them.

"Please understand. I know I won't really be needed, but I want to be on hand as the painting progresses. I promise not to interfere." He grinned, and looked a bit sheepish. "Well, not often. You have everything you need to complete the work, but I may want to make some last-minute adjustments. How can I do that if I'm not there?" He shrugged, and the grin widened.

They couldn't argue with that, and his charm won them over.

* * *

At the regular Wednesday-night open meeting of United American Artists, Local 60 of the CIO's United Office and Professional Workers of America, about a hundred members were in attendance, and Stuart Davis was holding the floor.

"Brother Bolotowsky is lying in Flushing Hospital in a coma. His fall was no accident!" he shouted, as his fist slammed down on the lectern. "Browne and his vigilantes are responsible, and they must be made to pay for their crime!" There was no microphone on the stand, but he didn't need one. His voice, booming with indignation, carried to the back of the meeting room in the UAA's headquarters at 162 West 48th Street, which had become their new home early in 1938.

Moving to Midtown from the rather shabby Artists Union offices at 430 Sixth Avenue in the West Village had been meant to affirm their recently acquired status as bona fide members of the labor-union fraternity. Not all 1,200 members were comfortable with the move, and even some of those in favor of CIO affiliation had argued against it. The rent was higher, the ceilings lower, and the atmosphere decidedly less free-wheeling bohemian. Instead of passing the hat, dues were paid at a teller's window. Nor was it conducive to the popular post-meeting parties, staples of the old Artists Union's agenda, where contentious issues were tabled in favor of drinking, dancing, and flirting.

There would be no genial socializing on this evening in late March. Davis' harangue set the tone for a militant response to what he considered a sinister effort by the United Scenic Artists of America to replace UAA muralists with their own men.

"Notwithstanding our often adversarial relationship with the police," he continued, and was interrupted by spirited booing and cries of "you said it" and "damn right." Many in the audience were remembering the picketing and sit-down strikes at Federal Art Project headquarters on King Street, where workers protested the periodic layoffs and funding reductions that threatened their jobs. The WPA was under constant attack by Congressional cost-cutters who considered federal work-relief to be nothing but a boondoggle—a waste of money on useless programs—and targeted the arts projects in particular as hotbeds of left-wing radicalism. The Artists' Union was at the forefront of efforts to counteract those attacks and even make the Project permanent.

Their tactics were not always appreciated by the New York City Police Department. When picket lines blocked the sidewalks and disrupted traffic, the cops often used their nightsticks and mounted officers to disperse the crowd. When strikers occupied the Federal Art Project offices and refused to leave until their demands were met, the cops waded in, forcibly dragged them away, and threw them in the tank overnight. As far as the artists were concerned, the police were no better than the hired goons who attacked striking coal miners and auto workers.

"All right, all right, I know how you feel," said Davis, waving his hands to quiet them, "but we must give them every cooperation in their search for whoever nearly killed brother Bolotowsky and committed other acts of sabotage. How many of you are working at the World's Fair?" Several hands went up. "Have you had any run-ins with the scenic artists?"

Lucienne Bloch rose and faced the meeting. A former assistant to the Mexican muralist Diego Rivera on his ill-fated 1932 fresco for Rockefeller Center, which was censored and removed after the artist inserted a portrait of Lenin, she was an experienced WPA alumna, respected for her mastery of the demanding true fresco technique.

"I was hired by the managers of the Switzerland pavilion to paint an interior mural," she told the crowd. "I was pouncing the cartoon when Browne sent a representative to protest. Even though it was inside the building and a foreign government was paying for it, he told the manager my UAA membership didn't count, and that if I wasn't taken off the job, his union would picket the building. Members of the other unions would refuse to cross the picket line, so all the work would stop.

"Rather than argue and possibly cause a delay, I created the composition in oil on a wood panel, in my own studio. It has a musical theme—in honor of my father, Ernest Bloch, Switzerland's foremost composer—derived from some of my studies for the frescoes I painted in the music room at George Washington High School last year. It was shipped to the Fair and scenic artists installed it. I'm happy with the way it turned out, though I would have preferred to work in situ, using fresco secco directly on the wall. It's actually better on a panel, since it can be relocated after the Fair closes. The building will be torn down, but my painting may survive. It's not terribly large, only seven by ten feet, so they should be able to find a home for it, maybe in the Swiss Consulate."

"You should have filed a grievance," scolded Davis. "They had no right to kick you out, and our attorney would have prevailed, as he did in my case." He looked around the room. "Anyone else have a beef with Browne's gang?"

"Like Lucienne," said the UAA president, Rockwell Kent, who was on the dais with Davis, "I avoided a dispute by not painting my mural on the fairgrounds. It's going in General Electric's building, and they rented a loft for me. It was actually a practical matter. For one thing, it's far too big to fit in my studio upstate. And I've been working on it for six months, so I couldn't have done it in the G-E building even if I'd wanted to. The wall it's going on is only now ready for the scenic guys to install it. I can oversee the process, but let them handle the thing."

A painter of stylized figure studies and landscapes from his extensive travels to remote regions, Kent was a charismatic and popular artist whose illustrations for *Moby-Dick* and other literary works were well known and admired. With a long history of political activism in support of workers' rights, he was an articulate spokesman for the artists' cause.

Davis turned to address him. "With all due respect, brother Kent, that doesn't answer my question. You didn't hear from Browne's henchman because you weren't there. And with all due respect to sister Bloch, she backed down before things got out of hand. I want to know if anyone here has been personally threatened or menaced."

Michael Loew stood up. "I got a warning from one of Browne's men. So did Bill, who's not here tonight," he said, referring to de Kooning. "We both have exterior murals on the Hall of Pharmacy. We got our contracts at the same time, late last fall, and we worked together on the designs so they would harmonize. Mine is a big wall on the north façade, about twenty by seventy feet. Bill's, on a long curving wall around the corner, is even bigger. We each needed several assistants, and were recruiting from Local 829's roster when the guy in charge asked if we were union members. We showed him our UAA cards, and he had a fit, said they weren't valid, threatened a Fair-wide work stoppage, the usual intimidating bullshit. I didn't know then that we could appeal.

"Bill said, let's join their union, that'll solve the problem. But the initiation fee was a whopping five hundred bucks, and we could only scrape together enough money between us for one membership. We hit some of you guys up." He looked around the room and saw several heads nodding. "We flipped a coin, and Bill won, so I handed over my sketches to the scenic guys. I have to admit they did a good job, but it was a big disappointment not to be able to work on it myself."

"You should have contacted brother Kent, or me," growled Davis. "We would have walked you through the grievance process, and you'd have been able to join the crew. Of course, they might have given you trouble on the job, but it didn't come to that. Meanwhile, Bill has had clear sailing, if only because Browne's man forced the issue and coerced him into joining."

"To tell the truth," replied Loew, "Bill had no qualms about it. He feels right at home with the scenery painters and commercial decorators. After all, he was one of them for years, though he worked for private clients and never joined the union. The only stumbling block was the up-front money, but we solved that. I didn't mind chipping in."

"Dammit, brother Loew, that's not the point," Davis insisted. "Your UAA membership entitled you to work on your murals yourselves, as I'm sure Browne's man knew perfectly well. It was coercion, pure and simple. I know it's been tried on the mural painters' society members, too, but their group isn't a trade union, so they don't have the same rights as we do. I don't think any of them joined, unless the Fair paid for it. Most of those stuck-up Beaux Arts hacks would rather walk away than stoop to such a degrading compromise."

Chapter Fourteen

Each day on his regular patrol, Fitz made it a point to stop into Communications to check on Davis' progress. He usually dropped by at lunchtime, so as not to disturb the artist at work, though Davis admitted that if Fitz hadn't shown up, he'd probably have gone right on painting and forgotten to eat.

Over sandwiches and a thermos of coffee, Davis reported on last night's union meeting. "I read a letter from Detective O'Toole. He wants the members to be on the lookout for any talk or actions that might point toward a culprit. Seems like his inquiries haven't had any results, so it's up to us to do his work for him." His tone told Fitz that was not a popular prospect.

"He's one of the best investigators we have," said Fitz, whose loyalty to the force overrode his personal dislike of O'Toole, "but when there's so little evidence, he needs all the help he can get. I'm sure your members know it's in their best interest to cooperate with him."

"Sure, they know it, but they're not happy about it." Davis took a swallow of coffee. "Listen, Fitz, you have to understand about the union. We've had several run-ins with the cops when we've exercised our constitutional right to demonstrate peacefully. Let's just say they haven't been sympathetic to our cause. And nobody likes a snitch, even in a case like this. It may not make sense to you, but that's the way they see it."

Fitz chewed on his sandwich and on Davis' information. "You know I'm sympathetic, Stuart. Maybe they'd be more willing to talk to me. O'Toole tends to come on a bit strong."

"To say the least. He grilled me as if I were the criminal. But wouldn't you be stepping on his toes?"

"Well, yes," admitted Fitz, "but maybe I could do it informally, like after a meeting when everyone is just mingling and chatting, then get one of my buddies to pass the word along."

"When we were headquartered downtown, we used to socialize after the business meeting," said Davis, "but the new offices don't have the right atmosphere, so people don't hang around. So now, once a month on a Saturday, we throw a party at someone's studio. We have a few drinks, put on some records, and dance. The next one's this Saturday. Our president, Rockwell Kent, has a big loft on Great Jones Street, so that's where it'll be. Tell you what. Why don't you and Mary come as my guests? You're more likely to get folks to open up after they've had a couple."

Fitz thought it was a great idea, but with a catch. "You'd have to tell them I'm a cop, so you don't get in trouble. I don't think it would be right to sort of infiltrate."

"That won't be a problem," Davis assured him. "Word is out. Lots of them know who you are, that you believe it's sabotage, and you're determined to find out who's responsible."

"Okay, then. I'll ask Mary if she's game and if she says yes, we'll be there."

* * *

"Where's Feinie the Heinie?" asked Frank Olsen as he and the Marine Transportation mural crew returned from lunch break.

Insisting that he wasn't tired or hungry, Feininger had continued working while the others dismounted from the scaffold and went inside the building with their lunch pails. Olsen had assured him that his newly minted union membership guaranteed him half an hour off for lunch, but he decided to stay on the job. Like Guston and the other so-called fine artists, he said the artificial night lights distorted the colors, so he wanted to take full advantage of all the available daylight.

Feininger hadn't hesitated when Grover Whelan offered him the option of joining Local 829 at the Fair's expense. At the Bauhaus, no distinction had been drawn between fine and applied arts, so he had no qualms about being classified as a scenic artist. Besides, it was the only way he could get permission to paint on the mural. When he reported for work and presented his card to Olsen, the foreman shook his hand and welcomed him into the brotherhood. Due to his advanced age of sixty-seven—a couple of the crew had grandfathers that old—his status as the mural's creator, and a work ethic that would have done credit to a much younger man, they showed him some deference, though it didn't prevent them from indulging in a bit of good-natured ribbing. Hence his nickname—perhaps inevitable, given his long history in Germany, even though he was a native-born American.

Despite his enviable diligence, at that moment Feininger was not on the scaffold. The sun was shining with full force on the mural in progress, but the artist was missing.

"Maybe he got hungry after all," speculated one of the crew. "Coulda brought his lunch and left it in his car." He walked over to where Feininger's vehicle was parked, but it was empty and locked. "Maybe he's in the can."

"We woulda seen him come in," said Olsen. "Any of you boys see him?" Several heads were shaken, and murmurs of not me, nope, and uh-uh were heard. "Guess he's just takin' a break. He'll show up soon. Let's get back to work."

With Olsen in the lead, they walked the length of the façade to the stationary ladder at the far end that led up to the scaffold, which sat on an overhang some twenty feet above the ground. As they turned the corner, they saw a man lying flat on his back at the bottom of the ladder.

"Holy shit, it's Feinie!" Olsen rushed to where the artist lay and pressed two fingers against his neck, feeling for a pulse. He couldn't find one. "Jesus, I think he's dead. Musta fallen off the ladder on his way down. Step back, guys, nothin' you can do for him now." He motioned to one of the crew. "Jerry, get yer ass back inside and call the cops."

Although not known for his sensitivity, Olsen pulled a bandana from his overalls pocket and covered Feininger's face. It seemed like the right thing to do.

* * *

"Hey, Fitz, here's another one for you," Nancy called out to him as he checked in at the City Building lobby on his way to afternoon patrol.

"How's that?" he asked.

"Call just came in. Another artist casualty. Fell off a ladder at the Marine Building. Looks like he's dead. You know the guy, Feininger. You settled his dispute with the foreman, remember?"

"Of course I remember! Sorry, I didn't mean to be rude. It's just a shock. I'd better get over there." He wheeled out a scooter and took off.

As he approached the scrum of men at the building's far end, Olsen stepped out to meet him. "Over here," he said, and led the way to the artist's body. Anticipating Fitz's initial question, he added, "I was the first to spot him on the ground. I checked his pulse, but he was gone, so I put the hankie on his face."

"Other than those actions, has he been touched or moved?"

"No. I kept everybody back and sent one of the crew to call it in."

"Good man. An ambulance is on the way." Fitz took out his notebook. "Any idea how it happened?"

"I can't say for sure. Nobody saw him fall. We broke for lunch, but he stayed behind, said he wanted to keep going in daylight as long as he could, so the rest of us went inside to eat. Maybe he got tired—he was no spring chicken, you know—or had to take a leak, decided to come down after all, and lost his balance mounting the ladder. Or maybe he slipped and fell on his way down."

"So you think it was an accident?"

Olsen gave him a quizzical look. "What else would it be? Climbing the ladder can be tricky, and you're out of your safety harness. I've seen plenty of men slip, especially when they're new on the job, like him. They grab hold and right themselves, but an older guy ain't got such quick reflexes."

"Maybe not," said Fitz, "but I won't rule out foul play. There've just been too many so-called accidents happening to muralists, one in the Aviation Building right across the way, as you probably know. This is number five, and the first fatality. It's beginning to look like a pattern of sabotage."

Olsen's expression morphed into one of disbelief. "That's crazy. Who the fuck would want to do something like that?"

"We have a detective investigating the other incidents," Fitz told him, "and I expect he'll add this one to his list, especially since there are no witnesses. This end of the building isn't visible from the courtyard, so anyone climbing up or down the ladder wouldn't be seen. Just suppose someone went up, with some pretext to get him to unhook and walk to the ladder, then pushed him over as he was turning around to step on. A straight fall from twenty feet up would certainly finish him."

"Yeah, okay, something like that coulda happened, but why? Nobody had a beef with Feinie since he joined the union. He's one of the brothers now. I mean, he was. I really respected the guy, liked him, too. So did the rest of the boys."

"So did I," said Fitz. "After we left here to get him squared away, he took me to see his murals in the art museum building. He told me about working in Germany and getting kicked out by the Nazis. He was convinced that Hitler is going to attack the rest of Europe. I hope he was wrong, but he knew a lot more about the situation there than I do. Anyway, I felt a lot of sympathy for him, so I need to know if his death really was an accident or not."

"Sure, I can see that," said Olsen, "especially with the other accidents looking suspicious. How do you figure it?"

"I was pretty sure Browne, your union boss, was behind it, since all four muralists were in the rival union. Intimidating or disabling them could open the way for his members to take over their jobs. Stuart Davis put that idea in my head right from the start. But if this case is tied to the others, that theory's out the window. Mr. Feininger was a fully paid-up member of United Scenic Artists Local 829, so Browne would have no reason to get rid of him."

* * *

Clarence O'Toole was frustrated, if not surprised, by the wall of ignorance that surrounded his inquiries. Having tracked down and interviewed every Local 829 member assigned to the Communications, Aviation, and Medicine and Public Health buildings, he had found no one willing to admit more than knowledge of the incidents. Nor did the building managers and night watchmen have anything to add beyond their assurance that they had neither seen nor heard anything suspicious. The WPA Building mural's outdoor location meant anyone passing could have done the job. Tracing the alleged sabotage back to its perpetrators was going to depend on plenty of persistence and not a little luck.

His interviews with the injured artists were equally unproductive, and in Bolotowsky's case, impossible, since he hadn't regained consciousness. Apart from being sure they were victims of the rival union's deliberate attempts to get them off the jobs, they had no idea who had actually done the deeds. All their scenic artist crew members were equally annoyed by their presence; no one stood out as especially hostile. Gorky had only one assistant, West, who was not only a fellow UAA member but also his lover, and had no motive for disabling him. Guston's assistants were all in the UAA, so that wasn't the issue. Since the tampering was on the exterior ladder, it could have been done whenever no one was watching.

Revisiting the locations was equally unproductive. With opening day approaching fast, work had commenced immediately at all four, so any trace evidence was either contaminated or obliterated. Trying to collect fingerprints from any of those places would be a waste of time and effort. The rope that held Guston's ladder had been replaced by metal clamps welded in place. New clamps had been installed on Bolotowsky's scaffold. The broken step on the staircase under Gorky's mural had been repaired. And there had been no damage to Davis' scaffold—only to Davis himself.

O'Toole figured he'd need to rely on the UAA artists to keep their ears open for any loose talk or bragging that might point to whoever was responsible. If it involved Local 829, they would likely have no qualms about reporting it. He had asked Davis to advise vulnerable muralists to be on the alert, police their own work sites, and report any suspicious behavior, like someone lurking around during lunch break or after hours. They could also be diligent about checking equipment for evidence of tampering, as Guston had done, before anyone got hurt.

But just as O'Toole was about to turn his attention to other cases, he got another call from the Fair. One more muralist mishap, this time a fatality, whether accidental or deliberate to be determined. Did Feininger slip and fall from the ladder, or did someone push him to his death? Certain he knew who was calling for an investigation of what was probably a simple case of carelessness, he cursed Fitz under his breath and ordered a patrol car to take him to what might or might not be a crime scene. At least he was on top of this one, while it was still fresh.

Chapter Fifteen

The floor-through loft, a former sweatshop, at 5 Great Jones Street proved to be an ideal space for a muralist's studio and a dance party. To ensure that the latter didn't have disastrous consequences for the former, a line of sawhorses had been stationed in front of Kent's enormous canvas, which ran nearly the entire length of the room.

"Electric Power," fifteen feet tall and fifty feet long, depicted electricity in archaic and modern guises, from its magical properties and early chemical experiments to contemporary power plants and electrical machinery. On one side, where superstition ruled, alchemists and conjurers turned their backs on the modern world. On the other, trailblazing women and bare-chested workmen marched toward a utopian future. Hand tools were discarded in favor of mechanization. In a gesture lifted straight off the Sistine ceiling, the idyllic World of Tomorrow was illuminated by a spark generated from a high-tension wire to a symbolic couple floating in the night sky.

The host was happy to give his fellow artists the opportunity to admire his magnum opus, which was scheduled to move out the following week. The canvas would be dismounted from its stretcher, rolled on a tube, shipped to the General Electric pavilion, re-stretched, and installed in a prominent position in the Exhibits Hall, where a model appliance store, a fully operational television studio, and an X-ray machine showing the innards of a genuine Egyptian mummy were the featured attractions. Technically, it wasn't a mural at all, but a giant portable painting, independent of the wall. Like Bloch's much smaller painting for the Swiss pavilion, it could be removed and relocated after the building was demolished. G-E had paid Kent a handsome fee for his huge allegory, and they intended to get as much mileage out of it as possible.

By the time Mary and Fitz arrived, a little after nine p.m., the party was in full swing. There must have been close to a hundred people, but the loft was plenty big enough to handle the crowd. A makeshift bar had been set up at the back—each member had chipped in fifty cents to stock it—with a stack of paper cups and a bucket of melting ice anchoring either end. Kent's two assistants had been recruited to bar-tend and make sure no one hogged the liquor.

Those who weren't glued to the bar were clustered in animated groups, smoking and joking, while couples danced to selections playing on Kent's General Electric H-708 radio-phonograph console with an automatic record changer, one of the perks that came with his commission. It was getting a workout tonight.

Fitz and Mary spotted Davis, who was deep in conversation with Kent, in front of the section of his mural dominated by a giant turbine and a surging crowd. One of the leaders strongly resembled Kent himself.

Davis was chuckling. "Last time I saw this painting, that guy lunging forward had a full head of hair and a round nose. Now he's bald, and his nose is pointed. Reminds me of someone I know."

"You caught me, Stuart. It'll be our secret."

"I see you didn't change his flat belly to more closely resemble the middle-aged paunch that goes with the new head."

"I'm not a realist. The whole composition is idealized."

"Then you should have left the hair."

Fitz and Mary interrupted their banter. Davis had forewarned Kent that one of his guests was an off-duty police officer. As he introduced them, Mary looked distracted. She apologized for her rudeness. "I'm sorry, Mr. Kent, but I can't take my eyes off your painting. It's just amazing."

Charmed by her guilelessness, and pleased by the compliment, Kent replied, "As Stuart has been telling me, the painting is much better looking than I am, so I don't blame you for preferring it to me."

"Oh, I didn't mean that," she flustered. "It's just that it's so impressive. And so complicated. How did you put it all together?"

Now it was Kent's turn to dish out a compliment. "Putting it together is exactly the right way to describe the process," he told her. "It's not unlike what Stuart did with his communications theme, though his style is very different. It involves finding appropriate subject matter by looking back in history and bringing it up to the present, but also looking toward the future. Electricity's potential to improve human life is enormous. Look at what the Tennessee Valley Authority is doing to bring power to rural communities all over the South. Look at Boulder Dam, with its huge generators powering the West. Incredible engineering feats, showing what we can achieve if we have the resources and, above all, the will to dream big. That's what the Fair is all about."

As the charming young woman hung on his every word, Kent decided to devote some personal attention to her aesthetic instruction. "You fellows won't mind if I steal Miss Dolan for a few minutes," he asked rhetorically. "I'd like to explain why I included some of the more obscure imagery, like a witch's cauldron, in a painting about electricity."

"Watch out for him, Mary," cautioned Davis. "He's between wives."

"Not true, Stuart. Frances and I are amicably separated, but I'm not a free man. Mary is perfectly safe with me."

"Glad to hear it," interjected Fitz drily. "I'll leave her in your keeping while I get us both a drink. Be back before you know it."

"I'll go with you," said Davis. "I could use a refill."

* * *

Making their way toward the bar, they passed a small group in earnest conversation, dominated by a shrill female voice.

"Goddamn it, Balcomb, why did you volunteer to finish Ilya's mural? You knew I was up for the job!" This from an auburn-haired woman whose curvaceous figure was topped by a homely face, now distorted in anger.

"I knew nothing of the sort, Lee," answered the tall, rangy man she called

Balcomb, whose tone was level to the point of condescension. "Besides, it's not up to me. Diller is in charge of assignments, and I'm already working on a mural for that building, so I was the natural choice. He asked if I'd do it, and I said yes. Simple as that." Burgoyne Diller, head of the Federal Art Project's mural division, was an abstract painter himself and worked hard to get assignments for his fellow abstractionists—no easy task when the sponsoring locations could be counted on to prefer pretty pictures of things they could recognize.

Balcomb's dismissive answer didn't satisfy the woman he called Lee. "Don't hand me that. You *knew* because I *told* you I wanted that job, and you could have told Diller. You also know I was passed over for that mural and two others, and the one I'm supposed to be getting at the radio station is stalled. And you know damned well that I'm the go-to artist for finishing other people's murals when they get fired or quit."

"Poor Lee, always a bridesmaid."

That unsympathetic wisecrack prompted Lee's boyfriend, Igor, to leap to her defense. With a few drinks under his belt, he was ready to make it physical.

"You will apologize to Lee," he began, his heavy Russian accent made even thicker by alcohol, "or I will, as you Americans say, knock your block off."

Balcomb recognized a bluff when he heard it. Although also tall and well built, Igor was far too vain to risk a punch that might disrupt his handsome features. A black eye or broken nose would seriously compromise his seductive allure, and he couldn't afford to have a cracked tooth repaired.

"Take it easy, Igor. No offense, Lee. Just stating the obvious. Don't worry, Diller assured me he's pushing ahead on the radio station project." The WPA had chosen five muralists to work on decorations in the lobby and studios of WNYC, New York City's municipal radio station, on the top floor of One Centre Street. And more spaces might become available as the project progressed.

"They have no objection to abstract art, fits in perfectly with their music programming," Balcomb said. He spotted Davis and gestured to him. "Hey, Stuart, aren't you painting a radio station mural? Come and reassure Lee that the work is underway. She seems to think it isn't happening."

Davis approached Lee with a friendly smile. "Balcomb's right, WNYC is going ahead, though I had to put my assignment on hold while I'm working on the World's Fair mural. I'll be able to get back on the WPA payroll after I finish creating an art-filled future for the World of Tomorrow."

Lee was not pacified. "Don't sound so smug, Stuart. You have so much work you need to keep your WPA job on ice while you get paid four times as much by the Fair. Igor and I are each getting a lousy ninety-one bucks a month on the Project. It's a good thing we're living together, or we wouldn't be able to afford to live at all."

She turned to Igor. "Get me another drink, will you?"

"Always at your service, lyubimaya," he replied with a suave bow, then turned and headed to the bar, weaving slightly as he made his way through the crowd.

"A peace offering, Lee," said Balcomb as he held out a pack of Camels. She took one, and he lighted it for her. "I prefer Chesterfields," she announced.

"I've waited four fucking years to get a decent wall," she continued, still nursing her bitterness. "Why couldn't Diller have got me into the WPA Building? Okay, it wouldn't have paid as well as a commission from the Fair, but think of the exposure. And why not a Fair commission? Diller could have recommended me. Even in a boring place like Medicine and Public Health, you'll have more visibility than I'll ever get at WNYC, where only the broadcasters will see my mural—if it ever gets painted, which looks like a big if to me, despite what you and Stuart think. You've already got your assignments, but all I have is a definite maybe."

Standing behind Davis, Fitz was taking in Lee's rant with interest. With so few opportunities for abstract painters to get WPA mural assignments, she was envious of those who had them, and even more resentful of those with Fair commissions. With a history of equal pay for equal work, the WPA was a model of parity for male and female artists, yet here she was being sidelined. Was it because she was a woman, or had she been just too good at damage control, making her more valuable in that role than as a muralist in her own right?

Fitz began speculating silently. *What lengths would she go to for a shot at a Fair mural, even if it were only a mop-up operation on someone else's painting? Like Bolotowsky's, or Guston's, or Gorky's, or even Davis'? And if she were the saboteur, how could she have gained access to the fairgrounds? Maybe her union card would be enough to get her through the gate. She could have made up a story about being assigned as an assistant to one of them, then...*

His thoughts were interrupted by Davis himself, introducing him to Lee Krasner, Balcomb Greene, Greene's wife Gertrude—who had observed Lee's verbal attack on her husband with amused detachment—and the recently returned Igor Pantuhoff, brandishing two paper cups of rye on the rocks. He decided not to mention Fitz's employer, the NYPD, and instead presented him as a friend who worked at the Fair. True, but hardly the whole story.

When asked what his job was, Fitz tactfully took Davis' hint and said, "Security patrol. I have to keep an eye on Stuart to make sure he doesn't fall off the scaffold again." That got a laugh all around. "Right now, my job is to rescue my girlfriend from Mr. Kent, and I promised her a drink, so please excuse me," he said, and headed toward the destination Igor had just left.

Chapter Sixteen

"Who is that good-looking redhead at the bar?" asked Elaine Fried. "I've never seen him before. Do you know him?" Her questions were addressed to Mercedes Carles, who quickly sized up her friend's motive.

"If you're hoping for an introduction, I can't help you. He's a stranger to me, but if I'm any judge, he won't be a stranger to you for long. Just don't let Bill catch you making eyes at him."

"Oh, Merci, you know better than that." Elaine turned toward the room full of partygoers.

"Right now, Bill's over there, making eyes, as you put it, at the pretty young thing standing next to Rockwell. I'd say she's about my age. The old goat just may charm the pants off her, and she wouldn't be the first. I certainly wasn't."

Elaine Fried and Willem de Kooning had been a couple for over a year. Studying at the Leonardo da Vinci Art School and already determined to be an artist, she had only just turned twenty when she set her cap for him. Fourteen years her senior and not long beyond his commercial art career, Bill was already a respected up-and-coming modernist who had blossomed under WPA auspices. Elaine had been told he was one of the two best artists in New York—Gorky being the other—and she was determined to meet him. She freely admitted that she threw herself at him, ostensibly wanting to become his student but really looking for romance, and she found it. Turned out the feeling was mutual. The sparks that flew between them were as powerfully electric as anything in Kent's G-E mural.

Bill had had a couple of live-in relationships before Elaine came along, and she had been shacking up with a fellow painter before moving in with him. Technically, she was still living at her family's home in Brooklyn, but she often stayed over at Bill's studio. He really was giving her art lessons, but when it came to sex, she needed no instruction from him.

Their flaming love affair, still burning brightly, did not inhibit either of them from playing the field. Monogamy was alien to them, so Elaine was not at all surprised to see Bill making a move on a pretty young woman. Nor would he have been shocked to find her cozying up to the attractive stranger, in whose direction she now headed.

* * *

Things at the bar were not going smoothly. There were no soft drinks, not even seltzer. The only mixer seemed to be ice, and that was quickly running out. Fitz certainly wasn't going to offer Mary straight rye or bourbon, and the only alternative was gin, also a definite no. He wasn't teetotal, like his father, but hard liquor had been the family curse, and he'd made a deal with himself not to fall victim to it, much less offer it to Mary, who would assume he was trying to get her drunk.

This provided Elaine with just the opening she needed. Edging up to Fitz, she touched his arm in a friendly way and confided, "There's some beer in the back room. I've got a private stash. Would that solve your problem?" Actually, the beer belonged to Kent, who had hidden it away before the party, but Elaine had spotted it while looking for the toilet.

Fitz turned to reply, and had the same sort of momentary paralysis he'd experienced with Corinne West. This unknown woman was, if possible, even more beautiful. Her strawberry blonde hair fell to her shoulders in waves, framing the exquisite features that looked up at him with an impish expression. Her amber eyes sparkled with mischief.

Used to this sort of reaction from men meeting her for the first time, she took Fitz's silence as affirmative. "Grab some cups and follow me," she said, and guided him to a side door that led to a storeroom, the former shop manager's office, and the toilet. If any of the other visitors to that facility had noticed the cases of beer resting against the office wall, they were too polite to raid them. Elaine, on the other hand, thought nothing of helping herself and sharing the spoils with what she hoped would be her next conquest. She was a year younger than Fitz, but far more experienced in seduction.

A few steps behind her, Fitz took in a rear view that was almost as alluring as the front one. Elaine's slender body, admired by the artists and fashion illustrators for whom she modeled, swayed gracefully under her clothing. A sheath skirt showed off her perfect legs, and a soft wool sweater invited a caress. The need to rescue Mary from what were now two male admirers suddenly seemed less urgent.

"I'm Elaine, by the way," she said over her shoulder as she opened the side door.

Fitz found his voice. "Nice to meet you, Elaine, I'm Brian, but my friends call me Fitz."

"Hello, friend Fitz. Come this way."

Most of the space was in shadow. The only light was a bare bulb hanging from the ceiling outside the office, and another inside the toilet, where an open door advertised its purpose. A musty smell permeating the room did not invite them to linger, but Elaine appeared to be in no hurry. "Over here," she said, pointing to some wooden crates, marked Ruppert Knickerbocker, inconspicuously stacked in a dark corner.

"New York's own beer, made right here in Yorkville. Do you like it?" she asked. Fitz said he did. "I never drink anything else," she lied. "Rockwell was kind enough to order some just for me, but I'm happy to share with you, friend Fitz." She pulled out a bottle, expertly popped the cap on the office windowsill, did it again, and handed one to him.

If Fitz had been thinking straight, he'd have wondered why their host would order four cases of beer for a single guest, but right now he wasn't thinking straight. Elaine had that effect on men. Her natural magnetism drew them to her, and she seldom took the trouble to repel them. Never mind that Fitz had left a date outside who was probably wondering what had happened to him. That was of no concern to Elaine. Her preoccupation at the moment was how to jump his bones.

She raised her bottle and asked, "What shall we drink to?"

"The union," he suggested.

"The union it is," she agreed, savoring his unintended endorsement of her intentions, and their bottles were ritually clinked.

"I haven't seen you at the meetings," she said. "I certainly would have remembered a handsome face like yours." She tilted her head and moved a little closer to him so she could get a better look. "Are you a new member?"

He explained that he was Stuart Davis' guest, and that the two had met at the World's Fair, where he worked in security. He started to tell her about the series of artists' mishaps, but she cut him off.

"Yes, I heard there'd been some trouble. Frankly, the whole thing leaves me cold. I've never been there, and don't plan to go." Another fib. Bill had taken her a couple of times to see how his Hall of Pharmacy mural was progressing. Now it was done, and he planned to start work on Gorky's Aviation mural on Monday.

Fitz was surprised by her attitude. "Really, Elaine, you should take a look. I'll be glad to show you around. Once you're there, I know you'll be impressed. It's a fantastic vision of the world to come. You can't help but feel uplifted."

She gave him a look that said different. "It's nothing but a giant salesroom disguised as a utopian dream, which anyone who reads the papers will tell you bears no resemblance to the future we can expect. Peel away the platitudes and what's left is pure hucksterism."

"Honestly, I'm sure you'd change your mind if you saw it for yourself. Can't I persuade you to let me be your guide?"

Of course you can, you April fool, she said to herself. And out loud to him, with a sigh and a squeeze of his arm, "Oh, all right. I guess I can give you a chance to convince me."

There was a little extra tick in his chest. "How about tomorrow?"

They exchanged last names and arranged to meet at the IRT/BMT gate at one o'clock on Sunday. She said she'd be coming up from her parents' house in Sheepshead Bay after morning Mass, but she hadn't set foot inside

St. Mark's in years, and she'd be leaving from Bill's place on West 22nd Street. She had moved in with him.

* * *

Trying to sound sincere, Fitz apologized to Mary for the delay and explained why it took him so long to bring her a drink. His account of the nice lady—didn't catch her name—leading him to the beer did not include a description of her.

Kent took the news in stride. "I should have thrown a blanket over those crates," he said. "Someone was bound to spot them. Can't blame her for helping herself and sharing the bounty with a needy soul."

Now it was Fitz's turn to apologize to Kent. "She told me you ordered the beer especially for her. I guess I should have realized she was just saying that so I wouldn't feel guilty."

The news delighted de Kooning. "I could use a beer chaser for my viskey. Is that okey-dokey vit you, Mr. President?"

Kent clapped him on the shoulder. "Go ahead, Bill, help yourself. Just leave some for me and my assistants. Painting a mural is thirsty work."

De Kooning nodded earnestly. "Ja, I know that for sure."

"It's hard to resist Bill," said Kent as de Kooning headed toward the storeroom. "I must say you did an admirable job, Mary. He tried all his best moves on you, and I've seldom seen them fail."

"He was very charming, with his cute Dutch accent, but I'm spoken for." She smiled up at Fitz and slipped her arm through his, making him feel even more guilty about his flirtation with the woman who, unknown to him, was de Kooning's lover.

"He offered to show me his Pharmacy mural, and I think he was a bit disappointed when I told him I'd already seen it the day you took me around. I just said you work at the Fair, not what you do there."

"I know you're a police officer," Kent told Fitz. "Stuart filled me in. He said you agree that someone is targeting muralists, especially since Feininger's death, which you think was no accident. He told me you offered to nose around informally, to see if you could pick up anything that might point to the saboteur without directly questioning people. He didn't announce it to the membership, but it's no secret. Some of them have seen you on the fairgrounds. Philip over there knows you're a cop," he said, pointing across the room toward Guston, dancing cheek to cheek with Mercedes Carles; his marital status notwithstanding, they were rumored to be an item. "So does Corinne. I'm surprised to see her here on her own. She's devoted to Gorky, but he's nursing a broken ankle. No dancing for him tonight."

"Speaking of dancing," said Mary, "I'd love to. How about it, Bri?"

They finished their beers, thanked Kent for them, and headed over to the record player, which was working hard to be audible over the general hubbub. As they approached, someone called out a request. "Put on that new Johnny Messner platter." The disk dropped, the tone arm swung into place, and the strains of a fox trot were heard. Fitz took Mary in his arms, and they began to dance to "Dawn of a New Day."

"Hey," said Fitz, "that's the World's Fair theme song! The Gershwins wrote it specially for Grover Whalen. He plays it over the loudspeaker whenever he has guests. I know it by heart." When Bobby King's vocal began, he sang along:

"Sound the brass, roll the drum
To the World of Tomorrow we come
See the sun through the grey
It's the dawn of a new day"

This coincidence provided the perfect opportunity to explain his need to visit the fairgrounds on Sunday.

"That reminds me. Grover has a special V.I.P. group coming in tomorrow, so I'll have to run over there right after Mass. Hope it won't take too long." He found it was easier to lie to her while they were in motion than it would have been standing still.

Chapter Seventeen

They left the party just before midnight. It was a mild night, and a light drizzle had begun to fall. Fitz grabbed a newspaper from a corner trash can and held it over Mary's head as they made their way to the Bleecker Street subway station's uptown entrance.

"Did you learn anything useful, Bri? Come on, I'm dying to know."

"Maybe I did, but I'm not sure. Wait 'til we get inside."

He ditched the paper in the station bin. As they approached the turnstiles, he fished two nickels out of his pocket and handed her one. There were several other people on the platform, and they recognized a couple of them from the party, so they walked down to one end where they wouldn't be overheard.

He told her about eavesdropping on Lee Krasner's argument with Balcomb Greene. "She was really angry about not getting a World's Fair job. Said she's been passed over in favor of other WPA muralists. I guessed she was talking about Gorky and Bolotowsky, or maybe people working in the WPA Building. She wanted to finish Bolotowsky's painting, but the supervisor, a guy named Diller, gave the job to someone else. It made me wonder if she could have engineered those accidents in the hope of taking over."

"I had a little run-in with her myself," said Mary. "That tall, dark, and handsome Russian guy who cut in on us turns out to be her boyfriend, and she wasn't happy about him dancing with me. He was holding me entirely too close and whispering in my ear."

"Right, Igor. I met him when Stuart stepped in to calm Lee down. You're too smart to be swept off your feet by a smooth operator like him."

"He didn't even get to first base before Lee spotted us and cut in on us herself! I've never seen a girl do that before. He took it in stride, actually seemed more amused than annoyed. He probably picked me up just to get her goat."

"Seems like it worked. Young, beautiful, a dynamite dancer, who wouldn't be jealous? Especially a girl with at least ten years on you and, as Mom would say, ill-favored."

Mary giggled. "What a quaint expression. But you may have noticed that, from the neck down, Lee has plenty going for her. I wouldn't mind having a figure like that."

"You're perfect just as you are," said Fitz earnestly. "Curves in all the right places. Igor certainly admired them." He put his arm around her and gave her an affectionate squeeze, reminding himself how much he cared for her, even though he knew where to draw the line.

The train pulled in and they headed up to Grand Central, where they'd change for the Long Island City train. Once they were seated, Mary circled back to Lee as a suspect.

"If she wanted the jobs Diller could have got her, what about Stuart's mural? That's not the same kind of deal as the others. She wouldn't have been in line to finish it, so why sabotage him? She's even less likely to have pushed Feininger. He wasn't on the WPA."

"Yeah, you're right, she is a long shot. It's just that what she said made me think the motive might be envy. Someone who got passed over and wants revenge. I'm sure there are plenty of WPA muralists who'd jump at the chance of a Fair job, with much higher pay and far more visibility. Even if the paintings are only temporary, millions of people will see them."

"Or maybe it isn't a WPA artist. How about that other group, the snooty one that won't let their members join the scenic union?"

"No, I don't see that. They can't work on the murals unless they join, so what would they gain? It has to be someone who would benefit. I wonder how many UAA members tried to get Fair jobs and failed. You don't have to be on the WPA, though I guess most of them are. Corinne West told me she's not. Maybe I can find out who got rejected, then check with Stuart to see which of them belong to the union."

Mary narrowed her eyes at him. "That would mean going to the Fair office and rummaging through the files. How do you think O'Toole would like that? You're already snooping around behind his back, but that would really be trespassing on his territory."

"I guess you're right," Fitz admitted, "but Stuart might have some ideas. He's convinced Browne is behind it, and I don't know how he'd feel about the idea that one of his own union members might be responsible. He could be reluctant to point the finger at anyone, but then again, he really wants to find out who's guilty, especially now that someone's been killed."

"Or slipped and fell," Mary reminded him. "You told me there was no evidence to point one way or the other. Maybe Feininger's death has nothing to do with the other injuries. Suppose it really was an accident."

* * *

It was still drizzling on Sunday morning when the Fitzgerald and Dolan families emerged from St. Patrick's after Palm Sunday Mass. Fitz repeated his lie about doing escort duty for Grover Whalen and took the el to the Fair, where he waited in the station for Elaine to appear. His uniform and gear were in his locker in the City Building, but he wouldn't be needing them today.

Not known for punctuality, Elaine arrived twenty minutes late, without apology. She was used to having men wait for her and considered it her due.

Fitz's annoyance vanished at the sight of her. "I was afraid you'd forgotten our date," he said by way of letting her know his concern, which she brushed aside.

"Well, here I am, ready to be impressed, though not necessarily favorably. I'm going to take a lot of convincing."

"Let's get to work on that," he said. The man at the gate recognized Fitz and waved them through, with an appreciative smile to Elaine.

The light rain had let up when they left the shelter of the station's canopy, and the sun peeked out briefly, making the damp pavement sparkle. Fitz took it as a good sign, though he had been looking forward to huddling close to Elaine under his umbrella. She hadn't bothered to bring one, relying on a chic belted raincoat and a wide-brimmed rain hat. She took off the hat, pocketed it, fluffed her hair, and gratified Fitz by slipping her arm through his.

"Lead on, friend Fitz," she exclaimed, contradicting herself by taking the lead.

He steered her toward the Theme Center, describing the concept behind the Fair and how the Trylon and Perisphere symbolized the present and the future. Her response was to question why a giant statue of George Washington was looming in the background.

"What's a dead president got to do with the World of Tomorrow? Or even the World of Today?"

"It's the hundred and fiftieth anniversary of his inauguration, here in New York City," Fitz explained. "That was the original excuse for the Fair. It'll open on the actual day, April thirtieth, less than a month from now. The way I see it, Washington represents our democracy. That's the foundation of our future, isn't it?"

"Not if Hitler has anything to say about it," she countered. "Quite apart from which, that style of sculpture is as dead as Washington. And that goes for the rest of these statues." She swept her arm toward Paul Manship's fountain figures, "The Moods of Time" and their companion sundial, "Time and the Fates of Man," John Gregory's "Four Victories of Peace," and Carl Milles's "The Astronomer," and pronounced them a bunch of academic throwbacks. "They couldn't be more retrograde. Hitler would certainly approve."

She was equally dismissive of most of the murals, which she called glorified posters, not real art. She made an exception for Fernand Léger's abstraction, some thirty feet tall, on the north wall of the Consolidated Edison building. Simplified chimney stacks of Con Ed's East River power plant and schematic transmission towers, set off against a cubistic New York skyline, were topped by a kite-and-key motif representing Benjamin Franklin's famous experiment to demonstrate the electrical power of lightning.

"I happen to know the artist," she told Fitz. "He's fascinated by all things mechanical, so it was the perfect fit for him. He's a famous French modernist who came to this country last year to escape the Nazis. The Rockefellers hired him to paint a mural for their apartment. Their architect designed this building, and he gave Léger the commission. He couldn't join the scenic artists' union because he's a refugee, so he had to turn his design over to them to do the actual painting."

"How do you know him?" asked Fitz.

"Through a mutual friend, an artist who looks up to him and speaks some French. Léger speaks hardly any English, so he needs people to translate for him, and my friend Bill volunteered. The Dutchman you met last night at the party.

"As a matter of fact, Bill painted a mural here, too. It's not as abstract as Léger's, but it's much more modern than most of what we've seen. He showed me his sketches, and I'd love to see the finished product. It's on the Hall of Pharmacy. Do you know where that is?" Not that she didn't, but she couldn't tell him that.

He knew every inch of the fairgrounds and took her straight to it. They stood in front of the huge wall, and Elaine enthused over the design.

"See how he's balanced the curves and angles, so the organic and the geometric elements are in perfect harmony. Of course, the subject matter has to reflect the building's theme, so the imagery needs to be appropriate. You can't just paint whatever you like. But Bill has worked like that before, on commercial jobs, so he didn't consider it a handicap. He says it doesn't matter what you paint as long as you paint it well. I wish I were that practical."

Chapter Eighteen

The damp weather had not slowed the pace of work as opening day approached. With almost all the building construction, exterior murals, and outdoor sculpture installations finished, scores of landscapers were putting in the greenery and floral plantings, including the million tulip bulbs donated by The Netherlands.

The most intensive activity was now happening indoors, where thousands of displays were nearing completion—some of them highly complex, like General Motors' Highways and Horizons exhibit, with its Futurama ride over an imagined landscape of twenty years ahead, filled with radio-controlled cars cruising along high-speed motorways, engineered farms, and cities with separate routes for pedestrians and motor traffic. Fitz offered to show it to her, but she wasn't interested. Nor was she enthusiastic about visiting Democracity, with its optimistic vision of progress and prosperity.

"To tell the truth, I don't want to think about the future, whatever it's going to be. I guess I have a pretty gloomy outlook, considering the political situation. What will happen to me, with a German last name, when we go to war with Hitler? Will I be ostracized, or worse, like my father was during the last war? The Frieds have been here for generations, but he was treated like the enemy."

"That worried Mr. Feininger, too. He was a native New Yorker, but his wife and kids are German-born, and anyway their name would mark them. He believed war is coming soon. Do you?"

"I hope not, but everyone I know says it is, and we'll be dragged in again." She shook off her mood and brightened up. "I want to live for today, and take all it has to offer. Show me something I can enjoy right now."

"I know," he said. "Let's go see Mr. Feininger's murals in the art building. They're really beautiful, and he told me what they represent, places from his European travels. How about it?" He decided not to share Feininger's fears of what would happen to those places during the war he had been sure was imminent.

They walked past the City Building along Front Street, which led straight to Masterpieces of Art. Movers were unloading crates from trucks parked near the entrance.

"They have loans worth millions from museums in New York and all around the country, even from overseas," Fitz explained. "This is going to be one terrific exhibit." They climbed the steps to the loggia, he flashed his shield to the guard at the entrance, and they were let into the courtyard.

Even under an overcast sky, the paintings' warm, earthy tonality brightened the walls. Elaine responded favorably. She walked slowly around all four sides of the courtyard, observing the compositions close up and at a distance. Fitz admired her focused attention, as well as the graceful sway of her body as she moved along the walkway. While she studied the murals, he studied her.

"I've seen some of his work at the Modern," she told Fitz, "but I think of him as a printmaker and illustrator, not someone capable of work on this scale. These scenes must have had deep meaning for him. It's almost as if he wanted to paint them as large as life, so he could enter them in his imagination."

"What a lovely way of putting it," said Fitz, amazed by her intuition. "He talked about his nostalgia for those places, and how the fragmented areas might represent the way memories are never complete. I thought that was very poetic." He paused, uncertain how far to go with Feininger's musings.

Elaine completed his thought. "He was probably afraid he'd never see them again, and now he never will."

* * *

With typical impulsiveness, Elaine took Fitz's hand and pulled him toward the entrance. "Let's go inside. I'd love to see how they're arranging the masterpieces."

"Hold your horses," he cautioned. "I'd better check with the guard before we go barging in. You wait here, I won't be long."

He returned a few minutes later with a smile on his face. "It's okay, we can go in. I told him you need to use the restroom, and that I'll make sure you don't walk off with a priceless painting."

"And he believed you?"

"The part about the restroom, yes. He doubted I could keep you honest."

"That man is a good judge of character. One look at me and he knew a hardened criminal when he saw one."

The single-story, flat-roofed building—shamelessly echoing Mies van der Rohe's German pavilion at the International Exposition in Barcelona a decade earlier—was laid out on a rectangular plan, with projecting wings for the loggia and rear galleries. The restrooms were at the back. After the building opened to the public, they would be accessible from the courtyard, but the guard said, for now, the only way to them was through the galleries. They were also told that the ladies' lounge was still under construction, so only the men's lounge was open. This was a matter of indifference to Elaine, though Fitz offered to prevent embarrassment by standing watch outside. When they were out of the guard's earshot, Elaine reminded him that she didn't really need to use the restroom at all.

The exhibition spanned five centuries of European art, from Gothic to Baroque. The first gallery they entered was actually the last chronologically, French 18th century. Installers were busy positioning paintings around the room. They passed an open crate marked "Musée du Louvre, Paris," in which Jacques-Louis David's portrait of Marquise d'Orvilliers was cradled. Elaine stopped to admire it.

"I must tell my friend Arshile to come see this. He's crazy about David."

"You mean Arshile Gorky, the guy who's painting the abstract aviation mural? That is, he was, until he broke his ankle, or had it broken for him. This doesn't seem like something he'd go for."

"It has nothing to do with the style or the subject. Whether it's figurative or abstract, the building blocks of art are the same. This painting is superbly organized, and the handling of texture is fantastic. You'd be surprised how much modern artists learn from studying works like this."

"I'm sure I would be," he admitted as they continued through the galleries. "Do you think the other abstract painters will want to see this exhibit?"

"Of course they will. Before the Depression, artists went to Europe to study and to visit the museums, but most of the people I know didn't have the money to do that. Now, great paintings from those collections are coming to us. Just look at the labels on these crates. A Rubens and a Rembrandt from Switzerland, a Vermeer from Amsterdam, a Fragonard from Paris, even an El Greco and a Goya from Cuba, and a Van Eyck from Australia. Just because we don't paint like that doesn't mean we don't admire them."

As they walked and talked, Elaine kept a firm grip on Fitz's arm and took every opportunity to hold him close while they navigated the installation work in progress. He did nothing to discourage her, enjoying the enthusiasm she radiated, as well as the pressure of her body against his. He also appreciated the way she talked about the paintings that were already hanging or leaning in place, ready to go up on the wall.

Having told her that he knew nothing about art, he was surprised when she said it didn't matter. She had a way of offering information in straightforward language, explaining without talking down to him. She even threw in interesting details about some of the artists' lives—like the facts that Goya went deaf, and Vermeer never left his home town—which made them seem more like real people than characters from a textbook.

"How do you know so much about this stuff?" asked Fitz. "Did you go to college?"

"Better than college," she replied. "I go to the Metropolitan Museum with Arshile and Bill. Looking at the paintings with them and listening to their discussions is like getting an art history degree."

* * *

After navigating a dozen galleries, they arrived at the restrooms. A sign on the ladies' lounge said CLOSED.

"You know," said Elaine, "I think I'll take advantage of the facilities after all." She opened the door marked Gentlemen, and Fitz told her he'd stand guard outside.

In addition to the plumbing, the room had a couch, a few armchairs, occasional tables and standing ashtrays—the lounges were the only places in the building where smoking would be allowed. This pleased Elaine on two counts. She was dying for a cigarette, and she could cozy up to Fitz on the couch.

Just for show, she flushed one of the toilets, then stuck her head out the door and said, "Come on in, let's take a break. My feet could use a rest, and there's a nice place to sit."

Fitz stepped inside and saw the upholstered seats, which did look inviting. "Are you sure it'll be okay? What if someone wants to use the toilet?"

"Just for a few minutes. Anyway, I'm sure the men can think of an alternative if they're desperate. There's always the reflecting pool." She locked the door behind him.

She took off her raincoat, settled on the couch, and patted the seat, inviting Fitz to join her. She offered him a cigarette, but he said he didn't smoke, so she reluctantly decided not to, afraid it would interfere with her romantic intentions.

He apologized for tiring her out. "I'm used to covering a lot of territory on my rounds, so I sometimes forget just how big the fairgrounds are." Then he decided to level with her. "I told you I was in security, but I don't work for the Fair. I'm actually a city police officer on assignment here, which is how I got involved in the suspected sabotage cases. They didn't look like accidents to me."

Elaine laughed. "I can picture you in uniform, a typical Irish cop. So, Officer Fitzgerald, tell me all about your investigations." She put her feet up and snuggled close. "Do you have any suspects?"

The room suddenly seemed very warm to Fitz, and he was having trouble organizing his reply. Without thinking, he unbuttoned his jacket and loosened his tie.

Elaine twisted on the couch to face him, leaned across his chest, removed his tie and opened the top button on his shirt. "Here," she said, "Let me help you get comfortable. It's a bit stuffy in here, don't you think?" Her voice was low and soothing, but it had the opposite effect. He felt a bit light-headed as she put an arm around his neck and drew herself toward him. Desire kicked in, just as she had planned. He embraced her, and his passionate kiss was returned with interest.

The small couch was not ideal for lovemaking, but her experience minimized the difficulties, as did her lack of underwear.

Cuddling in the afterglow, as Elaine whispered compliments on his prowess, a disquieting mix of emotions swept over Fitz. He was not a virgin, but his other substitutes for Mary had always left him feeling that something was lacking. Not this time. He had been completely swept away, which was both thrilling and troubling. Had he actually fallen in love, or was it purely sexual attraction? Elaine was beautiful, smart, intriguing, fun to be with and, as far as he knew, available. And she had just proved she was strongly attracted to him. But where could it go from here? He asked himself if he was just another of her conquests, or whether her feelings went deeper, like he felt his were going.

She sat up, kissed his cheek, and interrupted his disturbing and contradictory thoughts. "I'm famished. Is there someplace nearby where we can get a bite to eat? Let's get cleaned up, and then we can let the men have their restroom back."

Chapter Nineteen

Seated in the Administration Building cafeteria, Elaine tucked into a tuna salad sandwich while Fitz nursed a cup of coffee. His appetite had gone the way of his scruples.

On the short walk from Masterpieces of Art, he had tried to reassure her that, though his actions were impulsive, he wasn't trying to take advantage of her. She had laughed off his concern.

"I wanted you to make love to me, silly, because I wanted to make love to you. I fell for you the moment I saw you last night. I was itching to run my fingers through your gorgeous red curls. I hoped you were thinking something like that about me. Seems like you were."

"Well, not just then," he admitted, then tried to revise. "I mean, I was attracted to you, but I didn't know how you'd react if I put the make on you. We'd only just met."

"And you had a very pretty date," she reminded him. "I saw Bill hanging around her, and that wolf Igor couldn't wait to get his hands all over her, under the pretext of dancing. Are you two engaged?"

He explained their relationship as best he could. "Marriage is out as long as I'm on the force. I love her, but it's hopeless."

"Love can be so inconvenient. Let's worry about feeding our faces instead."

* * *

Her sandwich finished, Elaine refilled her coffee cup and finally indulged in a smoke. "You should eat something," she told Fitz. "How about a donut?

They look good."

"Yeah, I guess I should put something on my stomach."

"Other than me."

He groaned. "Seriously, Elaine, what are we going to do? I don't want this to be a one-time thing. I don't mean just, you know—"

"You don't mean just screwing, is that it? I agree with you. Let's do it again soon."

"No, no, that's not what I mean. That is, I do mean that, but not only that. Jesus, I can't think straight."

She put on a serious face. "Listen, Fitz, I told you I'm not interested in the future, and I meant it. I don't think about what might happen tomorrow, where the next meal, or the next boyfriend, is coming from. The truth is, right now I'm involved with Bill, but I'm a free agent and so is he. No strings." She was playing down the depth of her affair with de Kooning, her teacher and mentor as well as her lover, trying to make her revelation more palatable.

He was shocked. Maybe this was normal in her bohemian circle, but not in his world, where young people went steady, got engaged, and married in a straight line. Yet he had to admit it was no different from his own behavior. She'd cheated on Bill, and he'd been untrue to Mary. Worse, he was afraid he was in love with Elaine and would have to break it off with Mary, but it didn't seem likely Elaine would reciprocate. No strings probably meant no change to the status quo.

She declined his offer to take her home, since she was going to her uncle Carl's place in Yorkville for Sunday dinner with the family. That was true, but she also told him her parents had no telephone, which was not. She would need to call him from a pay phone to arrange further meetings, she said. He gave her his home number and said if someone else in the household answered, she should identify herself as a UAA member who was helping him with his inquiries. It was far too presumptuous to tell them he had a new girlfriend.

"Please don't keep me waiting, Elaine. I want to see you again soon, maybe for dinner or a drink after I clock out, just to talk more and get to know each other better."

"Don't you think we know each other pretty well already?" she teased.

They embraced as they rode the Flushing line to Queensborough Plaza, where they exchanged a last, lingering kiss before he got off. She stayed on, crossed the East River, connected to the Second Avenue el and rode uptown. After dinner, she said goodnight to the family, walked over to Lexington Avenue, took the downtown train to 23rd Street and went home to de Kooning's loft at 156 West 22nd Street.

But before she got there, she went into the all-night drugstore on Sixth Avenue and used the phone booth to make a call.

* * *

When Fitz got home, he decided to take a shower and change before confronting the family, since both he and his clothing were tainted with trace evidence. He called out to the house in general as he headed upstairs to the bathroom. Twenty minutes later, he was ready for inspection.

He found his mother and sister in the kitchen, where he was greeted by the delicious aroma of roasting leg of lamb studded with rosemary sprigs. "How did escort duty go? Were you able to get some lunch before they arrived?" asked Bridget. He gave her a peck on the cheek, and one to Alice, who was slicing carrots.

He had worked out a plausible story, seasoned with a few grains of truth. "It all went off fine, Mom. I ate in the Admin lunchroom. Thank goodness the rain stopped before we went out."

"Where did Mr. Whalen take them?"

"Masterpieces of Art. It was a group of the rich collectors who've lent paintings to the exhibit, and they wanted to check on how the installation is going. They were really pleased to see their things hanging next to pictures from famous European museums. Makes them feel even more important." Elaine had explained how collectors and artists alike want their works to be shown in good company.

"It sounds wonderful, Brian. I hope you'll take us to see it."

He gave his mother a hug. "You'd better buy a good pair of walking shoes, 'cause I'm gonna take you to every exhibit in the whole Fair, including the Amusement Zone. I know you're dying to see Mr. Dolly's naked mermaids." He kissed her blushing forehead. "Not all on the same day, I promise. Need any help with dinner?"

"You can peel the potatoes. Your father and Andy are out back tinkering with the motorbike." That disclosure gave her an idea. "Do you think they'd let Tim take me to the Fair on it? Then I wouldn't need those walking shoes."

"Sorry, no unofficial vehicles allowed, even for one of New York's Finest. I'm afraid you wouldn't be comfortable on my scooter, but they'll have sedan chairs and tractor trains roaming the grounds, even full-size Greyhound buses you can hop onto. Visitors certainly couldn't be expected to cover the whole place on foot. There are sixty miles of paved roads and pathways. Believe me, I know, because I've walked and ridden on all of them."

When he and Alice finished their chores, Bridget asked him to tell the men out in the yard that dinner would be ready in half an hour.

* * *

After dinner, Andy went to a friend's house, and the remaining four settled down to a game of Hearts. They were on their second round when the phone rang. The instrument sat on a table in the hall.

"I'll get it," said Tim, who was used to receiving calls at odd hours on police business. He returned to the living room a few moments later.

"It's for you, Brian. One of the artists you're working with behind Hammer's back. She's got some information for you." His look said he didn't approve of his son's interfering with O'Toole's investigation. Regardless of his personal dislike of the detective, he disliked a protocol violation even more.

Tim might have expected a sheepish look in response. Instead, he got a surprised smile. Fitz couldn't believe she'd called him so soon. He tried to hide his excitement and keep his voice level.

"Thanks, Dad. I was hoping to hear from her. If it's anything useful, I'll make sure O'Toole gets the information." Not that O'Toole would be needing to know when his next date with Elaine would be. He picked up the receiver, and was surprised again when she told him her call really did involve the Fair, though not the sabotage cases.

Dinner at Carl and Greta Fried's apartment had included a couple of their East 83rd Street neighbors. The wives were friends, and their kids went to school together. After the meal, the husband, a fellow named Schultz, took Carl aside. He started going on about the glories of the German-American Bund, which had its headquarters a couple of blocks away, and urged Carl to join. Schultz said he'd attended the Madison Square Garden rally, which he described as inspirational and exciting, especially when their private security guards, the Order Police, beat up the stinking kike who tried to jump Bundesführer Kuhn, their courageous leader.

Elaine overheard him, and decided to eavesdrop.

"Uncle Carl was definitely not interested," she said. "He tried to steer the conversation in another direction, but Schultz was on a soapbox. He was incensed that Germany wouldn't be represented at the World's Fair. Uncle Carl pointed out that, according to the papers, Germany had been invited but declined to participate. Schultz said the Bund should step up and rent space for a German exhibit in the Government Zone. There were a few unoccupied spaces, and he was recommending a last-minute effort to secure one."

"How did he know about that?" asked Fitz.

"That's what Uncle Carl asked him. Schultz told him he worked for the Fair, as a clerk in the Exhibits and Concessions Department."

He'd been furious when the empty Czech pavilion was given to a group of American supporters who had raised money to open it. By rights, he said, it belonged to Germany, which had reclaimed its ancestral territory in the Sudetenland, part of Czechoslovakia. Not only did Germany not have a presence, but the Czech exhibit stood as a rebuke to Hitler's territorial ambitions, which Schultz and the Bund viewed as a legitimate reunification effort.

Finally, Carl had had enough, and politely asked Schultz to change the subject or leave. He chose the latter option, with a parting announcement that the Bund was thinking of staging a rally at the fairgrounds and possibly marching in and occupying one of the vacant spaces, which he was encouraging them to do. Elaine thought Fitz would want to know what might be coming.

"I sure do, Elaine. I can't thank you enough for this warning. I'll pass it along to the chief first thing on Monday, and let him notify Mr. Whalen's office. They may want to put some of their own security people on alert. They'll have an internal police force once the Fair opens, and they're already in training. This could be their first test."

Elaine was having second thoughts. "Well, I don't know how serious his threat was. He'd had a few beers, so maybe it was all bluster. Just because he's pushing the Bund to rally at the Fair doesn't mean they will. Could be a false alarm."

"No, you did the right thing. Maybe we can find out what the Bund's plans are, if any."

"How could we do that?"

"Go to the next meeting."

"How would we get in?"

Fitz had been thinking furiously. "Not we, just me. You said this guy Schultz is Carl's neighbor, right? Find out where he lives, get in touch with him, and tell him you heard what he said about the Bund. You told your boyfriend about it, and he's interested in joining."

"Oh, my God, Uncle Carl would kill me! He hates the Bund. Schultz apparently thought he'd be a supporter because he has a German name, but he was dead wrong."

"Let Carl in on it. I'm sure he'll approve of you helping the police infiltrate them."

Chapter Twenty

Elaine was on it like a terrier on a rat. She fished out another nickel and called Uncle Carl, who was all for it. He had Schultz's number and gave it to her with his blessing. She had told Fitz that, if she got it, she was going to wait until Monday to call Schultz, since tonight seemed a bit too soon to fit in with the concocted boyfriend story. It would be more credible tomorrow evening.

She let herself into the loft, and found de Kooning at his easel, working on a study of a seated man. The painting bore evidence of numerous adjustments—some minor, like corrected folds on a trouser leg, some major, like the position of the head. He had used a friend to model for the initial pose, but the refinements, dictated by his perpetual dissatisfaction, sprang from his imagination and the painting's internal logic. He'd been working on the canvas for months, while most of his time was taken up with the mural, and he was eager to finish it. Elaine wondered if he ever would.

She kissed the top of his head, which barely broke through his concentration. "Oh, hi," he muttered. "Did you have a nice time at your uncle's?" She had told him she'd be out for dinner, but not about her date at the Fair. He had no idea where she'd been all day and wasn't especially curious.

"I'll tell you all about it in the morning. You're busy, and I'm bushed. Are you hungry? I brought you some of Aunt Greta's strudel." She opened a brown paper bag, removed a hefty slice of pastry wrapped in waxed paper, looked around for a plate to put it on, and didn't see one. "I bet you didn't eat dinner."

"The ice box vas empty, except for a couple of beers, so that's vat I had."

The idea of interrupting his work to go out and buy food hadn't occurred to him. He was hopelessly undomesticated, and unfortunately so was she. The only provisions she ever made sure they never ran out of were whiskey and cigarettes. His World's Fair commission meant they had enough money to keep them well stocked.

He had been given clearance to finish Gorky's mural, so he'd be heading out to the fairgrounds in the morning. He'd been looking forward to an uninterrupted stretch of work on his own canvas, but he couldn't refuse his dear friend in need. Corrine had promised to get Arshile there by ten, so he'd need to be up and out by nine. He felt a twinge of envy toward Elaine, who would have all morning free to work on her painting, a still life of objects she'd found lying around the studio, embellished with a few evergreen leaves picked up off the street in the nearby Flower District. Like Cézanne's apples, the objects had been chosen for their formal properties and compositional potential rather than for any illustrative purpose. She was still learning the basics, and de Kooning had helped her select things that would challenge her ability to deal with shapes, textures, and surfaces. He was pleased to see how well she was getting the hang of it.

* * *

The morning of Monday, April third, was sunny, for which Corinne West was thankful. She'd been dreading the prospect of getting Gorky up and down the subway stairs in the rain. Even a drizzle made them slippery, and his crutches would have been an extra hazard. To be sure he was ready on time, she had stayed overnight at his place, and while they lay in bed together, he had proposed to her once again. Once again, she refused him. As much as she loved him and was captivated by his artistic genius, she was fearful that his needs would overwhelm her.

She had seen too many of her fellow female artists who married male artists forced to put their careers on hold. It was even worse if they had children. Then their careers would evaporate altogether. They might teach art or work as illustrators, but not compete for art-world recognition. And

God forbid if they did.

She knew one up-and-coming painter whose husband said his easel was broken, asked to borrow hers, and never returned it. The wife got the message. Another one, who was being promoted by an important gallery, had a child which her husband threatened to take away from her if she continued. West wasn't aware of any artist couple who stood on equal footing, and in spite of Gorky's enthusiastic encouragement, she didn't think they would be the exception.

Right now, however, her role as his assistant was the priority. Her job was to get him to the Fair, then finish the mural with his supervision and de Kooning's help. The first task was likely to be more challenging than the second.

She made coffee and fried eggs on the gas ring while he washed and dressed, grumbling about the difficulty of getting his plastered ankle into the leg of his one-piece overalls and complaining about the situation in general. She decided not to point out that he didn't need to wear his work clothes, since he couldn't get onto the scaffold. That would only dampen his spirits even more.

The sun was making a valiant effort to penetrate the tall studio windows. Their perpetual coating of urban grime was actually beneficial, acting as a diffuser, so even on the brightest days, there was never glare in Gorky's workspace. He had been in that studio for nearly a decade, and his friends often observed how perfectly illuminated it was.

"Looks like a beautiful day," she remarked as she served their breakfast, hoping the good weather would cheer him up. His response was a grunt. She soldiered on. "Eat up, darling. We should get going soon. Bill can't start without you." Not strictly true, since all the color studies and materials were at hand, but she was sure that, out of courtesy, he wouldn't do anything until Gorky arrived.

The subway trip was not as difficult as she'd imagined. He had been practicing with the crutches, and managed the stairs quite well. The station attendant let him onto the platform through the gate, so he didn't have to deal with the turnstile. The long walk from the Fair entrance to Aviation was a daunting prospect, but one of the tractor trains drove by on a test run, and the driver gave them a lift.

De Kooning was already there and had everything set up, including an upholstered armchair, positioned opposite the mural, from which Gorky could observe the work in progress.

Gorky was touched by his thoughtfulness. "Where on earth did you get this, Bill?" he asked.

"The manager's office. A nice guy. He vanted you to be comfortable. Sit, please. Now, let's get to verk lickety-split!"

* * *

Fitz dropped by around eleven to see how things were going, but really to see West again and to get a better handle on de Kooning, whom he'd met only in passing when he rescued Mary from him at the union party.

Dressed in a housepainter's white bib overalls and cloth cap, he was on the scaffold with West, applying paint to outlined areas while she prepared the colors according to Gorky's studies. Fitz watched as de Kooning painted, deftly following the design like the seasoned professional muralist he was, with none of the hesitation and second-guessing that marked his personal work. The job was going so smoothly that Gorky had dozed off.

Apart from his obvious technical skill, de Kooning didn't seem like such a great catch to Fitz. *So this is the guy Elaine's involved with, as she put it,* he said to himself. *He's not bad looking, but she's way too young for him. Maybe she's ready to trade in a short, old Dutchman for a tall, young Irishman. I sure hope so.*

He caught West's eye and waved her down. Once again, he was struck by her beauty and poise as she hopped off the scaffold and approached him. He felt his pulse quicken just a bit. *God Almighty,* he thought, *what's the matter with me? I could fall in love with her, too. Get hold of yourself, Brian, and stick to business.*

He motioned her to the side so as not to disturb Gorky, who was snoring lightly in his comfy chair.

"Glad to see you back at work," he said. "Looks like it's going well."

108

"Arshile seems to think so," she said, with a glance toward the napping artist.

"So I see. Listen, I hope you don't mind me interrupting, but I need your advice."

"Really? What about?"

Fitz told her he'd been at the UAA party. "Stuart invited me," he explained. "I saw you there, but I didn't get a chance to say hi, and then you were gone."

"I was worried about Arshile, so I left early," she said. "He's doing better than I expected, though, to hear him tell it, he's crippled for life. What a big crybaby."

"Anyway," Fitz continued, "I overheard a conversation that got me thinking about a motive for the sabotage that has nothing to do with Browne's union. An artist called Lee Krasner was complaining that she got passed over for possible WPA jobs, and it seemed to me like maybe a disgruntled WPA artist might be behind it. Most of them are in the UAA. I was wondering if you'd heard anyone express bitterness or resentment over losing out."

"Haven't you asked Stuart about that? He's both WPA and UAA, so he should know if anyone has a grudge."

"If he does, he hasn't told me. He's so focused on the scenic artists that he may not even have considered that someone in his own ranks might be responsible."

Then Fitz has another thought. "Say, how did artists get Fair jobs? Was it a competition?"

"There were a few different ways," West told him. "Those who're working directly for the Fair, like Arshile, could send in a design for a specific building and hope it was accepted. Actually, he applied for the Marine Transportation mural first, but got rejected. Then he tried for Aviation and got it, on the strength of his Newark Airport murals. It's a much better fit for him anyway, though it's not as prominent. So, that's one way. Then some artists were hand-picked by the architects or designers who already knew their work. That's how most of the mural painters' society members got their jobs. Others were recommended by outsiders, like Bill was by the head of the WPA mural program, for the Pharmacy mural. Of course, whatever the route, they had to submit proposals and get approval from the Board of Design."

"Just for argument's sake," said Fitz, "let's say someone makes a proposal and gets rejected, like Arshile did the first time, then tries and fails again, maybe even tries a third time, strikes out. Do you know anybody like that?"

"Not offhand, but what about Lee Krasner? Didn't you say she'd been turned down?"

"I thought she meant for WPA jobs, but maybe she was talking about the Fair. She said Diller didn't recommend her, but she might have submitted proposals on her own."

"I don't know Lee well," said West, "but she's active in the union. Very aggressive, always urging us to sign a petition or march on a picket line, a real live wire. She's not shy about pushing herself, and I bet she'd be really angry if she was rejected, especially if it was more than once."

"Mad enough to take revenge against those who got the jobs she wanted?"

West stared at him, then looked doubtful. "How could she have done it?"

"One thing that struck me about all five so-called accidents is that none of them took a lot of strength. Stuart was simply rolled off the scaffold while he was asleep. A child could do it. The rope securing Guston's ladder was untied. How hard is that? Same with Bolotowsky's ladder, just unclip the brackets. Catching Feininger off balance and pushing him off the ladder would be easy. Okay, it's a bit more work to saw partway through that top step," he pointed to the staircase under Gorky's mural, "but even a woman could manage it."

"*Even* a woman? I know a few who could arm-wrestle you and win, Officer Fitzgerald."

Fitz tried to dig himself out. "I mean, a small, slender woman like Lee Krasner. What I'm getting at is, there was no fighting, no struggle, and, except in Feininger's case, no confrontation with the victim. Whoever pushed him must have been facing him, but the others didn't see who was responsible, and he didn't live to point the finger. That's one reason why Detective O'Toole hasn't been able to identify a culprit. That and the fact that there's no physical evidence, no fingerprints, no nothing. It would have been really helpful if there'd been a dropped glove or a footprint, but no such luck. And O'Toole believes they probably were accidents after all, so he's not giving it his best effort."

West was still doubtful. "Okay, suppose Lee wanted to do it. How would she get into those places?"

"How do you get in?"

"When we started, we showed our union cards at the gate and told them where we were going."

"Don't you need a Fair I.D.?"

"No. They had our names on a list in the guard's booth, but later they recognized us, and now they just wave us through. It's getting pretty hectic with opening day so close, so maybe they're not as careful as they were at first. And they might not be as strict with a woman if she said she was subbing for someone off sick or was a new assistant. In that case, her union card alone might get her in."

"Do they check you on the way out?" asked Fitz.

"We check in and out with the manager here in the building, but not at the gate. We don't get overtime, so they don't keep track of our hours. If we work late, we just let ourselves out."

Fitz was taking notes, and he stopped to review them. "Here's the way I see it. Someone—could be Lee Krasner, could be a different person, man or woman—comes to the gate, shows a UAA card, and says Mr. Davis needs another hand, so the WPA sent me over. He or she hangs around until quitting time, goes into the building and hides until the right moment, does the deed and slips out."

"How would they know that Davis is in there overnight?"

"It has to be a WPA artist or a union member who would've heard him talk about staying on after the crew left. Same for Bolotowsky. They would need to know when he's going to install the mural, because he didn't paint it in place like Stuart is doing. In Guston's case, it could be done any night during the work. But again, if he's the target, they'd have to find out that he goes to the job earlier than the rest of the crew."

West nodded. "I see what you mean. After they got in the first time, the guy at the gate would recognize them and let them through. But how would they know enough to doctor that step? Arshile doesn't go around telling people he jumps off the scaffold onto it."

Their speculations were interrupted by a shout from the scaffold in question. "If you're done flirting vit that cute cop, I could use some more cobalt blue up here."

Chapter Twenty-One

"Hello, Mrs. Schultz? May I please speak to your husband?"

"Who's calling, please?"

"My name is Brian Fitzgerald. I'm a friend of Elaine Fried, Carl and Greta's niece."

"Oh, yes, Elaine. We met her last night when we were at their place for dinner. Hold on a moment, I'll fetch Gustav."

Gustav Schultz, couldn't be more German, thought Fitz. *At least he's not an Adolph. The wife doesn't sound like she's from the old country. Maybe he isn't either. Could be from a German immigrant family like Mr. Feininger. And look at me, a Queens boy born and bred, but from a long line of Irish New Yorkers.*

When Schultz came on the line, his accent confirmed that he was a New York City native. "What can I do for you, Mr. Fitzgerald?"

Fitz trotted out his prepared story, expressed his sympathy for the Bund's cause, and asked about joining. Schultz was not surprised that someone of Irish extraction should be interested, since the leader of the Irish Republican Army had been cozying up to German intelligence for years. The IRA had expressed willingness to support Germany in military conflict with Britain and had already launched its own bombing campaign in English cities.

"I'm delighted to hear from you, Mr. Fitzgerald. We're always eager to welcome recruits to the growing ranks of those who want to protect our beloved country from the forces that threaten to destroy it from within." He was on his soapbox again. "The Bolshevik-Jewish conspiracy must be must be exposed and rooted out. Our great leader, Fritz Kuhn, needs men of action like yourself to carry forth his bold plan to return white Christians to power in America."

Schultz assured Fitz that he would be accepted. Never mind that members were supposed to be American citizens of German descent. The time had come to relax that restriction. The Bund was struggling to regain momentum after the Garden rally, which had backfired and alienated many New Yorkers. The ugly spectacle painted the movement as a potential threat to democracy rather than its savior, and it was widely denounced.

They arranged to meet at Bund headquarters at 7:00 the following evening, when Schultz would introduce Fitz to the man in charge of recruitment. The devil on Fitz's left shoulder told him he was doing a noble deed, while the angel on his right whispered that he was asking for trouble. He, a rookie patrolman, had no business taking it on himself to go undercover, however worthy the cause. Why not just report what Elaine overheard and let the detective branch handle it?

He didn't need the voices of good and evil to answer that question. If it turned out to be a false alarm, O'Toole would find a way to punish him for wasting police time. He was already down on Fitz over the sabotage investigation. If the threat was genuine, the warning didn't have to come from him. He could ask Elaine to report it as a tip from a concerned citizen.

* * *

Bund headquarters, at 178 East 85th Street, boasted nothing to distinguish it from the rest of the largely residential block. No swastika banners hanging outside or pro-Nazi posters in the windows. They had wisely chosen not to call public attention to their location.

Fitz arrived a little before 7:00 p.m. and found Schutz waiting for him at the door. He had pictured a formidable embodiment of Teutonic bombast, but instead saw a man as unremarkable as the building. Medium height, clean shaven, wearing glasses, a grey fedora and an overcoat that looked a size too big for him, he was every inch the clerical worker who went through life largely unnoticed. *Perhaps,* thought Fitz as he approached, *the Bund is Schultz's compensation for being overlooked and undervalued, but maybe I'm reading too much into appearances. Inside that innocuous exterior, the guy might be a real go-getter, the star of the Fair's Exhibits and Concessions Department.*

Schultz greeted him warmly. "Ah, Mr. Fitzgerald, what a pleasure. I'm so glad Miss Fried put you in touch with me. I've alerted Director Kunze, and he's eagerly awaiting you in his office. Allow me."

He rang the bell and stood in front of a peephole in the door. He was recognized, the buzzer sounded, and he and Fitz were admitted to the entrance hall, where a uniformed member of the Bund's Order Police, known as the Ordnungsdienst, stood watch. Schultz introduced him, and instead of shaking hands, the officer thrust his right arm straight out and up in the Nazi salute. Fitz decided not to return it and simply said, "Glad to meet you."

"You should have seen Sergeant Wagner and his men at the Garden rally in February. Highly disciplined, very efficient," said Schultz proudly. "It was a huge crowd. They kept everyone in line, and made short work of the few who came to heckle."

"I heard about the man who ran on stage and tried to attack one of the speakers."

"A dirty Jew. Don't know how he got in, certainly not under his own name. We must tighten our admission policy at the next rally, which I'm sure will be even bigger, as our ranks swell with patriots like you, eager to join our crusade."

Fitz was working hard to suppress his true feelings. Schultz's views disgusted him, and the idea that the Bund's ranks might be growing made him deeply uneasy, even a bit frightened. He hoped it was just empty boasting. Otherwise, the peaceful and prosperous future promised by the World of Tomorrow—the vision that so captivated and inspired him—was an illusion.

Sergeant Wagner announced, "Director Kunze is expecting you." He opened a door marked PR-Direktor, where Gerhard Wilhelm Kunze, the Bund's national publicity director and head of recruitment, sat behind an enormous oak desk with a row of swastikas carved on the front panel. A large American flag hung limply on a stanchion behind him, with a portrait of George Washington next to it. He rose courteously, and invited the men to take chairs in front of the desk. Dressed in a three-piece suit and tie, with a fresh haircut and a neatly trimmed moustache, he looked more like a salesman than a militant Nazi. It was only when he opened his mouth that his true colors were on display.

"Thank you for coming, Mr. Fitzgerald. Please explain what motivates you to join our organization. Your name tells me you are not of German descent, though perhaps on your mother's side?"

Fitz had decided to give an honest account of his background, if not of his reason for joining the Bund. The truth of that would not be acceptable to Kunze.

"No, my family is a hundred percent Irish, but we've been here for generations. My great-grandfather came over during the Hunger. This truly was the land of opportunity for him, and he succeeded like he never could have in the auld sod. I love America, and I'm prepared to fight for its founding principles. From what I hear, that's what you're doing." So far, he hadn't needed to lie, but he knew he would soon enough.

"Indeed it is," said Kunze, pleased with Fitz's spirited delivery. "Our purpose is to restore this country to the true Americans. All sincere men and women of white Gentile stock, provided they are United States citizens, are encouraged to join our struggle against Communists, atheists, and the international Jewish cabal. We must crush the menace of anti-nationalist Jewish Bolshevism, which pervades our government, our financial institutions, the press and the entertainment industry."

His father had told him the Bund's real purpose was to stir up sympathy for the Nazi cause by equating it with American patriotism, so Fitz was prepared for Kunze's rhetoric. "I'm with you all the way," he affirmed. "I want to join, if you'll have me."

Kunze raised a cautionary hand. "I admire your enthusiasm, Mr. Fitzgerald, but you have not yet heard the requirements. First, the initiation fee is a dollar and fifty cents, plus twenty cents for the membership card. Annual dues are nine dollars." Fitz said he was happy to pay those costs. "Second, you must be able to devote a certain amount of time and effort in service of the Bund's program, including attendance at meetings and rallies, as well as canvassing to spread our message. Are you prepared to do that?"

"Certainly, sir. My hours are flexible."

"Are you a married man with family obligations?"

"No, sir, I'm single. Didn't Mr. Schultz mention that it was my girlfriend who told me about the Bund?"

"Yes, forgive me, it slipped my mind. What is your occupation?"

As Fitz saw it, this was the decisive question. Hoping the truth would work in his favor, he said, "I'm a New York City police officer, currently assigned to the New York World's Fair."

A smile cracked Kunze's stony face. "Splendid. You can be extremely valuable to us. We are considering staging a rally at the Fair to protest the lack of German representation, and you could help us with logistics." He didn't give Schultz credit for the idea.

Fitz mirrored Kunze's smile. "Count me in. I know exactly where and when it would be most effective."

Now Schultz spoke up. "What a wonderful coincidence. I also work for the Fair, and it was I who suggested that the Bund rally there, even enter the grounds, take over a vacant space in the Government Zone and set up a German display. Do you think something like that could work?"

"Sure, it could," said Fitz, ignoring Kunze's scowl at Schultz for having asserted himself. "As long as the protest is peaceful, I could get the cops to hold back while you exercise your rights to free speech and freedom of assembly. Aren't those some of the things we're fighting for?" He didn't mention that unauthorized entry to the fairgrounds and occupation of a building were acts of trespass, not sanctioned by the First Amendment.

Kunze composed himself. "Very well, I'll discuss it with Bundesführer Kuhn and let you know if we want to proceed. Meanwhile, welcome to the German-American Bund, Mr. Fitzgerald." He rose, came out from behind his desk, and shook hands with the new recruit. "Schultz here will see to the formalities. There is an oath of allegiance, and of course, the initiation fee and dues. You can take care of everything in the secretary's office across the hall. She will issue your membership card."

He dismissed Fitz with an energetic Nazi salute.

Chapter Twenty-Two

At 11:00 a.m. on Wednesday, Clarence O'Toole was cooling his heels in the president's office at Local 829 union headquarters, 251 West 42nd Street, just off Times Square in the heart of the theater district. United Scenic Artists of America had greatly expanded its portfolio in recent years. In addition to its traditional membership of stage, film set, and lighting designers, it had added muralists and diorama artists to take advantage of the plentiful job opportunities offered by the Fair and was well known for its militant policing of the closed-shop rule.

Browne's secretary had informed O'Toole that her boss's meeting at Radio City Music Hall was running late, but he'd be returning shortly. Apparently, an appointment with a New York City police detective was not a priority. Just as O'Toole had tired of reading back copies of *Stage* and was ready to bail out, Browne appeared.

Central Casting could not have sent a more perfect union boss: a cigar-chomping, six-foot-one, 250-pound specimen of well-marbled beef, with a foghorn voice that carried across the negotiating table. The only touch that softened the effect was a pair of wire-rimmed spectacles, but behind them were dark, piercing eyes that could stare down pretty much any adversary. He advanced on O'Toole like a street fighter ready for a brawl.

The detective stood his ground. He had been prepared for an unfriendly reception, but was surprised when Browne greeted him cordially and extended his hand.

"Sorry to keep you waiting, Detective O'Toole. Just a minor dispute over at Radio City. Easily settled when the parties see reason, but that's not always the case," he said, hinting that there'd been some head-knocking and/or arm-twisting required. "Please come into my office, and let me know how I can help you." He instructed the secretary to hold his calls, opened the door, and stepped aside politely to let his visitor enter first. *Why the charm offensive?* O'Toole wondered, but he decided to play along.

Instead of putting a desk between them, Browne chose a comfortable armchair and offered one to O'Toole, suggesting a man-to-man chat rather than formal questioning. He offered a Robt. Burns Corona, which was accepted, and both men sat back for a moment to savor their smokes.

O'Toole got straight to the point. "I've been looking into some recent incidents involving muralists at the World's Fair. Reports of possible vandalism, three injuries, one serious, and a fatality. I'm sure you've heard about them. They may be accidental, but we can't rule out the possibility of sabotage."

Browne blew a smoke ring. "Why would you think that?"

"There's evidence of tampering, and one of the artists is convinced that Local 829 is behind it. All but one of the victims are members of United American Artists Local 60. You filed a jurisdictional grievance against them, and from what I'm told, the arbitration didn't go in your favor. Are any of your members sore enough about the outcome to want to take revenge?"

O'Toole was expecting a vehement denial, but he was surprised again when Browne's response was reasonable. "I can see why that might seem to explain the rash of accidents, but I'm inclined to doubt it. I can't speak for every Local 829 worker at the Fair, but once the dispute was settled, I personally instructed all of them to abide by the ruling. It isn't brotherly to bear a grudge."

This struck O'Toole as disingenuous. He had done his homework. The scenic artists versus fine artists rivalry was overshadowed by bitter hostility between the venerable American Federation of Labor, with which Local 829 was affiliated, and the upstart Congress of Industrial Organizations, Local 60's parent. So, as the detective knew, there were hard feelings on two levels.

"The fatality you're talking about was Lyonel Feininger, is that right?" Browne continued. O'Toole confirmed it. "One of our newest members.

The Fair signed him up in March so he could work on his mural. I know he had a run-in with Olsen, the foreman, but that was before he joined, and Olsen was very much within his rights to bar him from the job. But once he got his card, it was a different story. I heard he was well-liked by the crew, so none of them would have a reason to kill him. Besides, they were all together at lunch when he fell. Olsen thinks he lost his grip coming down the ladder. We've had a few other accidental deaths at the Fair, so his isn't the first, though I hope it's the last."

Despite his own doubts, O'Toole wasn't quite ready to let it drop. "I agree that Olsen's men are in the clear, but it's possible that another Local 829 member had it in for Feininger. If there was foul play, I'm sure you'd want to get to the bottom of it. If you hear anything suspicious, get in touch with me." He rose, and handed his card to Browne.

"Count on me," said Browne, though O'Toole had the feeling he couldn't. Pointing the finger at one of his own would not endear him to the rank and file.

Browne showed O'Toole to the door, shook hands, and offered a parting thought. "Why don't you talk to the head of Local 60? Maybe one of his boys wasn't happy about Feininger joining us instead of them."

* * *

Fitz had been eagerly awaiting Elaine's Wednesday night call. When the phone rang, he said, "I'll get it, Dad," and jumped to answer it.

Tim looked up from his evening paper. "Probably that gal you're in cahoots with. Just be careful how you play this. It's dangerous."

After he returned from his swearing-in the night before, Fitz had decided to let his family in on his plan to infiltrate the Bund. He'd had to fill in his address and telephone number on the membership form, so there would be calls from the Bund office asking him to show up for duty. Their reactions varied from Andy's wholehearted support—"Gosh, Bri, you're a secret agent!"—to shocked concern from Bridget and Alice and stern disapproval from Tim. But it was a fait accompli, and he had to admire his son's initiative even as he feared for his safety, not to mention the prospect of O'Toole's wrath. If Hammer found out, he would come down on him with a vengeance.

"Isn't it enough that you're sticking your nose into his sabotage investigation?" Tim scolded. "Now you have to get yourself involved in spying on a bunch of Nazis who may or may not be planning to invade the Fair. Two completely separate issues, both of which are way outside your territory. If you're not very lucky, when this is over you're going to find yourself patrolling the Staten Island Snake Farm."

"Are you going to have to hang out with those horrible people?" his mother wanted to know. "I suppose they'll make you wear one of those disgraceful uniforms, like the Nazi storm troopers in Germany." She had seen the pictures in the *Daily News*.

"Oh, no, Mom, nothing like that. No one outside the Bund is supposed to know I'm a member. I'll probably have to go to a few meetings, especially if they decide to go through with the Fair rally, but that's it. I told them I had to be under cover, otherwise I couldn't get the inside information they need to pull it off."

Bridget was not reassured. "I'm afraid of them, Brian. They seem to be a lot more popular than I imagined, and some of them are violent. Look at what they did to that poor Jewish boy. If the police hadn't stepped in, they would have beaten him to death."

The papers had shown graphic images of NYPD officers rescuing Isadore Greenbaum, a 26-year-old plumber's assistant from Brooklyn, who had snuck into the Garden rally. Incensed by the anti-Jewish hate speech, he ran on stage, pulled out the microphone cable to silence Fritz Kuhn's poisonous tirade, and shouted, "Down with Hitler!" Quickly overwhelmed by the Ordnungsdienst thugs, he was punched and kicked and had his clothes nearly torn off before help could reach him. Ironically, Greenbaum was promptly arrested for disturbing the peace and ordered to pay a twenty-five dollar fine or spend ten days in jail. He paid the fine and had no regrets.

Alice was more philosophical. "They rented the Garden and had a permit for the rally. LaGuardia was criticized for not blocking it, but he said denying them the right to assemble and have their say, however odious, would put him in the same camp as Hitler. Like it or not, the cops actually had to protect them from the protesters. Suppose they get a permit to march outside the Fair. You could tell them that's all they need. But if they march in it'll be illegal, and they could be arrested for trespassing. That would sure turn the tables. If you can pull it off, Bri, you might help send them to jail."

* * *

Elaine wanted the whole story, and Fitz was eager to give it to her.

"Why didn't you tell me what Schultz looked like? I thought he was going to be a big blowhard, but he's just a, well, a nonentity. He spouts the party line, but I can't imagine him firing up a crowd, though he did persuade the higher-ups to at least consider his hare-brained World's Fair invasion scheme."

"Not so hare-brained, really," said Elaine. "It could get them plenty of press coverage, even if they don't get as far as the Government Zone. That's the crazy part. If they did set up a German exhibit, I'm sure the Fair would padlock it before it could ever open."

"Yeah, but they'd get their point across. I could see their publicity guy, Kunze, making hay out of them tangling with the cops and getting censored. He's the one who signed me up. A real creep. Anyway, I'm supposed to be their eyes and ears inside Fair security. Schultz was the idea man, but he doesn't know the ins and outs of policing the grounds and what sort of reception they could expect."

"What do you have to do?"

"For the moment, sit tight. They're gonna have a meeting of the top brass later this week to decide whether to go ahead with the Fair protest, and Kunze wants me there to lay out the logistics. He said he'd call and let me know where and when."

"Speaking of logistics, where and when will I see you again?" Her tone was suggestive, and Fitz felt a twinge in his groin. He peeked into the living room to make sure he wouldn't be overheard.

"Are you busy Friday? Maybe I could call in sick."

"I have a modeling job this week, but Friday is Good Friday, so I have the day off. I share a studio with Bill in Chelsea, and he's at the Fair finishing up Gorky's mural. Would you like to come over and see what I'm up to?"

You bet I would, he said to himself. He felt no qualms about two-timing Mary. His feelings were entirely directed elsewhere.

"Sure, that would be great. I need to check the roster. Call me tomorrow night, and I'll let you know."

"Do your folks know what's going on? With the Bund, I mean, not with us."

"I told them about how you made the Bund connection, but not the whole story. I needed a reason why you would call me, in case one of them answers the phone. I said I met you at the union party, and you offered to help me find out about the sabotage, but then you got wind of this rally and invasion plan and thought I should know. I had to tell them about joining the Bund, because they're going to call, too."

He lowered his voice. "I didn't tell them about Sunday."

Chapter Twenty-Three

O'Toole had decided to act on Browne's advice. His next destination was 5 Great Jones Street, where Rockwell Kent had agreed to see him on Thursday afternoon.

"I'm expecting the movers to pick up my G-E mural in the morning," Kent told the desk sergeant over the phone. "Packing it will take some time, and I need to supervise every step. If they're late, I may have to postpone our meeting. Please tell Detective O'Toole I'll call to let him know. I wouldn't want him to make the trip for nothing." His long history of interaction with the police in service of various labor and social justice causes had taught him that sometimes accommodation was the best policy.

Fortunately, the art movers showed up on time, and the weather was dry, both of which augured well. In spite of the logistical complexities of handling such a huge canvas, the process went smoothly. After the van pulled away, the artist went to the phone and notified the One Ten that O'Toole was welcome to come by at his convenience.

When he arrived at 1:00 p.m., Kent and his assistants were eating lunch, celebrating the painting's removal with sandwiches from the local deli and beer from the stock of Knickerbocker. Both were offered to him, and both were declined. Kent left the table and directed O'Toole to the office, where they could confer in private.

"As the sergeant told you," O'Toole began, "I'm investigating the string of so-called accidents that have happened to muralists at the Fair. It's been suggested that a member or members of the United Scenic Artists are trying to sabotage painters who belong to the union you run, since most of the victims are members of it and there's bad blood between you."

Kent interrupted him. "I assure you the bad blood, as you call it, is entirely on the scenic artists' side. Our members have nothing against them. But we see no need to go to the considerable expense of joining another union when we're already members of the United Artists of America, an equally bona fide labor union."

"I interviewed Browne, who assured me that none of his members were responsible," said O'Toole, to which Kent responded with a snort.

"What did you expect him to say? That his boys are out for revenge? He may not know exactly who's doing it, but you can be sure he knows they're from Local 829."

"I'm not saying I took his word for it," replied O'Toole somewhat defensively, "but the reason I'm here is that he did suggest an alternative. That's what I want to discuss with you. Let's assume, hypothetically, that these cases are sabotage, not accidents. Browne raised the possibility that one of your own members might be doing it out of envy. Someone who didn't get the Fair job or jobs they wanted, getting back at those who did. What do you think of that idea?"

That was the very possibility Officer Fitzgerald was investigating, and Kent almost let the cat out of the bag. Luckily for Fitz, before he answered, he remembered that Davis had told him the young patrolman was snooping around informally, without his superiors' knowledge. So he held back that information and saved Fitz from a severe reprimand. Instead, he acknowledged that it wasn't an unreasonable suggestion.

"I can see why Browne would send you in that direction, to deflect attention from his people. But it's worth considering, and we're already making inquiries on our own. There are a few disgruntled members whose proposals were rejected, but their resentment is against the Fair bureaucracy in general and the Board of Design in particular, not the brothers and sisters who won out." That was not strictly true, since Krasner was angry with fellow UAA member Greene for bypassing her, and about her radio station proposal in limbo while others were moving along. Kent considered her outburst to be the result of not enough WPA recognition and too much whiskey.

"You have to understand where we're coming from," he continued. "Almost all of us have been working for one or another of the New Deal art programs for years, and we're used to submitting mural designs only to have them sent back for revisions because someone objected to the subject matter, or having the job cancelled when the sponsor backed out. We don't expect everything to be accepted."

As he had done with Browne, O'Toole gave Kent his card and asked him to report any suspicions. Not that he was expecting promising leads, but at least he'd done all he could to make both union bosses aware that he took the investigation seriously. A detective to his bones, his ingrained tenacity outweighed his gut feeling that it was a wild goose chase.

* * *

Fitz arrived at the Fair on Thursday morning to find himself assigned to a four-man escort detail. "Here we go again," he announced to the locker room in general as he changed into his uniform, and his fellow sufferers moaned in response.

"Cheer up, fellas," said Smith, who was also on the list, "the sun is shining, the birds are singing, and trailing around after Grover beats patrolling the perimeter fence. Besides, it won't be for much longer. A few more weeks, and the Fair's own force will take over. Then we can go back to pounding the beat in beautiful downtown Elmhurst."

"Good point, Smitty," said Fitz. "I'm really gonna miss the Fair, though I've promised to bring the whole family and my friends as often as I can, so it's not like I won't be coming back to visit."

Smith finished buttoning his tunic. "Me, too. I heard a rumor that Grover's giving us free passes as a reward for following him and his guests around. I hope they include our own personal entourages."

"Who's he got coming this time?"

"A bunch of Belgians. Their ambassador is in town and wants to see the setup. They've had a lot of trouble with the unions, especially the electrical workers, and he's looking for confirmation that everything's been ironed out."

A sleek International Style design, the Belgium pavilion was built in the home country using native materials, disassembled, and shipped over in sections for reconstruction on site. Its one hundred and fifty-five-foot-tall carillon was fitted with thirty-six bronze bells cast in Tournai. The major attraction was to be a display of diamonds mined in its African colony, the Belgian Congo, which required high security, including armed guards and an elaborately wired alarm system. Delays, disputes, and arguments over installation costs had plagued the project for months, and Whalen wanted to assure the Belgians that their treasure, valued at two million dollars, would be properly protected.

The party assembled in the Administration Building reception area, where a row of blue uniforms stood at attention. There were about a dozen assorted dignitaries mingling and chatting, accompanied by the piped-in strains of "Dawn of a New Day." Presently, Whalen appeared, wearing a perfectly tailored three-piece suit, rep-striped tie, and homburg hat, with the Belgian ambassador, Count Robert Van der Straten-Ponthoz, similarly attired, in tow. The four blue uniforms saluted as one, and Whalen returned the gesture—a bent-elbowed delivery of the right hand to the temple, quite different from what Fitz had experienced at Bund headquarters.

His usual affable self, Whalen beamed his patented smile. But as he scanned the group and prepared to deliver his stock welcome speech, his smile froze, and he found himself momentarily at a loss for words. There in the crowd was a familiar face, one he'd been hoping never to see again.

Joseph F. Shadgen.

His first thought was, *how the hell did that bastard get in here?* Then he remembered that Shadgen was from Belgium. He had received his engineering training there, and no doubt knew the building's architect, who was present. Maybe even the ambassador. *One of them must have invited him,* Whalen decided, *and brought him in their car, otherwise he'd surely have been stopped at the gate. Christ Almighty, if he makes a scene, I'm up the creek.*

Whalen collected himself and held forth to the Belgians, thanking them profusely for their great nation's participation in this triumph of international cooperation and goodwill. If his words rang a bit hollow in light of neighboring Germany's current saber-rattling, the audience was too polite to snicker. For them, Fair participation was a public relations tool, a way to gain American sympathy and support in case the worst should happen. That was the cooperation and goodwill they were interested in.

A Greyhound tractor train, emblazoned with the company's trademark dog leaping over the Trylon and Perisphere, was waiting to ferry the group across the fairgrounds to the Belgium pavilion, which occupied a prime spot facing the Lagoon of Nations. Whalen took the ambassador to the front car and sat beside him. Glancing around casually while making small talk with His Excellency the Count, he saw Shadgen board one of the cars near the back, with the police escort bringing up the rear, and breathed a sigh of relief.

The carillon operator had been alerted to ring the bells as they approached—literally music to the Belgians' ears. The bell tower, finished in grey slate, contrasted dramatically with the building's red tile cladding. Sun glinted on its glazed surface and shone through a welcoming wall of glass, bathing the interior in natural light. As they left the vehicle, the ambassador congratulated the architect. "You've done us proud, Van de Velde," he said in Dutch, and received "Het was mijn eer" (It was my honor) in reply.

The tour, conducted by Belgium's official liaison to the Fair, Commissioner General Joseph Gavaert, initially went according to plan. Everyone admired the displays of fine linen and lace, photographic equipment, precision tools and other products for which the country was renowned. But the highlight was the Belgian Congo exhibit, which included the precious gems and equipment for diamond-cutting and polishing demonstrations. This was clearly going to be a crowd-pleaser, and the Count was eager to see it in operation. He had brought an official photographer and wanted plenty of publicity shots for the papers back home.

To his extreme displeasure, he learned that a dispute with the electrical workers' union had caused the building's current to be shut off. A temporary generator had been rigged up, but it wasn't powerful enough to run everything, so the equipment wasn't working. Amid profuse apologies from both Whalen and Gavaert, he demanded details about security for the gem collection in case the alarm system was also non-functional, and to know when the situation would be rectified.

While the ambassador fumed, Whalen's eye wandered to the lineup of blue uniforms, and he had an inspiration. "Please don't concern yourself, Your Excellency. The New York City police force is at your disposal for as long as their presence is required. I shall personally see to it that armed officers patrol the building day and night until the dispute is settled and full power is restored. Dr. Gavaert and I will keep you informed."

Oh, shit, said Fitz to himself. *There goes my day off.*

Chapter Twenty-Four

On the phone with Harvey Gibson, Whalen took pleasure in describing how he had averted what might have been a serious blow to international relations and a possible public relations disaster for the Fair. Gibson was used to his hyperbole and accepted it as part of the package.

"By the way," said Whalen, "you'll be surprised to learn that our old friend Shadgen was among the ambassador's guests."

Gibson was indeed surprised. "Good Lord, what was he doing there? I thought he swore he'd never set foot on the fairgrounds."

"That he did, back in November. But he is Belgian, you know, or was until he became an American citizen. He's an admirer of Van de Velde, who designed the building, and looked him up when he came over to check that everything was in order. Van de Velde invited him out to see it. At least that's what he told me."

"You mean you spoke to him? I thought you were afraid to go near him, in case he might assault you."

"I admit I was nervous when he approached me, but only a madman would have come at me with all those cops on guard, and whatever else Shadgen is, he's not crazy. Angry, yes. Bitter, certainly. But he was remarkably civil. In fact, he said he was glad to see me, especially under the circumstances, which were embarrassing to say the least. He was smirking when he told me how much he enjoyed watching me try to cover up the Fair's ineptitude, of which he had heard there was plenty."

Gibson grunted. "Damned nerve. I admit there've been some slip-ups, and quite a few setbacks entirely beyond our control, but all things considered, we're in good shape for opening day. Mind you, not every exhibit will be ready. Unless we can iron out that dispute with the electricians, Belgium's opening may be delayed. What the hell is the problem, anyway?"

"I believe it's about overtime pay. As you know, the Belgians aren't the only ones complaining about excessive labor costs. The unions have them by the short hairs, and they're not happy about it."

Gibson, the money man, had faced the same issues regarding Fair-financed construction and installation expenses. "I realize you've done your best to iron out those differences, Grover, and I appreciate your diligence, but in the end, it's up to the individual exhibitors to cover their costs. They knew the Fair was a closed shop when they signed on.

"Tell me," he continued, "did you find out why Shadgen called you a few weeks ago?"

"Yes. He'd had a change of heart about never visiting the Fair. He wanted to see the Belgium pavilion and assumed he'd need my authorization. He was right about that. When I wouldn't accept his call, he thought about asking in writing but was so offended by my snub that he decided to drop it. Then Van de Velde arrived and offered to take him along. So, he got to see the building and listen to the Count give me a dressing-down in front of the whole group and the cops. He said that gave him more satisfaction than getting the settlement check."

* * *

By the time Fitz's shift was over, Friday's extra duty roster for the Belgium pavilion patrol had been posted. He was relieved to see that his name was not on it. Whalen had wasted no time in making good on his promise. His call to Captain Consolla at the One Ten had gotten a few more officers temporarily assigned to the Fair. Congratulating himself on having the luck of the Irish, Fitz approached Nancy's desk, cleared his throat, blew his nose, and signed out for a sick day.

He did not share news of his good fortune with the family. As far as they knew, he'd be reporting for duty tomorrow morning as usual. When the phone rang, he hurried to answer and kept his end of the conversation neutral, so if they heard him, they wouldn't catch on.

"Hi, there. Thanks for calling. Have you got anything for me?"

"Yes, plenty. But you'll have to come to my studio to get it. Can you take off tomorrow?"

"Sure, that's fine. Let me have the details."

She realized why he was being vague and played along. "Here's the address. Take the IND to Twenty-Third and Eighth. How's eleven o'clock?"

"Perfect. Thanks a lot. Bye, now." Kind of a lame sign-off, but a necessary precaution. He knew she understood.

Bridget came into the hall on her way to the kitchen. "Was that one of those horrible Bund people? I wish you hadn't gotten involved with them. They scare me."

"They scare me, too, Mom. What they represent is scary. And to think that thousands of Americans agree with them, it makes you wonder how folks can be so gullible. But as long as they're within the law, it's hard to fight them. I'm hoping I can get them to break the law. Then we can nail them. But it has to be done from the inside, that's why I had to join."

He put his arms around his mother, whose head only reached as far as his chin, and gave her a hug. "You understand, don't you?" She stepped back from his embrace, drew herself up to full height, and gave her son a hard look.

"Brian Francis Xavier Fitzgerald, you cannot hope to understand how a mother feels when her child is in danger. It's bad enough that I have to worry about you and your father getting injured, or worse, in the line of duty, but what you're doing is beyond anything a patrolman is required to do. And you, a rookie at that! You always were headstrong, but this is too much. For my sake, please get out while you can."

Fitz displayed his stubborn streak again. "I'm sorry, Mom, but I have to go through with it. It seems like no amount of opposition is having an effect. Even Walter Winchell can't turn enough people against them."

With millions of nationwide listeners to his Sunday night broadcasts on the NBC-Blue radio network, Winchell had the public ear. The veteran journalist turned gossip columnist was a sworn enemy of the Bund, with a special animus for its leader, Fritz Kuhn, whom he reviled as Khunazi, the Shamerican, Chief of the Ratzis. His slangy, rapid-fire commentary denounced the Bund's cynical pseudo-patriotism and fanatical anti-Semitism, which was especially offensive to Winchell, who was Jewish.

But his diatribes, as well as universal condemnation by mainstream political and religious leaders, had done little to diminish the Bund's influence. It seemed they were gaining momentum among nationalists, xenophobes, anti-Semites and anti-Communists around the country, except perhaps in New York City, where the Garden rally had sparked a backlash and the mayor was already working with the District Attorney's office to find ways to go after them without violating any of their constitutional rights. The city was their headquarters, and if they were going to be undermined and ultimately put out of business, it would have to be done here, at the top.

As Bridget shook her head and walked to the kitchen, muttering, "I don't know what to do with that boy," the phone rang again. This time it was the Bund. A voice asked to speak to Brian Fitzgerald, and Fitz identified himself.

"This is Director Kunze's secretary calling. You are to report to his office tomorrow evening at seven. Do not be late. The meeting will discuss the proposed World's Fair rally."

Fitz's heart skipped a beat. Things were moving quickly. "Yes," he told the secretary, "I'll be there."

If they did decide to go ahead with the rally, would they want to do it before the Fair opened, or after? He needed to formulate a persuasive case for them to do it before, while the NYPD was still handling Fair security. No doubt, maximizing publicity would be desirable, suggesting a demonstration when the public was on the grounds. But the potential for success also had to be considered. If they planned to march in, they'd want as little interference as possible. Suppose the fairgoers turned against them? During the Garden rally, it was only the large police presence—and the Ordnungsdienst's wise precaution of hiding their Nazi-style uniforms under overcoats when they left the hall, which kept the huge crowd of protestors from attacking them.

He supposed that Schultz, who had insider knowledge of the Fair's workings, would be at the meeting, so he mustn't say anything he could contradict. He'd also have to avoid involving any other Fair personnel, who might spill the beans to their bosses, or other police officers, who might do the same to O'Toole. He didn't have time to find out which of them, if any, were sympathetic to the Bund. He hoped it was none. Some of his fellow cops had German last names, but that didn't make them automatically pro-Nazi. Look at Elaine's family, a hundred percent patriotic Americans, yet stigmatized during the last war only because their name was Fried.

That thought helped him focus on tomorrow's rendezvous with Elaine and put the Bund at the back of his mind. He could talk it over with her and get her advice, but that wouldn't be their first topic of conversation.

* * *

On Friday morning, Fitz rang the bell marked DE KOONING just before 11:00 a.m. The subway ride from Queens Plaza had taken less time than he'd allowed, and the loft was only a short walk from the 23rd Street station.

Elaine stuck her head out the third-floor window and shouted to him, "The buzzer doesn't work. Let yourself in. Here, catch!" She threw down a Spaldeen—the pink rubber ball used in Brooklyn stickball, of which she was a champion—with a key tied to it.

If he hadn't seen that she was on three, Fitz would have known it was the right floor by the odor. The studio door was open, filling the hall with the aroma of oil paint and turpentine. He knocked and called her name, and she answered, "Come on in, I'm at the back. Be right with you."

It was a floor-through loft, with north windows facing 22nd Street at the front, where de Kooning had his studio. A few surprisingly realistic drawings, including an exquisite portrait of Elaine, were pinned to the wall. There was also a large easel with an unfinished painting of a man on it, a palette table, a worktable on sawhorses, a low daybed and, against one wall, a large supply cabinet and a shelf unit holding numerous books and art magazines. With a mental picture of the bohemian stereotype, he was expecting a messy place, but it was remarkably neat and tidy.

To his left, a curtain separated the working and living spaces, and he could hear footsteps behind it as Elaine approached. She pulled the curtain aside, revealing a makeshift kitchen area, with a double sink and cooktop and a small table with two chairs. Beyond it, a screen partially concealed a double bed. The toilet was in the hall.

At the very back, separated by another screen, was Elaine's studio, with windows facing the alley to the south. Not the ideal orientation, but both she and Bill wanted privacy when they worked, so being at opposite ends of the loft was the best arrangement.

"Follow me," she said, and headed toward her studio. She wore a floor-length, V-neck dressing gown, made of grosgrain fabric that rustled as she walked. Its form-fitting cut emphasized her round, firm breasts and slender waist, and its short, slightly puffy sleeves flattered her smooth arms. When she turned to face him, he saw it was held closed by a self-belt; there were no buttons.

"Do you like my wrap?" she asked coyly. Hands on hips, she twisted this way and that to show off its flared skirt. "It came from S. Klein On The Square. I get all my clothes there. They have such lovely things, and the prices are so reasonable. I often go there for frocks and robes, like this one, to wear for modeling, and I leave the price tags on, so when the job is over, I can take them back. Here, I'll show you."

She slipped the dressing gown off to reveal the tag tucked inside. She was wearing nothing underneath.

They only got as far as the bed.

Chapter Twenty-Five

Now he was really hooked. His limited experience hadn't prepared him for Elaine's uninhibited sexuality, playful one minute and demanding the next. Her energy was as exhilarating as it was exhausting.

When they had satisfied each other, he was ready for a nap, but she had something else on her mind.

"Come on, sleepyhead. Time for lunch. Screwing always makes me hungry."

She said it so guilelessly that it seemed like the most natural thing, even though food was the last thing he was thinking about. What he wanted was a rest and then a rematch. She started to get out of bed, but he pulled her back.

"I want you for lunch."

"I was the appetizer," she said, and licked his bare chest. "It's time for the main course. I don't cook, so we'll need to go out for that. But leave room for dessert. We can have that here." She patted the bed. She was ready to come back for more, but was he? Maybe a lunch break wasn't such a bad idea. They got dressed and headed out.

* * *

In Stewart's Cafeteria on 23rd Street, they ordered Reuben sandwiches and celery soda, and Fitz told her about the meeting coming up that night.

"They want me there at seven, like last time. I think they're going ahead with the demonstration. The sooner, the better, as far as I'm concerned. I hope I can convince them that if they get a permit to protest at the gate, they can also march into the grounds. It is City property, after all."

"Do you think you should call the mayor's office and alert them?"

"Not a bad idea, once I find out the date. The D.A. is already after the Bund. He's looking for ways to press charges, and this might give him a great opportunity to nab some of them. Especially Kuhn."

He reached across the table and took her hand. "Meeting you, well, I can't believe my luck, Elaine. Even if we hadn't become what you call involved, your tip about the Bund has given me a chance to help destroy it. Okay, maybe not actually kill it, but at least cripple it, especially if the big boys get arrested. I have to persuade them that they must be there."

"You can do it, Fitz. Just let them take the lead. You may not have to work too hard to line them up. I can't imagine a bigmouth bully like Kuhn missing a chance to strut and bluster in public, especially with a bunch of reporters and photographers covering it."

"No doubt Kunze will see to it that there's plenty of press. I wonder how many demonstrators they'll be able to turn out."

"Judging by the Garden rally, it could be thousands. It's easy to get there on the el."

"Yeah, but that's not the entrance they should use," said Fitz. "If they want to get to the vacant exhibit space in the Government Zone, they'll need to use the Flushing gate. That way, they only have to march in a few yards instead of all the way across the grounds and risk being intercepted before they could reach the building."

"But that won't appeal to them if it cuts down on their numbers."

"I bet plenty of their members have cars, and they could hire buses for the rest. There's a big parking lot over there. Even a thousand angry Nazis would make quite a show."

"What if they decide to do both? Rally at the el station and the Flushing gate?"

Fitz had to hand it to her. Apart from being gorgeous and sensational in bed, Elaine was as smart as any of his Police Academy instructors. He gave the question some thought.

"I'm sure glad you brought that up. It would certainly boost their numbers if folks could get there on the el. But they have to specify where the rally will take place, so I'm pretty sure they'd need two permits, one for each gate. If they propose it, I'll tell them that the el station protest could be a diversion from the real aim of getting into the vacant building and setting up a German exhibit. Maybe that'll make it seem more likely to succeed."

Elaine squeezed his hand and polished off her celery soda. "How likely is it that you'll succeed in finishing that sandwich and paying the check so we can get back to the studio for dessert?"

* * *

She kicked him out at 4:00 p.m., with the excuse that she needed to get some work done before Bill got back. Her still life was progressing well, but she was having trouble with the reflective surfaces, which would be tricky even for a much more experienced painter. Besides, she told him, she needed a break before she could concentrate on the canvas. If he didn't leave, she'd be thinking about him instead. She promised to call him on Saturday morning to find out how the meeting went.

With a couple of hours to kill before heading uptown, Fitz decided to visit the library to read up on the Bund. He hadn't paid much attention to the press reports over the past couple of years; even the Garden rally hadn't registered strongly. It was only when his father brought it up that it began to sink in, and now that he was actually a Bund member, he felt he needed more background.

He walked over to the Muhlenberg branch on West 23rd Street and consulted the newspaper files. Checking through full copies of the City's many dailies was an overwhelming prospect, but fortunately, there was a large clip file of articles about the Bund. Columns from the *Daily News*, the *Times*, the *Mirror*, the *Post* and the *Journal-American* provided him with ample information.

Reports in the bilingual Yiddish-English *Jewish Daily Forward* were especially inflammatory, filled with dire warnings about Nazi influence at home and malevolent progress overseas. There were even copies of the Bund's own bilingual German-English weekly, *Deutscher Weckruf Und Beobachter and The Free American,* overflowing with the same vitriol spewed at its rallies. Articles railed against the pervasive Jewish influence and godless Communist ideology spreading through American culture, undermining wholesome values and promoting decadence in the arts.

The research was as depressing as it was revealing. He hadn't been aware of the Bund's symbiotic relationship with Father Charles Coughlin, the Roman Catholic priest whose weekly radio broadcast, *Golden Hour,* used the Sunday-sermon format to promote his so-called Social Justice agenda, heavy with anti-Communist, anti-Semitic, pro-Fascist, and pro-Nazi rhetoric. The Fitzgerald family weren't *Golden Hour* listeners, so Fitz had no idea that a man of the cloth was preaching such toxic propaganda from the pulpit. He was not especially devout, but the thought of a "radio priest" in league with the Bund revolted him.

He was also shocked to learn that no less a revered public figure than the aviator Charles A. Lindbergh was favorably inclined toward the Nazi regime and had even accepted a medal from them. Not that Lindbergh was alone in warning European and American leaders that Germany was far better prepared for conflict, but his sympathies seemed to go beyond admiration for its superior air power. The *Forward* had been quick to pick up on his anti-Semitic attitude and advice against aiding countries threatened with Nazi invasion, which, as Kristallnacht had vividly demonstrated, would have dire consequences for their Jewish populations.

Reading these accounts made Fitz feel like a sleepwalker. How had he missed so much consequential information? Why had he paid so little attention to world news, breezing through to get to the sports page and the comics? But, however ignorant he had been, he was now wide awake and fully aware. And determined to play his part, however small, in preventing Nazi ideology from infecting America.

* * *

Fitz was still at breakfast when the phone rang. Bridget was on her way to answer it when he breezed past her. "I'll get it," he announced. "I'm expecting a call." His mother's disapproving silence followed him down the hall.

Elaine skipped the greeting. "How did it go? What did they decide?"

"It's going ahead," he told her. "I convinced them that a pre-opening demonstration would be more effective, since there are lots of other mass gatherings planned for the first few weeks, and the police force will be much bigger after the Fair opens. And you were dead right about them wanting to double up. They want a big rally at the el station entrance and a smaller one at the Flushing gate, right by the vacant exhibit space. They're gonna go with Schultz's idea of a German display, and they can bring stuff right to the gate in a van."

He chuckled. "You know what? They didn't invite Schultz. Can't say I was surprised. Kunze took credit for the whole scheme, so he couldn't risk the real idea man shooting off his mouth in front of Kuhn and a couple of high-ranking members of his private goon squad, the so-called Order Police."

"So the big boss was there?"

"Sure. He had to approve the final plan. They'd already decided to go ahead, but they needed an insider's take on logistics, so that's where I came in."

"Did they set a date?"

"Saturday the twenty-second, a week before opening. It'll take 'em a week or so to get the permits. If they apply on Monday, they'll have approval in plenty of time. That blowhard Kuhn was crowing, in his thick German accent, that the man he called Fiorello 'Jew Lumpen' LaGuardia wouldn't dare deny their right to hold a peaceful protest. That's true, but I need to talk to someone in the mayor's office to make sure the permit wording makes it seem like they'll be okay entering the grounds, when in fact they won't be. Dad will know who to call."

"Mind if I offer a suggestion?" Elaine asked, and went ahead before he could answer. "I don't think you should be the one to deal with the mayor's office. You're only a rookie patrolman, and what you're doing with the Bund is highly irregular, or as Kuhn might say, verboten. Why should they take you seriously? And even if they do, you told me yourself that if O'Toole gets wind of it, your goose will be cooked."

"Well then, what's the right move?"

"You should hand it over to your father. He can say he got a tip from an insider. Coming from a police captain, it's likely to get the result you want."

Goddamn, she did it again. It should have occurred to him, but the fact that it hadn't only made it clearer that he wasn't cut out to be a detective.

Chapter Twenty-Six

Fitz found his father in the back yard, working on his motorcycle. Tim was very proud of his 1938 Indian Chief, a model favored by police departments around the country. Bought on the recommendation of his friends in the Motorcycle Squad, this was his new toy, and he was looking forward to getting it on the road now that spring had come. He'd been saving up for a sidecar so he could take Bridget to the beach.

While Tim tuned the brakes, Fitz grabbed a chamois and started polishing the front mudguard, which was already spotless. Sensing that his son's real purpose was not cleaning the bike, Tim asked, "What's on your mind, Brian?"

"I didn't tell you why I came home late last night. I went to a Bund meeting. They wanted me there because they're going ahead with the rally at the Fair, and I'm their inside man. I told them they should do it before the Fair opens, and they agreed. They want to split it into two, one bunch at the el station and another at the Flushing gate. The plan is to enter one of the vacant exhibit spaces in the Government Zone and set up a display glorifying Nazi Germany, which doesn't have a pavilion. They'll have to get two police permits, or one permit that covers both locations. They know they have to apply to my precinct, and they want me to facilitate it. Do you think LaGuardia will let it go through?"

"Hizonner won't block it," said Tim. "When people criticized him for allowing the Bund's rally in Yorkville last year, he limited the parade route and imposed other restrictions, but he wouldn't deny their right to free speech, however obnoxious and even personally insulting to him. He could do something like that again, but it would be against his principles to pressure

Consolla to turn them down. Frankly, I'm not sure he actually has the authority to do that. Maybe Commissioner Valentine does, but on what grounds?"

"So you're saying the mayor could influence the terms of the permit, even if he couldn't veto it?"

"Damn right he could. Let 'em march, but with limitations."

Fitz reminded him of their Wednesday night dinner-table conversation. "I'm thinking of Alice's idea about getting them a permit that's not valid on the fairgrounds, but they believe it is. Do you think LaGuardia could come up with something like that?"

"Gotta hand it to Alice. I'm glad one of my kids inherited my brains as well as your mother's beauty."

"Ouch, Dad, that hurt! I'm trying to use what brains I did get from you to figure out how to make the Bund break the law so we can arrest them, but I don't know what to do."

A bald-faced lie. Thanks to Elaine, he knew exactly what to do, but he wanted it to come from his father.

"You're sure this is for real?" Tim asked. Fitz nodded. "What's the date?" Fitz told him. "They'll have to wait until Monday to apply. It will go directly to Consolla, but Joe can be given, shall we say, guidance on the wording."

Fitz decided to play the impetuous card. "Who should I call to get the ball rolling?"

His father took the bait. "Not you, you lunkhead. Use those brains! If you call the mayor's office and hand them that line, they'll get straight onto O'Toole to check on it. Then you'll learn personally why they call him Hammer."

"I guess you're right, Dad. But I have to get the information to the right people."

"Leave it to me," said Tim, and Fitz silently congratulated himself. "Let's go inside and work out some wording that I can pass along to Newbold Morris. He has LaGuardia's ear." As president of the New York City Council, Morris sometimes served as the mayor's surrogate, which he had done during the Bund's Madison Square Garden rally while Hizonner was out of town. A graduate of Yale Law School, Morris had no sympathy for the Bund's cause, and could be counted on to create a document that would hold up in court.

* * *

From his office at the Five Nine, Tim put through a Monday morning call to the City Council. He explained his purpose to Morris's personal assistant and was connected.

"Good morning, Captain Fitzgerald. My assistant tells me you have a rather interesting request. Please let me know the details."

"I received a tip that the Bund is planning to apply for a permit to rally at the World's Fair a week before the official opening day. Their aim is to protest Germany's exclusion and set up an ad hoc German exhibit in one of the empty spaces in the Government Zone. I've confirmed that this information is legit, and I see it as an opportunity to arrest the Bund leaders, who will very likely be there. They plan to assemble at the el station entrance and the gate off Rodman Street. The question is, if they enter the fairgrounds, will they be trespassing?"

Morris considered the question. "All the land leased to the Fair Corporation is owned by the City of New York. If they have a permit to rally at the Fair, it could be limited to the property outside the perimeter and exclude the grounds themselves."

"But in that case, sir, they'd know that entering was prohibited. We want them to think that going in is legal, so they won't realize they're breaking the law." He and Fitz had come up with a draft that made the permit ambiguous. He was about to read it when Morris interjected.

"As I said, the fairgrounds and surroundings, such as parking lots, access roads, and rapid transit stations, belong to the City. The point, however, is that while the land is City property, the buildings on it are not. They belong to the exhibitors or to the Fair Corporation itself. Unauthorized entry into any of them would be an act of trespass."

"I see," said Tim. "So the permit could allow the Bund access to the grounds and just not mention that the buildings are off limits. Once they go inside the exhibit space, they'd be breaking the law."

"Yes, that is correct. Let's hope they don't realize that the building is private property and therefore not covered by the permit. I'll be glad to ask my clerk to draft it and send it to the relevant precinct, which I believe is the hundred and tenth. Please advise the officer in charge to expect my clerk to send it over. The precinct will issue it, and will also be responsible for any arrests, if the Bund falls into your trap."

Tim couldn't see Morris' smile, but he heard the equivalent in his voice. "I must congratulate you, Captain Fitzgerald, for coming up with a possible means of hobbling the Bund. As you may know, the District Attorney's office is working along similar lines, looking for grounds on which to charge them. So far, they've been unsuccessful. I hope your plan will succeed."

* * *

Tim's next call was to Captain Consolla at the One Ten to let him know the plan. Then he called the precinct outpost in the New York City Building and asked Nancy to have his son call him when he checked in. An hour later, his intercom buzzed to let him know Fitz was on the line.

"Great news, Brian. Morris is all for it, and even came up with a better way to nail them. I'll give you the details tonight, but I wanted you to know that his office will handle it."

Fitz couldn't talk freely on the desk phone. "Thanks a million, Dad. We'll discuss it when I get home. Meanwhile, there's been another incident involving a muralist, and this time there's no question it's vandalism. Someone splashed house paint on a couple of murals in the WPA Building. Another one for O'Toole."

"I don't suppose you're going to butt out and let him handle it."

"He hasn't made any headway so far."

"That's not an answer. What happened, anyway?"

Fitz went over what was known so far. The deed must have been done overnight on Sunday, when the artist and his assistants were off. The building manager discovered the damage on Monday morning. Someone had climbed the scaffold and thrown enamel paint on the two canvases that had just been installed. The interior was being finished, so there were plenty of cans of it lying around.

When Fitz arrived at the scene, the artist, Anton Refregier—a founder of the original Artists Union, active UAA Local 60 member, and vocal supporter of workers' rights—was distraught. The results of three months' intensive work had been horribly disfigured, and there was no time to repaint the vandalized murals before the Fair opened. It took a while for Fitz to calm him down enough to get a coherent statement.

As Refregier explained it, the plan called for five vertical canvases, each eight feet wide and thirty feet tall, and three shorter over-door panels, filling half the wall space in the sixteen-sided theater lobby. Two had gone up, and the other six were rolled and awaiting installation. He had painted them in the Brooklyn scenic workshop the WPA had rented so the work could proceed while the building was under construction. The theme was "Cultural Activities of the WPA," illustrating various aspects of Federal One, as the visual, literary, and performing arts projects were collectively known, and how they benefited the public.

After several false starts on developing a unifying scheme, as well as coping with an unusually tall, narrow format, Refregier had hit on the motif of a brick wall as an anchoring device. It made perfect sense, since construction was a primary WPA function. The wall was shown in perspective, winding its way up each of the panels. In one of the two already installed, a muralist was painting on the wall—a highly appropriate self-referential device. In the other, a hole in the wall served as the proscenium for a children's puppet show, courtesy of the Federal Theatre Project. Both compositions were now defaced by random splashes of semi-gloss enamel, which was being used to paint the blank walls between the mural panels.

Just as Refregier's anger and indignation were descending into despair, Philip Guston had turned up. After the incident with the ladder, he took the precaution of requesting a WPA worker to stand guard overnight. The assignment was approved, so his façade mural was progressing without further interference and was nearly finished.

Once past his initial shock at confronting what seemed to be irreparable damage, Guston took a close look at the empty paint cans and reassured Refregier that all was not lost.

All the WPA Building muralists used Glyptol, a synthetic casein resin paint developed by the art project's technical workshop. The novel formula was durable, fade-resistant and water-based. The vandal had used oil-based house paint. Guston said it should be possible to clean the murals with turpentine or mineral spirits without damaging them, since the solvent wouldn't work on Glyptol.

Overwhelmed with relief, Refregier embraced Guston, pronounced him a genius, and kissed him on the lips—a traditional gesture of man-to-man camaraderie in his native Russia but shocking to Fitz and the assembled crew. Guston, whose family had emigrated from Odessa, was unfazed. He asked the building manager if he could use the phone to call Project headquarters and request a clean-up detail. While they worked, Refregier and his assistants could get on with installing the other six panels.

The director, Audrey McMahon, assured Guston that a group of experienced muralists would be sent over immediately, and an overnight guard would be stationed inside the building. More interior murals extolling the WPA's social, cultural, and economic contributions were scheduled to go up in the next few days, and she wanted to ensure that no further damage would be done to the Federal Art Project's crowning achievement.

Chapter Twenty-Seven

O'Toole was not pleased to add yet another mural incident to the already long list, though he was grateful that this one didn't involve personal injury or death. It was a clear case of vandalism, and it strongly suggested that the others were also not accidents after all. Someone really did appear to be sabotaging muralists, and his investigation was getting nowhere.

Fitz turned over his notes to the detective and beat a hasty retreat. More convinced than ever that an envious WPA muralist was the culprit, he had an idea of how to gain access to the Board of Design files and identify a likely suspect. But first, he wanted to pay a call on Stuart Davis in the Communications Building, which was directly on his way.

"Glad to see you, Fitz," said Davis as he climbed down from the scaffold. "I missed you at lunch on Friday."

"Sorry, I was out sick. Must have been a twenty-four-hour bug. I'm fine now." He wasn't going to tell Davis the truth about either his tryst with Elaine or his Bund meeting. What he did tell him was the story of Refregier's murals being defaced.

"Jesus, what a mess. At least no one was hurt," said Davis, unconsciously massaging his healing left shoulder. "I hope the clean-up crew can get the oil paint off without damaging Ref's work. From what you say, Phil thinks it won't be a problem. I've never used Glyptol, but he loves the stuff. The fact that it thins and cleans up with water makes it much nicer to use, and they tell me the colors are just as brilliant as oils. Dries a lot quicker, too. But it's not available commercially. Only WPA artists have access to it."

"Would everyone on the WPA know that it's different from oil paint?"

"I doubt it. It's still experimental, and only people with big jobs would be using it. It really speeds up the work. I think all the WPA Building muralists were given it. The Project supplies their materials. The Fair bought the paint for my mural, and disappointed me plenty when they wouldn't spring for the expensive phosphorescent stuff. I'm happy with the way it's turning out, but it would have been a real eye-catcher if it glowed in the dark."

"The reason I asked," said Fitz, "is that I was having second thoughts about a disgruntled WPA artist being responsible. If they knew the oil paint wouldn't ruin Refregier's mural, they'd have found a different way of sabotaging him. But what you've told me has me back to thinking I was on the right track. Sure you haven't heard anything that might point the finger?"

Davis pursed his lips and looked thoughtful. "If I had, I'd be struggling with my conscience, unless it was a dead cert. As it is, my conscience is clear. I can bring it up again at Wednesday's union meeting, but I very much doubt you'll get anywhere with that line of inquiry."

"I understand. As it happens, I have another way to investigate that possibility, one that may not occur to O'Toole."

"Think you can outsmart the ace detective? Don't suppose he'll thank you for your effort if you do."

"You ain't kiddin', Stuart. If I do get a lead, I'll have to find a way to tip him off without him knowing where it came from."

* * *

Fitz said goodbye to Davis and walked across Main Street to the Administration Building. At the reception desk, he asked the way to Gustav Schultz's office in the Exhibits and Concessions Department. The receptionist said she'd ring him, which she did, and received the okay to send the officer in.

The department occupied a suite with several desks, at which men and women were busy on phones and typewriters, and a few individual offices with glass walls, one of which belonged to Schultz, whose name and title, Senior Clerk, were lettered on the door. Fitz had imagined him as a lowly functionary, but evidently his rank was fairly high. Just goes to show, he said to himself, you can't always judge by appearance.

Schultz opened the office door and greeted him. "Please come in, Officer Fitzgerald. How may I help you?" Once inside with the door closed, he said, "I heard you had a meeting on Friday. Please sit and tell me the latest news." Schultz was trying hard to keep his voice neutral, but Fitz heard an undertone of disappointment at having been left out. He decided to revise the minutes a bit.

"Your plan was praised as an excellent way to further the Bund's cause and get plenty of publicity. Everything you suggested was approved. It's scheduled for the twenty-second. There'll be a large rally at the el station and a smaller one at the Flushing gate, which will march to the vacant building and set up the German display. I'm responsible for seeing to it that the door is unlocked and the police don't block their access. My precinct will issue the permit, and I'll make sure it's approved." That was far outside his authority, but he already knew it would go through.

A satisfied smile spread across Schultz's face. "I'm delighted to hear this. I only regret that my position in the Fair administration will prevent me from participating. But I'll be cheering them on in absentia."

His remark helped Fitz transition to his real reason for visiting Schultz, whom he could easily have informed by phone. "As far as the Fair is concerned, it wouldn't be advisable for either of us to reveal our ties to the Bund. Better to work quietly from the inside. Which reminds me, in your position dealing with exhibits, do you have access to Board of Design records?"

The question caught Schutz off guard. "Yes, to some extent. Why do you ask?"

"As you no doubt know, there's been a series of incidents involving muralists, including one fatality. We're treating them as possible sabotage, but so far we haven't identified any likely suspect or suspects. It's been suggested that a rival union is behind it, but I think a rejected muralist may be responsible, someone who didn't get the jobs and wants to punish those who did. If I can look at the applications, maybe I can find an artist who fits the bill."

Schultz looked intrigued. "I see what you're driving at. An artist who applied but never won a Fair commission. Those records would indeed be in the Board of Design files, which are up on the second floor. There are two different classifications—applications submitted for Fair Corporation buildings and private exhibitors' submissions for approval—amounting to hundreds of individual proposals. It would take you quite a while to sort through all of them."

"I'm only interested in Fair-sponsored murals and the WPA Building. There were two incidents there, one just last night."

"That narrows it down a lot, but it's still a large number. The WPA file will include only the final designs for approval, so you'd have to go to the Federal Art Project office in Manhattan to find out who was rejected, but the files upstairs will have all the submitted proposals for the Fair's own buildings."

"Can you arrange for me to see them?"

"As part of an official police investigation, which I'm aware is underway, I don't think it'll be a problem. I'll call Baker, the office manager. I'm sure he could authorize it without having to go through Kohn or Teague." The architect Robert D. Kohn, chairman of the design board's Committee on Theme, and the industrial designer Walter Dorwin Teague were in charge of implementing the Fair's futuristic concept and ensuring that all architectural and decorative elements conformed to the board's guidelines. With opening day only three weeks away, their work was finished. Soon, the public and the press would judge whether they had fulfilled their mission.

Schultz's request received a favorable response. As he and Fitz climbed the stairs to the second floor, he asked, "Have you considered Joseph Shadgen as a suspect? The Fair was his idea, and he never got proper credit for it. He used to work in the design board's drafting department, but he was fired, and he's very bitter over his treatment."

"Interesting you should think of him," said Fitz. "He actually showed up here last Thursday, with the Belgian ambassador's delegation. Grover had been afraid he'd come around and make trouble, so he told the gate guards and the cops to keep a lookout for him and not let him on the grounds. But he was with the ambassador's party, so he came in by the back door, so to speak. I was in the escort detail. We were on the alert in case he tried something, but he was well-behaved. I even saw him and Grover having a chat, so I guess they decided to patch things up. Anyway, I don't see him sabotaging muralists. More likely to go after one of the higher-ups who got him canned. That's why Grover was spooked."

* * *

With not much to occupy him, Fred Baker was grateful for the company and glad to help Fitz find the relevant information. He directed him to a seat at a table opposite a bank of filing cabinets and flat files.

"The Fair Corporation commissioned seventy-four artists, thirty-nine of whom are muralists working on our own buildings for the various zones," Baker explained. "Some of them were recommended by the architects, and six were subsidized by an outside group, but most were chosen from submitted designs. I guess those are the ones you're interested in."

"Yes," said Fitz, "in particular, any cases where a few artists were under consideration, and especially if the same artist was rejected more than once."

"That should narrow it down quite a bit." Baker opened a file drawer marked C. "As I recall, Communications and Community Interests were both competitive." He removed several folders and handed them across to Fitz. "Why don't you make a start on these, and I'll pull the rest for you."

In the folder marked Communications-Mural-Exterior, correspondence indicated that Eugene Savage had been recommended by the architect and was unanimously accepted. The folder for the interior mural held cover letters from four artists, including Davis, describing their proposed designs. One of the other three was Lee Krasner. Fitz made a note of their names.

"Excuse me, Mr. Baker. Do you have the actual sketches that came with these proposals?"

"Yes, they're in the flat files, alphabetical by artist. Come to think of it, if you search them, you'll find those with multiple submissions, if there were any, for all the Fair-built buildings. The board held onto the sketches in case they wanted to consider the artist for something else, unless they specifically asked for them to be returned."

Fitz stood and approached the stack of flat files. "Okay if I take a look?"

"Help yourself," said Baker, "But please keep them in order."

"I don't need to remove them. I just want to check on how many jobs each artist may have put in for."

There was only a single proposal on file for Davis; the sketch, very similar to his final Communications design, was stamped accepted. Two of the other contenders for that job had also submitted only once. But Krasner had sent in no fewer than three proposals for different murals. All three were among the saboteur's targets.

For Communications, she submitted a montage of stylized telephones, telegraph keys, radio tubes and other modern messaging apparatus. For Medicine and Public Health, an arrangement of beakers, test tubes, and other laboratory equipment. For Aviation, a survey of aircraft, from hot air balloons to the Pan American Clipper. They were done in the cubistic style favored by followers of Hans Hofmann, the influential German émigré teacher who was training a generation of young American modernists. Krasner had been his student for a couple of years and had thoroughly mastered his abstract approach.

Having confirmed his suspicion that Krasner had reason to resent the muralists who had won out over her, Fitz was tempted to end his search there and then. Proper police procedure, however, dictated that he check for other potential suspects, so he reluctantly went back to the folders. In Marine Transportation, he found Feininger's acceptance, as well as Gorky's letter marked rejected, with a follow-up note from Diller recommending him for Aviation. There were also a couple of other rejections, and he noted the artists' names in case they popped up in other files.

Several submissions included letters of recommendation from Diller or McMahon, indicating that the artists were, or had been, on the WPA payroll. In fact, the Medicine and Public Health group were still active Federal Art Project employees, saving the Fair the expense of hiring them. The same was true of the WPA Building muralists, though Guston's façade mural was subject to Board of Design approval, which it received without revision.

It took Fitz a little over an hour to finish his search. Of the scores of artists who submitted proposals for Fair Corporation commissions, four had tried for more than one job. Krasner was the only one who had failed each time.

Chapter Twenty-Eight

"How well do you know Lee Krasner?" Fitz asked Elaine when she called that night.

"Better than I'd like to," she answered tersely.

"Can you be a little more specific?"

"She's pushy. Has an opinion about everything and doesn't mind sharing it, whether or not you want to listen. To hear her tell it, Cubism is the only real modern art and Hans Hofmann is its true prophet."

"Who's Hans Hofmann?"

"He's a German painter who runs an art school in the Village. It was originally in Munich, but when Hitler came to power, he decided to relocate to the States. The Nazis don't tolerate his brand of abstract art. He studied in Paris and knew all the avant-garde hotshots, so he's a living link to the European innovators, passing their theories along to us poor, benighted yokels."

"I take it you're not a fan."

"Actually, I am, with reservations. So many of my friends were raving about him that I went to a couple of his classes. It's very different from conventional art training, where you learn to depict a model or a still life realistically. He looks at things in terms of pictorial organization, so all parts of the composition—the subject and the background—are given equal treatment."

"You're way over my head."

"You'd know what I mean if you saw one of Krasner's paintings or drawings. What I have against it is that it's a rigid system you have to conform to. It doesn't leave room for individuality. And getting the message hidden in his thick German accent was a struggle. The class monitor had to translate for me. So that put me off, plus the fact that he thinks American art is second-rate. Pretty arrogant, though it's true that the most important modern trends have come from Europe. Lee has the same attitude. She has no use for anyone who doesn't toe the Hofmann line, except Igor, that good-for-nothing boyfriend of hers. He's an academic portrait painter who brags that he sleeps with every woman he paints. Why she puts up with him, I'll never know."

Fitz bit his tongue. That was pretty rich, coming from a woman who thought nothing of cheating on Bill with him and who knew how many others, not to mention that Bill was far from faithful.

"Now I know what Igor was up to at the union party when he told my date he wanted to paint her. I think she was wise to him, but in any case, Krasner stepped in. And I overheard her giving one of the other artists hell for taking a job she wanted. Seems to me she has a pretty short fuse."

"That, and a gift for harboring a grudge. Not long before I met Bill, she made a play for him. From what he told me, she wanted to give Igor a taste of his own medicine, but Bill wasn't interested. That rascal is used to women throwing themselves at him, so he shrugged it off, but I don't think she's got over it. She's cordial to him, but she only speaks to me if she has to."

Now came the crucial question. "Temperamental, opinionated, resentful. Do you think she's also the vindictive type?"

Elaine guessed where this was leading. "You think she's the saboteur?"

He told her about his visit to the Board of Design office. "Our friend Schultz got me in. The manager let me look through the files for muralists who'd been rejected, and it turns out Krasner failed three times. A few others, like Gorky, for example, also tried and failed but got a job the second time around. Not Krasner. Three strikes for her. Her sketches were in the files, and they're pretty much like you described the Hofmann style. Flat shapes, very simple and angular, I guess that's what you call Cubism. I kinda liked them, but the guys who decide liked something else better."

"Which buildings were they for?"

"That's the point. All three were for buildings that were hit."

On the other end of the line, Elaine was quiet for a moment. "I don't like Lee, but I have a hard time imagining her wanting to harm fellow artists. You say she lost out to three others, but six have been targeted. One failed sabotage attempt, one act of vandalism, three injuries, and one fatality, Feininger. Did she apply for his job?"

"No, his was Marine Transportation," Fitz told her. "She went for the Communications job Davis got, Gorky's Aviation job, and Medicine and Public Health, which has six muralists. She may also have tried for the Guston or Refregier jobs in the WPA Building, but those proposals aren't in the design board's files. I'll have to go to the art project office to see them."

"Okay," said Elaine, "let's say you find out Lee tried for a WPA Building job and failed. Maybe she's hopping mad and decides to get back at the artists who beat her out. She figures out how to gain access to the fairgrounds. She's physically capable of the various acts of sabotage. She goes after Stuart, Phil, Arshile, Ilya and Ref. But why does she target Feininger? She's not in line for his job. And why kill him? Surely she'd know that pushing him off such a tall ladder would be fatal."

"His case has been bothering me for a while," Fitz admitted. "It just doesn't fit. All the other incidents involve members of UAA Local 60. Stuart blames it on the rival union, but Feininger was a member, so they had nothing against him."

"Bill told me most of the mural painters are scenic artists scaling up other people's designs. He joined their union so he could work with them on his own project, and he has nothing but praise for their skill. But it's not creative. They're just enlarging someone else's original."

"That's why it doesn't make sense to get rid of Feininger. Even with him dead, there's no replacement. The job is going ahead according to his sketches, like it would have if he hadn't been there at all."

The call ended on a downbeat note. When Fitz tried to make another date with Elaine, she put him off. She was only free during the day, when he was on duty. Evenings and weekends were out, and while she wouldn't give a reason he wasn't an idiot. Having spent several hours at the loft, he had realized she was living with de Kooning. She could hardly bring another lover home while he was there. And as soon as he finished Gorky's mural, probably this week, he'd be there all the time.

He wasn't ready to invite her to dinner with his family, who already disapproved of her for helping with his unauthorized, possibly dangerous, investigations. Besides, the prospect of making small talk in the dining room instead of making love in the bedroom he shared with Andy didn't appeal to either of them. The only chance of privacy would be the Hotel Chelsea or some other rented love nest, which seemed sordid. So they agreed to put the brakes on for the time being.

* * *

By Tuesday morning, when Fitz checked in at the WPA Building, the clean-up crew was hard at work on Refregier's murals. Sure enough, as Guston had predicted, the solvent for the house paint had no effect on Glyptol, and while the removal process was tedious, it was progressing well. In addition to several buckets of mineral spirits and a large quantity of cotton rags, they had a supply of the casein resin paints in case touch-up was needed.

A couple of portable fans were trying to dissipate the odor, but the room still reeked of both the solvent and the adhesive Ref and his assistants were using to install another of the tall panels. More scaffolding had been brought in so they could get on with the job, and Ref was keeping a close eye on the cleaning procedure as he oversaw the tricky process of applying the canvas to the wall smoothly and evenly.

McMahon had assigned three artists to the repair work, and Fitz was not surprised to see that one of them was Krasner. By her own account, offered at top volume at the party, she was the mural division's ace damage controller, so here she was, once again, working on someone else's painting while she waited to get the green light for one of her own.

It occurred to Fitz that he might be able to save himself a trip to search the art project files if he could get Krasner to open up about her unsuccessful Fair proposals. He looked at his watch and saw it was nearly eleven. *They'll break for lunch in about an hour,* he thought, *so I'll stop back and question her then.*

Just then, Ref unhitched and climbed down with some difficulty. He seemed a bit off balance.

"Are you okay, Mr. Refregier?" asked Fitz as he steadied the artist and helped him to a seat.

"I'm feeling dizzy," said Ref. "The fumes are getting to me. We didn't have that problem in the workshop. Glyptol paint is water-based. What with the glue and the solvent, I'm glad I have a harness."

"Too bad there are no windows to open."

"It's Fair policy to have no outside windows. The government and private exhibitors didn't have to follow that rule, but the WPA opted to. It makes the buildings easier to air-condition. Unbroken walls also mean more space for exhibits and murals, so I can't complain. Look how much I have, over seventeen hundred square feet." He swept his arm around the room, then dropped it in his lap. "I think I'd better go outside for a few minutes. Maybe that'll clear my head."

They walked into the courtyard, where an outdoor amphitheater would be hosting free entertainment. On the outside wall above the entrance, "Recreational Activities," Ryah Ludins' three-panel polychrome relief, composed of cutout wooden figures of children at play and adults enjoying various sports, had already been installed. Refregier pointed it out to Fitz.

"Would you believe that such a massive mural was done by a woman who barely comes up to my nose? She had two assistants, but she did much of the physical work herself. Watching her handle the wooden shapes with such skill was inspiring. I tell you, Officer, the positive energy and cooperative spirit in that studio were incredible. It was like a Renaissance workshop, though we're working for the people, not the Church. Or for some fat cat like Rockefeller, who can dictate what even a distinguished muralist like Diego Rivera is allowed to paint on his wall."

"Do you mean to say the art project has no control over what muralists paint?"

"The way it works, they try to match the artist with a sympathetic location.

The administration trusts us to respect the place and understand its needs. As long as the subject matter is appropriate, there's no interference. My friend Lucienne Bloch is a perfect example. Her father is a composer, so when a school wanted a mural for its music room, she was a natural choice. Schools, hospitals, libraries, public housing—any state or municipal building—can benefit from our free labor. They only have to pay for the materials.

"With federal post offices and courthouses, it's a different story. Those are commissions, like the competitive mural jobs here at the Fair. It's a Treasury Department program. Instead of wages, you're paid a fee and have to conform to federal rules and regulations, very restrictive. They want what one critic calls Chamber of Commerce pleasers, nothing controversial and certainly no abstracts. You're required to sign a contract, post a performance bond, like a plumber or electrician, and pay for your materials and any assistants you need. I know a few artists who've done those jobs, but most of us would rather get a WPA paycheck and have more creative freedom."

"Who are you kidding, Ref? You told me you're gonna enter the competition for that big post office job in San Francisco." This rebuke came from Krasner, who had entered the courtyard with her crew, also needing a break from the fumes. "Not that I blame you. Who knows how long we can depend on the WPA? At least the Treasury Department is here to stay, and so is the Postal Service. We all know the WPA is only temporary, like this building and the murals in it."

Krasner plopped down on a seat, lit a cigarette, and handed the pack to Ref, who took one and offered one to Fitz.

"No thanks, I don't smoke," he said, and turned to Krasner. "You probably don't remember, but we met at the union party. Of course, I wasn't in uniform then. I'm Brian Fitzgerald. Stuart Davis introduced us."

"I didn't remember your name, but who could forget that flaming red hair?" said Krasner. "You said you were in security, but didn't mention that you're a cop. That was wise, given the union's history with law enforcement." She took a deep drag on her cigarette. "Are you investigating the vandalism?"

Fitz was trying to judge her intention, but his lack of experience interrogating suspects made it hard. The question was straightforward, and she asked it in a neutral tone, no hint of anything more than interest. She didn't sound to him like someone concerned that he might be getting too close to the truth. If she was the saboteur, she was one cool customer.

He opted to pass the buck. "No, that's Detective O'Toole's department. I just reported the incidents to him." He turned to Ref. "I left before he questioned you and your crew."

"Not the most sympathetic type, is he?" asked Ref rhetorically. "He expected us to come up with a list of suspects, but we have no idea who'd want to throw paint on my work. Besides, we weren't even here when it happened."

"Look at it from his point of view," said Fitz, surprised to find himself sticking up for his nemesis. "Even though you weren't around, you may know somebody who has it in for you." *Might as well open the can of worms,* he thought. "Maybe somebody you beat out for the job."

Krasner piped up. "That would be all the other WPA muralists, me included. Everybody was vying for Fair commissions—even I tried a few times with no luck—but the murals in this building are WPA assignments. We were all eligible."

"Didn't it bother you that you were passed over?" asked Fitz, remembering her outburst at the party and trying to sound merely curious.

Krasner was adamant. "Of course it did! Nothing personal against Ryah," she said, glancing up at the entrance wall, "but her imagery is trite. I could have filled those spaces much more dynamically, and represented the abstract artists. We get too few opportunities as it is."

"If it weren't for Diller's support, you and your fellow Hofmann acolytes wouldn't have any work at all," Ref reminded her. "And McMahon made it clear that this building needed storytelling murals that illustrate the WPA's accomplishments. Your work wouldn't have been appropriate, Lee. You know that."

She started to protest, but thought better of it. "You're right, I don't mean to sound ungrateful. But when I see what you and the others have done here, you can't blame me for being a bit envious. And to think that someone would deface your wonderful murals! It makes my blood boil. I'm just glad they were too stupid to do the job right, and that I can help clean up the mess, even if it is making my eyes water and my head swim."

Ref smiled and gave her a hug. "That's the spirit, Lee. We're all in this together. The union makes us strong!"

"Speaking of cleanup," she said, "When I finish here, I have to get over to Hans' place. There was a fire at the school last night, and I promised to help there, too."

Chapter Twenty-Nine

Hans Hofmann. German refugee. Opposed to Hitler. *Could this be the Bund's work, Fitz wondered, echoing the Nazis' campaign against modern art? Or maybe, given the recent anti-Bund sentiment, part of a backlash against Germans in general?*

"Do you know what caused it?" he asked Krasner.

"It looks like a bunch of paint rags caught fire. That can happen if they're not stored properly. No one was there at the time, but people in the building next door smelled smoke and called the fire department. One of the other students came by this morning to tell me and ask if I'd lend a hand, but I'd already been assigned here, so I said I'd be there tonight."

"So you think it was an accident?"

Krasner heard the uncertainty in his voice. "What makes you think it wasn't?"

"I don't know, it's just that there's a lot of anti-German feeling in the city since that Bund rally at the Garden in February."

"Hans is vehemently opposed to the Bund. He left Germany to get away from what they represent, and he's as outspoken against the Nazis as Marlene Dietrich and Albert Einstein."

"Dietrich and Einstein are public figures, Lee," Ref pointed out. "Their anti-Nazi position is well known. That's not true of Hans and other ordinary people with German names. Their friends know where they stand, but not the general public. I read that there were a hundred thousand protestors outside the Garden, and you can bet not all of them are as smart as Einstein."

"Or as beautiful as Dietrich," quipped Fitz. "But I can see it either way. An anti-German vandal targeting Hofmann just because he's German, or the Bund targeting him because he's the kind of artist Hitler doesn't like."

"Whichever way," said Krasner, "he could be in danger, especially since the fire didn't do that much damage. They might go after him directly. I'm sure he'd pay no attention to me, or the other students warning him, he'd think we were being alarmists. Would you speak to him, Officer Fitzgerald? He'd be more likely to take it seriously coming from you."

"Sure, if you think it will help," said Fitz, who had been thinking of proposing it himself. He was asking himself if the attack on the school might be related to the Fair sabotage, though there was no obvious link. The only thing they had in common was modern art.

Oh, and possibly Lee Krasner.

* * *

They agreed to meet at the el station gate at 5:30 p.m., and for Fitz to stay in uniform so his warning to Hofmann would seem more official. He called to let his mother know he wouldn't be home for dinner. "I'm heading to the Village to help a friend clean up after a fire," he told her. "Not sure how long I'll be."

During the train ride, Krasner filled him in on Hofmann's background and the influence his teaching was having on the young artists who studied with him. She threw in a bit of her own background as well.

"Even as a kid, I was dead set on becoming an artist. But just when I finished art school, the Depression hit rock bottom, and no one wanted to buy paintings by established artists, much less unknowns like me, so I did odd jobs, like waiting tables and modeling, and moved in with my boyfriend to save money. I was kind of drifting artistically, doing half-baked modern paintings without any real idea of how to make them work. I was still struggling when the government starting hiring artists in thirty-three, and I got on the first work-relief project. Then the WPA came along, and so did a regular paycheck. That's when I found out about Hofmann's school, which had just moved downtown to West Ninth Street, right down the block from me. Last year, he moved a block south, to the place we're going to."

"What's so special about his school?" Fitz wanted to know.

"He's a direct link to all the most advanced concepts. He was in Paris for ten years before the war, hanging out with the Cubists, Orphists, Fauves and other ground-breaking painters. When the war came, he went back to Germany and set up his school in Munich, teaching the new theories to the avant-garde there. It's a completely different way of dealing with the basic elements of painting. It's still based on observation, but the way you experience what you see, and translate those feelings to canvas, is much more expressive."

"I probably wouldn't get the distinction."

"You would if you went to the Museum of Modern Art and saw the kind of pictures that blew me away when I was a student. Nothing like the academic pictures I was taught to admire."

"I did visit Mrs. Whitney's museum years ago, on a school field trip, but I've never been to the Modern. I think I need to take a field trip there before I can understand what you're talking about."

Krasner laughed. "The Whitney collection is pretty tame compared to the Modern's. If you're interested, we can go together."

"I think I'd enjoy that," said Fitz. "Then maybe I'll get why Hitler is so against modern art." Remembering one of the *Free American* articles, he continued, "I read that he put on a big display of it, billed as a freak show, so people would mock it. The paper said the artists were fired from their teaching jobs and their work was confiscated from museums and galleries so it wouldn't defile German culture. That's why Feininger left Germany. He was afraid of what Hitler might do to him and his family."

"It isn't only Hitler," she explained. "Stalin is just as bad. They want propaganda for their regimes and their vision for a perfect Germany and Soviet Union, full of happy workers toiling in their service. To tell you the truth, some of the WPA stuff isn't so different, but at least it's about uplifting the people, not glorifying some dictator."

* * *

It was a short walk from the Broadway BMT station to the Hans Hofmann School of Fine Arts at 52 West 8th Street, which also housed the Eighth Street Cinema and, in the basement, a country-themed nightclub, the Village Barn.

A blackened metal trash can, filled with a gooey mass of charred rags, had been dragged to the curb. Piles of waterlogged canvas and paper and a few singed easels had been dumped next to it. As Fitz and Krasner entered the building, the acrid smell of smoke and burned cloth greeted them at the door, on which a hand-lettered sign announced ART CLASSES CANCELLED.

They went up to the third floor, where they heard the voices of students who had volunteered to clean up the mess. Inside the studio, the windows were open and washing, scraping, and sweeping were in progress. Krasner was greeted with a cheer and a question.

"Hallelujah, it's Lee! Grab a bucket and help me over here," cried a young man in paint-stained jeans and a grubby sweatshirt. "Or are you under arrest?"

"Don't be silly, George. I brought Officer Fitzgerald to talk to Hans about the fire. He thinks it might be arson." She introduced Fitz to George McNeil, the school's monitor, and recounted their conversation at the Fair.

"Hans isn't here," McNeil told them. "We convinced him we could handle things, so he went home. He was pretty upset and depressed, and who could blame him?"

"How did the fire start?" asked Fitz.

McNeil pointed to a corner of the room that was especially damaged. Sections of paneling were burned through, and the ceiling was covered in soot. "There was a can of oily paint rags over there that apparently caught fire from spontaneous combustion. It should have been sealed tight, but it was open."

"Aren't you supposed to check those things, George?" said Krasner, whose disapproval was clear. "After all, you're in charge of the studio."

"That's just it, Lee. I'm sure the lid was on it when I left. No one but Hans and I have keys, and he said he didn't come back after hours. Even if he had, I can't imagine him being careless about something so basic. That's why I think Officer Fitzgerald may be onto something."

Fitz asked, "How would someone get into the studio at night?"

"People come and go to the movie theater and the nightclub at all hours, but the studio's always locked when no one's in here. They'd have to jimmy the lock, but the firemen broke down the door when they came in, so there's no way to tell."

"What did they think about the spontaneous combustion idea?"

"That's what they thought it was," said McNeil. "The can of rags was the obvious starting place, so they wrote it up as an accident. The rags are soaked with flammable oil and turp. They can easily go up all by themselves if they're not properly stored."

"So all you'd have to do is throw in a match, and it would look like that's what happened. You wouldn't know it was done deliberately," Fitz reasoned.

"Except that the lid was on when I locked up."

Chapter Thirty

"Do you think Hofmann's in good enough shape to answer a few questions?" asked Fitz. "I want to find out if he's had any threats or knows anybody who might have a grudge against him."

"I guess so," said McNeil, "but you won't be able to understand his heavy accent. I'll have to translate. I'll take you over to his place on West Fourth. Here you go, Lee." He handed over his mop and bucket.

Walking down Sixth Avenue, Fitz asked, "How come you speak German? With a name like McNeil, it doesn't seem likely."

"I grew up in Yorkville, picked it up on the street," said McNeil. "Not many Irish families in that neighborhood, but my dad works in the brewery. I don't really speak it, but I do understand what Hans is saying, which is more than most of the students do. He's been in this country for nearly ten years off and on, but his English is also off and on, so my work as a translator is as important as my monitor job, maybe more."

McNeil confided to Fitz that he'd been worried about some sort of trouble ever since the Bund backlash. "People don't draw distinctions. They assume all Germans support Hitler. Even native-born Americans with German or German-sounding names get lumped in."

"I know," said Fitz. "My friend Elaine said that happened to her family during the war. They're from Brooklyn, but with German roots. Their last name is Fried."

"You're friends with Elaine Fried? She's a pip, isn't she? I met her when she came to a couple of classes, but she didn't stick with it. Hans' methods don't suit her. She gets more conventional art lessons from her boyfriend

Bill, and that's not all he gives her, as you probably know."

Wincing inwardly, Fitz was sorry he'd brought up Elaine's name, but glad he hadn't called her his girlfriend. Evidently, her affair with de Kooning was no secret, but why should it be? They were both single and over the age of consent—in de Kooning's case, way over.

* * *

They climbed the stoop at 177 West 4th Street. McNeil rang Hofmann's bell and was buzzed in.

Instead of his usual ebullient greeting, Hofmann opened the door in silence. He seemed neither surprised nor pleased to see a police officer. He simply nodded and stepped aside to admit the two men, then led them to chairs in the front parlor. With a hopeful look, he finally spoke.

"Zo, Georg, ist gut? Ve haf class tomorrow, nicht vahr?"

McNeil shook his head. "I'm afraid not, Hans. We haven't finished cleaning up the smoke and water damage, and we'll need new easels and supplies that couldn't be salvaged. I don't think we can start up again for at least a few days."

"Mein Got, das ist terrible! Nicht fur me, but fur mein pupils, nicht vahr?"

"Please don't worry, Hans. They'll understand that it'll take a little time to get things back in shape. I'm going to ask them to chip in what they can to buy what's needed, and I'm sure the landlord will replace the damaged paneling." McNeil wasn't at all sure about that, but would try to persuade him to cover the repair costs. Needless to say, the school had no insurance.

Fitz was having no trouble following this conversation, though he didn't know why each of Hofmann's sentences ended in "nicht wahr?" It was one of those characteristically German turns of phrase, like "am I right?" in English, with which he almost always closed his remarks. It was familiar to his students, but it puzzled Fitz.

Hofmann turned his gaze on Fitz. "Vy are you here, officer? Ist dere a law vas broken, nicht vahr?"

"That's what I want to find out, Mr. Hofmann. Not by you, but by someone who wanted to harm you. Can you think of anyone who would do that?"

Hofmann looked stunned. Apparently, it had not occurred to him that the fire might have been set deliberately, even though McNeil had assured him that the paint rags had not been left exposed. His anguish stemmed in part from the feeling that his trusted assistant was covering up his own disastrous mistake.

He glanced down, and noticed that he was wringing his hands. Such an unusual gesture from someone whose self-confidence radiated from him like sunshine. He quieted them, and returned his eyes to meet Fitz's.

"Das ist ridikulis. Mein enemies are all in Chermany, among mein own people."

"That's what I'm getting at, Mr. Hofmann. I've been told you're very anti-Nazi, and I wonder if the pro-Nazi faction here in New York has it in for you. Have you ever had a run-in with the German-American Bund?"

"Schweinehunds!" exclaimed Hofmann. "Von uf dem came to me, vanted my support. I spit on him, said fick dich selbst, und he left."

"That means go fuck yourself," interjected McNeil, though Fitz had got the drift.

"You don't happen to remember his name?"

"Nein. Ein kriechen, how you say, a creep, nicht vahr? Vanted me to renounce modern art, say I vas misguided. Dummkopf!"

Fitz had started taking notes. "When was this, Mr. Hofmann?"

"Zince vun month, vielleicht, ich vergesse."

McNeil translated, "He says he doesn't remember exactly, but he thinks maybe a month or so ago."

Interesting, thought Fitz. *Right around the time the sabotage at the Fair started.*

* * *

Heading back to the school, McNeil suggested they stop for a bite at the Waldorf Cafeteria on Sixth Avenue and 8th Street, a favorite haunt of the neighborhood's many artists. The bare-bones eatery discouraged them from hanging out there, since they hogged the tables, nursed cups of coffee while they debated aesthetics and politics, and were lousy tippers. The management tried banning smoking and locking the toilets, but the other customers complained.

As McNeil and Fitz entered, heads turned, and the hubbub volume went down. The presence of a uniformed police officer caused a couple of men to rise silently and make their way to the exit.

McNeil filled him in on the scene. "We have to be careful where we sit. The Trotskyites have their own tables, far away from the Stalinists. The abstract artists don't speak to the realists, and the sculptors just speak to each other. The only time the rules relax is during baseball season, when the Dodgers fans sit together and snub the Yankees and Giants fans. It's a thinner crowd then, anyway. Hans has a summer school in Provincetown, so lots of us go to the Cape for the summer."

McNeil spotted Balcomb and Gertrude Greene. "That's a safe table," he whispered, "they're abstractionists." He greeted them and was about to introduce Fitz when Gertrude spoke up.

"Well, well, the redhead from the union party. You're even more handsome in uniform. Hope you're not here to make an arrest."

Disarmed, Fitz assured her that he wasn't actually on duty.

"In that case," she said, "please join us. You, too, George, and tell us what brings you here."

Fitz explained his interest in the vandalism at the Fair, as well as the Hofmann School fire. "Lee Krasner told me about it, and it made me wonder if there's any connection."

"I can't imagine Local 829 having any reason to sabotage Hofmann," said Balcomb. "Ilya and I and the other Local 60 members, yes, since they believe we're horning in on their territory. But none of the targeted muralists are affiliated with the school. So what's the link, if any?"

"You're assuming Local 829 is behind the Fair incidents," said Fitz, "but I have my doubts about that."

"Who else would have it in for us?"

"That's the question I'm trying to answer. By the way, do you know how Bolotowsky is doing? Is he still in the hospital?"

"I'm afraid so. He came out of the coma, but he's still recovering from his concussion and internal injuries. Gertrude and I visited him last week. I wanted to assure him that his mural has been installed properly. Mine is going up in the same building tomorrow."

"Aren't you worried about something like that happening to you?"

Balcomb shook his head. "After what happened to Ref's murals, the Federal Art Project assigned overnight monitors to the WPA Building and Medicine and Public Health. No chance of interference with someone on guard duty."

"That was a wise precaution," said Fitz. "I hope that'll put a stop to it. Meanwhile, we're no closer to finding out who's responsible."

"Why don't you think it was the scenic artists' union?" asked Gertrude. "Stuart's sure it's their doing, and we have good reason to suspect them."

"I understand why Stuart blames them for the sabotage, but why would they kill Feininger? He was a Local 829 member."

Balcomb and Gertrude exchanged looks. He said, "I didn't know that. Are you sure his death wasn't an accident?"

"Not a hundred percent sure, no. The detective who's working on the case thinks he lost his grip on the ladder and fell, but I can't shake the feeling he was pushed off, and it's part of the pattern of disabling muralists. But who's after them, and why?"

"If you can figure out why," said Gertrude, "you'll probably know who."

Chapter Thirty-One

"She put her finger on it," Fitz told McNeil as they walked down 8th Street toward the school. "It's the why I'm missing. Union rivalry doesn't work for Feininger, and I can't see the Hofmann connection."

"Maybe it's three completely separate things," said McNeil. "The rival union went after the Local 60 muralists. Someone had it in for Feininger, or maybe it was an accident after all. The Bund got even with Hofmann because he wouldn't play ball with them."

"I had another idea about the Local 60 sabotage," said Fitz, "and I'm still not convinced it's wrong, but it also doesn't fit with the Feininger killing or the Hofmann School arson." He didn't want to point the finger at Krasner, or any other rejected muralist, without more to go on. "Like you say, it may all be coincidence."

"But you don't believe that."

"Hofmann, maybe, but not the muralists. And there's a wild card. A guy who was fired from the Fair and might be out for revenge, though I can't for the life of me imagine why he'd go after artists. If it is him, I haven't been able to make the link."

"What's his name?"

"Joseph Shadgen. The Fair was his idea in the first place, but they kicked him out."

"I read about that," said McNeil. "Didn't he sue the Fair for a lot of money?"

"They settled out of court, but he was plenty sore, and the brass are scared he might try something. They put all the gate guards and the cops on alert in case he shows up and tries to make trouble. In fact, he did show up, but with a private tour group. I was on escort detail, and he behaved himself. So he's a long shot, but I can't rule him out altogether."

* * *

By the time Fitz got home, it was after 10:00 p.m. He had stayed to help with the mopping-up operation. They found one of Hofmann's overalls in the closet, so he hung up his uniform and pitched in with a scrub brush and 20 Mule Team Borax.

His father was in the living room, smoking and reading the evening paper. Fitz grabbed a ginger ale from the icebox and joined him. Tim was surprised to see his son in uniform; he usually changed into civvies before leaving the fairgrounds.

"I needed to look official," Fitz told him, "even though I was off duty. I told Mom I was helping clean up after a fire, which I did. I thought it might be arson, and related to what's happening to artists at the Fair. I wanted to question the victim, see if I could establish the connection."

He described the circumstances at the Hofmann School and outlined his suspicions. "The only common factor in all these incidents is modern art."

"What do you mean by modern?" asked Tim.

"It's the style, Dad. I don't know much about it myself, but some of the artists have been explaining it to me. It's recognizable but simplified, what they call abstract, the method Hofmann teaches. You don't try to paint a subject the way it looks, you use what you see as a jumping-off point. It's a kind of improvising, like the jazz musicians do.

"Davis, the first guy who got injured, is a big jazz fan. That's how he explained it. He's painting outlines of things like a man running, a big ear listening to the radio, a hand making sign language, stuff like that, but it's just flat, like a diagram, no details. Gorky, the guy painting the aviation mural, took aircraft parts and rearranged them to make a design. Guston and Refregier, the guys doing the WPA Building, paint figures overlapping each other in spaces that don't look real. Bolotowsky's mural has no figures at all, just colored shapes and lines."

"What about the guy who got killed? Feininger, right?"

"His mural is pictures of steamships and sailboats, sort of flattened and fragmented. You can tell what they are, but they're geometric, not realistic. And the pictures I saw at Hofmann's place were like that, too. They were pretty badly damaged, so we had to throw most of them out, but they were all abstract."

Tim wasn't convinced. "If that's the only common thread, it's a pretty thin one. If somebody's against abstract art, why aren't they attacking the Museum of Modern Art or the galleries that show the stuff?"

"Maybe they are, and we just don't know about it."

"I'm sure there would have been something in the papers, and I haven't seen anything," said Tim, who read the *Times,* the *Daily News,* and the *Post* every day.

"What I'm getting at is that it could explain why only abstract muralists at the Fair have been attacked. The whole union rivalry idea may be completely wrong. It may be about the style of the paintings. None of the traditional muralists have been targeted."

"Wait," said Tim, "didn't you tell me they're not actually painting their designs, that scenic artists are doing the work? If their union is responsible, they wouldn't target their own men, would they? They'd go after the artists in the other union."

Fitz was warming to his alternate theory. "That's the point. Union rivalry is most popular opinion, but it doesn't explain why Feininger was killed. O'Toole thinks he just slipped and fell, so I don't know how hard he's working on the case. As a matter of fact, until Refregier's murals were vandalized, he thought they were all accidents. Now he has to think again."

* * *

If anyone knew who might have it in for abstract artists, it would probably be Lee Krasner. Fitz had had plenty of time to size her up as they worked together cleaning the Hofmann studio. Her natural candor and enthusiastic support for her fellow WPA muralists had won him over. After reporting for duty on Wednesday, he decided to pay her a call at the WPA Building. He could also ask Balcomb Greene, who had mentioned that he'd be installing his Medicine and Public Health mural. Between them, they might point him in a new and more promising direction.

The two buildings stood next to each other along the Avenue of Patriots, on either side of Hamilton Place. On his walk from the City Building, Fitz reached Medicine and Public Health first, so he headed in to see what he could learn from Greene.

The artist and an assistant were on the scaffold preparing the ten-by-sixteen-foot wall above an entrance to the exhibit area, a location that matched Bolotowsky's. The mural, still rolled face inward on its tube, sat on the floor below them. As it was unrolled, the back would be in contact with the adhesive on the wall surface, which had to be perfectly smooth. The installation required careful coordination to ensure that the canvas rolled on evenly, with no creases or air bubbles. Two more assistants would be on hand when the time came.

"Good morning, Mr. Greene," called Fitz, and got the artist's attention. "When you're ready for a break, can I have a few words?"

"Be right down," said Greene. He unhooked and descended. "Good to see you again, Officer Fitzgerald. What can I do for you?"

"When we were talking last night, you wife said that figuring out the reason for the attacks would suggest who's responsible. It made me think maybe modern art is the common factor, since only artists who paint like that have been targeted. Do you know of anyone who's dead set against the kind of art you and the others make?"

A wry smile crossed Greene's craggy face. "I sure do. Just read what the critics say about us. There are several who think our work is half-baked imitations of European modernism at best, or pointless scribbles with no content or meaning at worst. Old fossils like Royal Cortissoz, who thought the Armory Show was an abomination, is the most anti-modern. His reviews in the *Herald Tribune* read like Nazi diatribes against so-called degenerate art."

That got Fitz's attention. "What's the Armory Show?" he asked.

"A big exhibition, held at the Sixty-Ninth Regiment Armory in Manhattan back in nineteen thirteen, that introduced the European avant-garde artists to America. A group of forward-thinking painters and sculptors put it together, as a challenge to the academy and what they considered the old-fashioned attitudes that dominated American art.

"The timing was perfect. European art was bursting with new movements, and the show brought them to us for inspiration. I was only a nine-year-old kid, but twenty years later, when I decided to devote myself to painting, its influence was still strong. Even today, we look back to the Armory Show as the watershed moment in American modernism. It showed us the way."

"So this critic guy, Cortissoz, who was so against it, would naturally feel the same about American artists like the ones who've been attacked. Do you think he'd be capable of putting his words into action?"

"When I called him an old fossil," said Greene, "I was referring to his age as well as his views. He must be at least seventy. I've never met him, but from what I've heard, he's not very robust. Bit of a hypochondriac, so I'm told. Still, it didn't take much effort to push Stuart off the scaffold, or to untie a rope or remove some clamps. I guess sawing partway through a step would require the most physical strength, but probably not a lot. Nor would it be all that hard to spill a bucket of paint on Ref's murals, or, for that matter, to push Feininger off the ladder."

Chapter Thirty-Two

Fitz wanted to talk over the latest developments with Elaine. But, unless she called him, he had no way to get in touch with her, except to go to de Kooning's loft and hope to find her there. Likely that de Kooning would be there, too, and how would he handle that?

In any case, he wouldn't be able to go until he went off duty, so he moved on to the WPA Building to ask Lee Krasner's opinion. She certainly was the next best thing. What she lacked in the looks department, she made up for in art-world savvy.

He stopped outside to admire Guston's mural, now finished, on the façade. The huge figures of the construction worker, surveyor, and driller made an authoritative statement about the dignity of manual labor, and the scientist in her laboratory announced that women were also contributing to public well-being. That this work was being carried on with federal government support for millions who would otherwise be idle, their skills wasted and their spirits broken, was the mural's underlying message—one that would not be lost on the many Fair visitors who had benefitted personally from WPA employment.

Why would someone want to harm an artist making such a positive statement, he wondered. True, some people were against the New Deal in general and the WPA in particular, but that would only account for vandalism at this building, where its achievements were being celebrated so explicitly. Also true, the attacks were against muralists who had worked for the WPA or were still on the payroll, so the motive could be opposition to federal support for artists. Except that didn't explain Feininger, the maddening anomaly.

* * *

In the theater lobby, he found Krasner gathering a pile of paint-soaked rags for disposal. After the Hofmann fire, she was ever more mindful of the danger they posed if not properly handled.

"Sorry I can't help you out today," said Fitz, "but I'm on duty. And my mother would have a fit if I got paint on my uniform."

"We can't have your mom mad at you," said Krasner. "Thanks again for pitching in last night. You were a big help. I hope it won't take more than a couple of days to get the place back in shape. I went over to Hans' this morning and told him to stay away until we can re-open. George said the same thing. We don't want him to have to deal with the mess. He's having a hard enough time coping as it is."

Fitz followed her to the dumpster in the courtyard. "Can you take a break for a few minutes? I could use your opinion about something that's bothering me."

"Sure," she said. "Glad of an excuse to get away from that stinky solvent. Let's sit over here." She pointed to a nearby bench.

He told her about his idea that the target was modern art, and about his conversation with Greene. "He mentioned a critic who's an anti-modern fanatic, guy called Cortissoz. Ever heard of him?"

She made a face. "Royal's his first name, and he's a royal pain. Acts like the ruler of the art world and wants it to stay the way it was when he started writing about it in the eighteen nineties. As far as he's concerned, Whistler and Sargent are the pinnacle of the avant-garde. If it were up to him, abstract artists would be banished from his kingdom."

"Has he written anything negative about the modern art at the Fair?"

"Not yet, but I'm sure he'll take his hatchet to it after opening day. All the critics will weigh in, especially since there's been a lot of publicity about how much art there is here. The administration made a big deal about how the Fair would represent a future in which art would play a vital part in everyday life, not hidden away in museums or for sale in snobby galleries. That's the whole point of the WPA's Federal Art Project, to bring art to the people, which is why the Fair is such a great opportunity for us."

"Have you ever met Cortissoz?" asked Fitz.

"As a matter of fact, I have, though it was only in passing, and we didn't speak to each other. It was at an exhibition by a group I belong to, the American Abstract Artists. We got together a few years ago to promote our work, which gets short shrift from critics and collectors who think we can't hold a candle to the School of Paris. I grant you that, until now, the breakthroughs have been made in Europe, but we want to show that advanced art can be done here, too. So, we rent a gallery space and hold an annual exhibition, and take turns monitoring it.

"At last year's show, I happened to be the monitor when he walked in. He didn't introduce himself, but I recognized him because he was on the cover of *Time* magazine when I was a student. It was right after the Modern opened, and he was the strongest opponent of everything the museum represents. *Time* touted him as the champion of conservatism and quoted his negative opinions of the artists who were knocking me out, like Matisse and Picasso.

"Considering his well-known attitude, I was surprised to see him at the Triple A show. I thought about saying something to him, like, are you sure you're in the right place, but I decided to keep my big mouth shut in case he'd had a change of heart. He did a circuit of the gallery and walked out without a word. His review was predictably scathing, calling our work sterile, distorted, technically deficient and worthless."

"Sounds pretty hostile," observed Fitz. "Do you think he'd be angry enough to go after modern art for real, instead of just in print?"

"Wow, there's an idea! You know, I wouldn't put it past him. After decades preaching against modernism to no effect, he may have built up such a head of steam that the Fair was the last straw. He probably approves of most of the murals, which are pretty academic, but the fact that there are some prominent abstractions could have inspired him to act."

Krasner sat back and gave Fitz a questioning look. "What gave you that idea, anyway?"

"Modern art was the only common factor," he said. "Union rivalry didn't work as a motive in Feininger's case, and Hofmann's school has nothing to do with the Fair."

"But you believe the attack on him is somehow related?"

"That's what made me think it was someone opposed to the kind of art they're all doing. Modern, abstract, cubist, whatever you call it. I asked Mr. Greene if he knew of anyone like that, and he said Cortissoz."

"He's not the only one," she pointed out. "He's the most extreme, but there's a lot of opposition among the critics, and the realist painters as well. Even though they dominate the WPA, they resent any attention we get, especially in a prime location like the Fair. One of them could have decided to retaliate. Might also be behind the arson at Hans's school, since he's the foremost exponent of everything they hate."

Fitz started considering logistics. "Anyone could attack Hofmann's school. Easy to get into the building through the theater or the nightclub, and it wouldn't take much effort to break into the studio and set fire to the rags. But how would an elderly art critic or a disgruntled WPA realist get into the fairgrounds? All the sabotage, except the attack on Feininger, happened overnight. The place is humming twenty-four hours a day, and the gates are manned all night. If it wasn't someone authorized to be there, he'd need to be let in several times."

"Or she," corrected Krasner.

"Right, thank you. Corinne West told me not to rule out a woman." He didn't mention that West's suggestion led him to Krasner as his prime female suspect. "She also said the guards weren't too strict about checking the artists' I.D.s. Did you have any trouble getting in?"

"No. The art project office phoned ahead to let the guards know to expect us."

"I wonder how hard it would be to talk your way in. Show your UAA card and say you're an assistant or a replacement for someone out sick. Miss West brought that up as well. Or let's say it's the critic. Maybe his press card would get him through."

***

Krasner agreed to keep thinking of any realist who might be angry, and crazy, enough to harm abstract artists, and Fitz decided to pursue the Cortissoz angle. Both seemed to them like long shots, but not outlandish. Besides, nothing more plausible had yet turned up.

The easiest way to eliminate or implicate the critic, thought Fitz, *would be to ask the gate guards if anyone with that unusual name had been admitted.* He did the rounds of the entrances, but none of the guards had a record of such a visitor. That didn't really surprise him, since if the guy was bent on mischief, he'd likely have used a fake I.D.

He could easily hide his name, but not his face, so the next step would be to show a photograph of him to the guards. But how to get a photograph? Wait, Krasner said his picture was on the cover of *Time,* though it was years ago. Where could he get a copy? The library, of course. His Queens Public Library card was valid at all the borough's branches, but they'd be unlikely to let him take it out. Back periodicals are strictly for reference, and he had no official reason to demand it. Still, better take a look. Maybe a description would be enough.

He chose the largest branch, Flushing, as the most likely to have a complete set of back issues. It was also the closest, so he headed there after his shift ended.

The Periodicals Division had bound copies of *Time,* dating back to volume 1, number 1, March 3, 1923. Krasner had told him the Modern opened in late 1929, so he started there. When he reached March 10, 1930, he found what he was looking for.

Under Cortissoz's cover portrait, a quote, "There have been arid epochs before this…" announced his position on modern art in no uncertain terms. Inside, the profile of him, headlined "Sterile Modernism," reinforced it at length. The article described him as "a small, chunky, lively gentleman with iron-grey hair, moustache and goatee," whose age was given as sixty-one. This helped flesh out the picture of a frustrated tastemaker swimming against the rising tide of "modernistic art," which *Time* noted was "undeniably fashionable."

After he finished reading, Fitz considered Cortissoz, despite his now being seventy, to be a promising candidate. Someone who'd been nursing deep antipathy to modern art, if not downright hatred for it, for over thirty years would be well primed for an all-out assault on its exposure to millions at a venue that hailed it as the trend of the future. The artists' union status was irrelevant. The only thing that mattered was their style. No wonder the academic muralists had been left alone.

This left Fitz wondering how to get a copy of the magazine so he could show the picture to Fair security. Did he know anyone who subscribed and might have back copies at home? Could he borrow his mother's Brownie camera to photograph it?

Then he had a brainstorm. Looking around de Kooning's studio before he and Elaine had their tryst, he'd seen some realistic drawings of her and others pinned on the wall. Why not ask de Kooning to draw a copy of the cover? He had finished Gorky's mural, so he wasn't on the fairgrounds anymore. That would be a legitimate excuse to show up at the loft and see Elaine again.

Chapter Thirty-Three

After he clocked out on Thursday, Fitz took the subway to 23rd Street and headed back to the Muhlenberg library to check that they had a copy of the issue in question. They did. Then he walked a block south to de Kooning's place.

He took his time. He'd spent the train ride framing his approach, deciding how he should act around Elaine, hoping he wouldn't say or do something to compromise her, but longing to show his affection. No, he couldn't kiss or embrace her, so he'd have to play it cool. Try to ignore her, as if that were possible. Now, with the encounter looming, he resolved to assume the plainclothes policeman role and hope he could sustain a professional demeanor.

He tried the doorbell, though he remembered it didn't work the first time he was there. Maybe it was fixed, but no such luck. He knew the New York trick of tossing pebbles at the window to alert the occupant to throw down the keys, but if he did that, would it give away the fact that he'd been there before? He was already a bit rattled or that wouldn't even have occurred to him. He could just say he tried the bell and got no answer.

The third pebble got a response. De Kooning opened the window and stuck out his head.

"Hello. Who is it?"

"Hello, Mr. de Kooning. It's Brian Fitzgerald, the cop from the World's Fair. Can I come up and talk to you? The bell isn't working."

"Ja, sure. Catch the keys." Down came the Spaldeen, and in went Fitz.

As he approached the loft door, it opened to reveal Elaine. She was wearing the grosgrain dressing gown and a captivating smile. His heart went to his mouth. He had to swallow hard and take a deep breath before the power of speech returned.

She stepped into the hall and stood on tiptoes to kiss him, lightly, on the lips. "I know you're not here to see me, friend Fitz, but I'm happy to see you. I do miss you. But let's not keep Bill waiting."

"I, I, ah, miss you, too," he stammered. "It might be better if you let me talk to de Kooning alone. So I don't lose my train of thought."

"Understood," she winked. "I'll make myself scarce." She let him in and headed back toward her studio with a toss of her head and another captivating smile as she pulled the curtain. As if that erased her presence. He took a couple more deep breaths and moved into the front studio.

De Kooning was seated in a tattered armchair, smoking and nursing a glass of whiskey as he contemplated the painting of the seated man. It didn't look much different than when Fitz was there a week earlier. Elaine had told him de Kooning was a slow worker, always making adjustments or even scraping off whole areas and repainting them, so he wasn't surprised that little progress had been made.

The artist rose to greet him. "Say, I recognize you. You're the guy I met at Kent's place, and I saw you making eyes at Corinne ven I vas painting Gorky's mural."

Fitz corrected him. "I was questioning her about the sabotage. We're anxious to get to the bottom of these attacks, which is why I came to see you, Mr. de Kooning. I could use your expertise, if you're willing."

"It's Bill, please, and my expertise is at your beck and call."

"And I'm known as Fitz. It's kind of an unusual request, but I think you're the perfect man for the job."

De Kooning directed him to an equally decrepit chair and offered him a cigarette and a drink, neither of which he accepted. He described his informal inquiries into the Fair sabotage and brought up the Hofmann School arson as well. He laid out his theory about modern artists being the target and his hunch that a rabidly conservative art critic could be responsible.

"Ever heard of Royal Cortissoz?" he asked.

De Kooning grunted. "That fool! He lives in the past. I know vere his head is, down in the ground like an ostrich. I vas there, too, until I vised up. I vas trained at Rotterdam Academy, and I learned pretty good how to draw and paint the old-fashioned vay. You just copy vat you see. They call it realism, but it's an illusion. Now I paint from my imagination."

He gestured at the canvas. "That man, he isn't real. He's made of paint. He's not in the room. He's on a flat canvas. Vat I'm trying to catch is the man's spirit, to make his image live, on its own terms. Does that make sense to you, Fitz?"

"I guess so. At least I can see why a modern artist wouldn't want to just repeat what others did in the past. Making it less realistic would be one way to do something new. Anyway, I'm wondering if this Cortissoz guy would be so against the modern art at the Fair that he'd attack the artists doing it. What do you think?"

De Kooning scratched his head. "That's pretty extreme, but those vere no accidents."

"My idea is to find out if he had access to the fairgrounds. I need a picture of him to show the guards. There's one on an old *Time* magazine cover, and they have that issue at the library on Twenty-Third Street. Here's where your expertise comes in, Bill. Would you draw a copy of it for me?"

To his surprise, de Kooning agreed readily. "Sure thing. Vant me to do it now?"

"If you don't mind interrupting your work."

"I can take a break," said de Kooning as he stood. He opened the supply cabinet and removed a sketch pad, pencils, and a kneaded eraser from a compartment tray specially designed to hold them. Fitz was again taken by how neatly his materials were kept.

"Ve can go to Stewart's for dinner after. Elaine can join us there." He called out to let her know their plan.

"I was listening," she told them as she emerged from behind the curtain. "You know what a busybody I am. So, Officer, do you really think an art critic is behind all this?"

Struggling to maintain his composure, he said, "I'm off duty, so please call me Fitz. And yes, I know it's far-fetched, but he has a motive for sabotaging modern artists, so I need to investigate. I hope an identity check will clear him."

"Bill will get you a good likeness," she assured him. "He paints like a devil, but he draws like an angel. I'll meet you at Stewart's around seven."

* * *

When they arrived at the library, the reading room was crowded. Often refuges for the unemployed and the homeless, libraries stayed open late during the Depression, when they were known as "the breadline of the spirit."

Fitz directed de Kooning to the Periodicals Division and asked the librarian to pull the *Time* volume he'd looked at earlier. He laid it on the table and opened it to the cover in question.

"Ja, that's the old fogey himself," sniffed de Kooning. "More gray in the hair now, but no more sense in the brain."

He opened his sketch pad and set to work. Fitz watched with admiration as he deftly copied the likeness, modeling Cortissoz's features with subtle shading and carefully reproducing the texture of his hair, moustache, and beard. Even his wire-rimmed glasses were perfectly rendered in perspective. After half an hour's work, he had drawn a portrait as accurate as *Time*'s cover photograph.

"He alvays dresses in a three-piece suit and tie," said de Kooning. "I can add a little so you see the clothes." He sketched in the shoulders and upper body to give a more complete picture of the man's appearance.

"Wow, that's amazing, Bill. I bet it takes a lot of practice to get that good. You could make a nice living as a portrait painter."

"That's not for me, Fitz. I leave that hack verk to Igor, God's gift to bored society dames. I get by okay vit my decorating verk, and maybe I'll get more jobs now that I'm in the scenic union. Maybe get to meet some chorus girls. Hotcha!"

Even with a corker like Elaine in his bed, he's got a roving eye, thought Fitz ruefully. *Well, for that matter, so does she. That's how I got lucky. Guess I'll just have to wait in line and hope she decides to move on.*

* * *

They rendezvoused with Elaine at Stewart's. Apart from the pleasure of spending time in her company, even though it wasn't going to end as he would have liked, Fitz wanted to hear what she thought about where his investigations were going. Over plates of the cafeteria's cheap and filling fare, the trio reviewed the various motives and suspects, from vengeance (Shadgen), envy (a WPA would-be muralist), and rivalry (Local 829) to hatred of modern art (Cortissoz).

"Don't forget the Bund. They're probably behind the arson at Hofmann's, since he wouldn't play along with them," said Elaine between bites of chicken pot pie.

"Vouldn't put it past them," agreed Bill. "Couple of the boys on my Hall of Pharmacy crew vere pro-Hitler. Think the Jews and Commies are taking over the vorld. I don't say they're in the Bund, but that's how they talk."

This pointed Fitz to yet another potential avenue of investigation. In line with Hitler's anti-modernism policy—of which Feininger had been a victim—which was praised in the articles he'd read in the Bund's newsletter, could they have orchestrated Nazi-inspired sabotage targeting the advanced artists? His Bund membership might make it possible for him to find out.

Chapter Thirty-Four

De Kooning's drawing of Cortissoz drew a blank with the attendants at the rail stations and the Corona and Flushing gates, but it was recognized by the guard at the Administration Building entrance.

"Yeah, I've seen that fellow," he said. "I didn't get his name, but I remember him. Dapper little guy. He came in with Commissioner Moses, who towered over him. The Commish had a car and driver laid on to take him on a personal tour. He was giving him an earful about the show of European masterpieces, so I got the idea he was some kind of art expert."

"When was this?" asked Fitz.

"Oh, maybe a week ago."

"And that's the only time you saw him? Never earlier?"

"No, just that once. I'm sure I'd remember if it was more. I have the nine-to-five shift, so I'm here all day."

"Who covers for you on lunch break?"

"I pack in," said the guard. "Cafeteria's too expensive, and my wife's a great cook. Course I go in to use the john, but I lock the gate when I'm gone. Anyone who comes when I'm out just has to wait."

"Thanks," said Fitz. "Maybe I'll come back later and check with the guy who's on the five-to-one shift." But his heart wasn't in it. The idea of an elderly art critic sneaking in with a fake I.D. several times to make mischief was always a long shot, and it now looked like a washout. Still, the motive, hatred of modern art, had legs if you looked at the Bund instead.

* * *

"The trap is set," Tim informed his son at dinner on Monday. "The permit was delivered to Bund H.Q. this afternoon. Consolla himself is going to head the team at the vacant exhibit space. He'll put you on duty at the other gate, so you won't be involved in the arrests."

That made sense, protecting Fitz from blame and possible retribution, but he was deeply disappointed that he wouldn't be in on the action he had orchestrated. He'd been looking forward to watching Kuhn, Kunze, and their goon squad marched off in handcuffs. No doubt they'd quickly be released on bail and would try to question him, and his absence would make it easier to deny that he knew anything about the arrest plan. He could say he never saw the permit, so he had no way of knowing it didn't include the building.

"I'm sure you noticed that Mary wasn't at church yesterday," said Bridget, changing the subject. "Her mother told me she isn't feeling well. I hope it's nothing serious." She turned to Fitz. "Why don't you call her? I'm sure she'd appreciate a kind word from you if she's laid up."

A little frisson of guilt caused blood to rush to his face, which he tried to hide by coughing into his napkin.

"Not you, too? Oh, dear, something must be going around."

"No, Mom, I just swallowed the wrong way." He cleared his throat convincingly and took a sip of ginger ale. "I'll give her a ring right now." He excused himself and headed to the phone. Just before he reached it, it rang.

"Brian Fitzgerald, please."

"Speaking," he replied.

It was Kunze's assistant. "The director wants to speak to you. Hold the line." Fitz took a deep breath as he was connected.

"Good news, Officer Fitzgerald," said Kunze. "Our rally has received a permit, so we will be going ahead with plans for this Saturday. There is certain to be a significant police presence, and I need to know how many, especially the number we can expect to encounter at the Rodman Street parking lot and Flushing gate. And will they attempt to prevent us from entering the grounds?"

How much could he tell him without revealing inside knowledge? Maybe Kunze would give him a clue. "I'll try to find out how many men they plan to assign. What does the permit say about restrictions?" he asked.

"It is only valid for the one day, April twenty-second, from noon to four p.m. The demonstration must be orderly. No weapons are permitted. We are not allowed to wear uniforms, display insignia that feature the swastika, or distribute literature supporting the Nazi cause. But as long as the protest is peaceful, we can exercise our constitutional right to free speech in support of Germany as a nation and against its exclusion from the Fair."

"Does it say anything about where you can march?"

"On property leased to the New York World's Fair Corporation by the City of New York."

"Well, that's the whole fairgrounds, including the rail stations and parking lots, so you definitely have the right to enter, at least on foot. I don't think they'll let vehicles through, so you'll have to take your exhibits in by hand."

"That won't be a problem," said Kunze, reassured. "It will largely be banners, photographs, and printed material dealing with German history, not current affairs. We want to steer clear of the censors. The idea is to highlight Germany's many important contributions to the world, especially in industry, science, and the arts. We have a proud past to celebrate and, by implication, a great future promised by Hitler's program to reestablish Germany at the forefront of civilization. We want our fellow patriotic Americans to know that Germany, a bulwark against the forces that threaten to undermine our shared values, deserves their wholehearted support."

Kunze's rhetoric was wearing thin on Fitz, but he had to endure it in silence. He was sure there would be no acknowledgment of the Jewish industrialists, scientists, composers, architects, writers and painters whose contributions were central to German culture. No banners touting their achievements, no books or pamphlets describing their work, no framed portraits of them on the walls. In fact, there would be no display of German greatness at all, since once the Bund protestors were inside the building, they'd be arrested and their exhibits confiscated.

Kunze may be a fanatic, said Fitz to himself, *but he's no fool. Surely he realizes that the Fair won't sanction the Bund's unauthorized pavilion.*

"I guess you can't display anything valuable, since it's really just a big publicity stunt," he said. "You haven't rented the space, so the Fair is bound to remove everything you install."

Kunze surprised him by replying, "Schultz is looking into that. He thinks they're desperate to recoup their investment, so they'll be glad to accept a last-minute tenant, especially in the Government Zone. In fact, they were hoping Germany would participate, so this will be the next best thing. I'm confident our supporters will step up with the necessary funds. And once we're in and have the lease, we can expand the installation and represent the new Germany as well."

An alarm bell sounded in Fitz's brain. *Christ, this could ruin the whole scheme! Schultz, Mr. Exhibits and Concessions, must know that the building belongs to the Fair Corporation, not the City. He could warn them that the permit isn't valid inside it.*

But how would Schultz know about that technicality, unless Kunze shares the permit terms with him? How likely is he to do that? The alarm bell's volume went down as Fitz recalled how Schultz had been frozen out of the planning process. *Kunze has no need to confer with him over logistics. And surely Schultz can't approve a lease agreement on his own. Okay, he's a senior clerk in the department, but he's not the boss. If he submits an application on the Bund's behalf, the director or some higher-up will have to approve it. If we let them know the plan, they can stall it, and Schultz won't be the wiser. Better get on that right away.*

Fitz relayed this information to his father, who called Newbold Morris's office first thing on Tuesday morning. Within an hour, he was informed that the Exhibits and Concessions executive office had received the Bund's application and had agreed to sit on it. Anyone inquiring about it would be told that more information was required or given some other plausible excuse for the delay. As long as they didn't have the lease by Saturday, if they went into the building during the rally they'd definitely be guilty of unlawful entry.

Chapter Thirty-Five

Saturday, April 22nd dawned with a light drizzle, but the sky cleared steadily as the day progressed and the temperature climbed into the low sixties—fine weather for a protest march. To keep Kunze believing that Fitz was their inside man, Tim had confirmed that fifty NYPD officers would be assigned, fifteen at each rail station and twenty at the Flushing gate. Nothing like the huge police presence at the Garden rally. Fitz had dutifully relayed this information.

Since few, if any, counter-protesters were expected, confrontations were unlikely. The Fair's own police force would be patrolling the grounds and could be called on if things got out of hand. Although they couldn't make arrests, they were authorized to detain any troublemakers.

* * *

No one questioned why Schultz was in his office on a Saturday. In the hectic weeks before opening, it wasn't unusual to find him about on weekends and in the evenings. Several concessions in the Amusement Zone were still behind schedule, and even at this late date there were vacant spaces to fill. Numerous latecomers had applied for exhibits in the theme buildings as well. It was now clear that the Fair wouldn't be a hundred percent finished by April 30th, but he was doing his best to process and refer everything that came his way. Especially the eleventh-hour German exhibit.

From his office window, he had an oblique view of the Long Island Rail Road entrance, which blocked his line of vision to the el station gate, where the largest turnout was expected. Nor could he see the Flushing gate on the opposite side of the grounds, the entry point for the contingent planning to occupy the vacant space in the Hall of Nations. Of the three available vacancies, he had assigned the one next to Italy, Germany's ally, as the appropriate place for the Bund to stake its claim.

An adjunct to Italy's grandiose stand-alone pavilion, which boasted a waterfall façade topped by a giant statue of the goddess Roma, the Hall of Nations display celebrated the outsized personality of Prime Minister Benito Mussolini, known as Il Duce, leader of the National Fascist Party. Surrounding the dictator's statue, maps rendered in black marble and copper depicted Italy's territorial empire. Schultz envisioned something similar for the German display—a laudatory tribute to Der Führer and evidence of the strides made under his leadership of the National Socialist German Workers' Party—once the lease was signed. He'd been assured that the Bund's application was moving forward.

He debated with himself whether to walk over to Bowling Green once the rally got underway so he could see what sort of turnout there was, but decided against it in case someone recognized him from Bund meetings and called him to join in. If he was identified as a member, it might put him under scrutiny and interfere with his ability to act on the Bund's behalf. As deeply devoted as he was, he believed his service was more effective when carried out in secret. Yet he longed for the day when he could openly proclaim his support for the cause.

This conflict quickened his pulse as the protestors gathered and the rally began in earnest. His open window admitted the sounds of chanting and the blare of a bullhorn exhorting the crowd to march on the Administration Building and demand German representation at the Fair.

Good Lord, he realized, *they're coming here, and my department will be their most likely target. I don't suppose they'll be able to get inside, but if they do, I'll have to make myself scarce.*

He took the precaution of locking the Exhibits and Concessions suite door and turning out the lights.

* * *

In full Bundesführer uniform, Fritz Kuhn stood on the flatbed of a pickup truck and deployed his loudspeaker to address the crowd gathered in the Rodman Street parking lot outside the Flushing gate.

"To all de loyal Americans who haf come out today in support of our cause, I offer tanks on behalf of de Cherman people, who are grateful for your solidarity. Deir glorious Führer und Reichskanzler, Adolph Hitler, has chust celebrated his fiftieth birthday, and ve vish him many more years of enlightened leadership."

A cheer went up from the roughly two hundred in attendance, among them Director Kunze, a few men with boxes containing the exhibit material loaded on hand trucks, and some two dozen Ordnungsdienst guards in plain clothes. The several reporters and photographers who were present muttered sarcastically or remained silent as they documented the proceedings.

"Vat more meaningful birthday gift can ve gif Der Führer," Kuhn cried, "den a presence at dis peaceful gathering of nations, dis vision of vorld harmony, to vitch he is committed?" followed by shouts of affirmation.

Waving his followers onward, Kuhn marched through the gate and along Federal Place to the Court of Peace, where two facing rows of buildings housed the smaller international exhibits. Scanning the faces of the police officers who followed them along the way, he didn't see Fitz and assumed he'd be at the building to ensure that the door was open. When he got there, however, Fitz was nowhere to be seen. But the pavilion was unlocked, so Kuhn led the way inside.

As the room began to fill with demonstrators, Kunze directed his men to set up their displays. While the reporters descended on Kuhn and the photographers' flashbulbs popped, an officer approached Kunze, introduced himself as Captain Joseph Consolla of the 110th Precinct, and asked to see the assembly permit. Kunze handed it over, only to be told that it was no good inside the building, where the entire police contingent was now backing Consolla up.

The ensuing argument resulted in the arrest for trespass of Kunze, Kuhn—

also for violating the permit's no-uniforms clause—and several of the Bund guards who had tried to intervene. More flashbulbs went off as the cops loaded their prisoners into paddy wagons that had been conveniently parked out back.

* * *

The Sunday papers were full of it. Headlines shouted, "Bund Boss Arrested at Fair," "Bund Exhibit at Fair Thwarted," and "Pro-German Fair Display Quashed." The *Daily News*, New York's Picture Newspaper, was especially thorough, with shots of Kuhn and Kunze in custody, cops disbursing the demonstrators, and piles of display material heaped on the pavement outside the building.

Grover Whalen's office had issued an official statement explaining the situation in suitably measured terms. The Mayor's office was more explicit, condemning the Bund for unlawful occupation of private property and trying to foist its poisonous propaganda on fairgoers. Always ready with a colorful quote, LaGuardia denounced Kuhn and his cohorts as "nothing but a bunch of cooties" and praised the cops for "getting the Flit."

The anticipated call to Fitz came on Sunday afternoon. Kunze's secretary wasted no time on formalities. When the director got on the line, his words were harsh, and his tone was glacial. Having spent the night as a guest of the New York City Department of Correction, he was eager to blame someone else for his misfortune.

"You bungling imbecile!" he fumed. "You were supposed to arrange everything. Why didn't you warn us that the building was off limits?"

Ready for this rebuke, Fitz had prepared his response. "You told me the permit covered the whole Fair. That's what you said. How was I supposed to know the Fair's own building wasn't included?"

Through clenched teeth, Kunze replied, "What I told you was that the permit covered all property leased by the City to the Fair. According to the arresting officer, it did not include anything built on that property. How could you not know that?"

"I'm just a patrolman. They don't tell me details like that. Why didn't Schultz tell you? He oughta know."

There was a pause on Kunze's end. "I did not discuss the permit with him. In hindsight, that was…" another pause, "regrettable. But his job was to get the lease. We knew that was unlikely to happen in time for the demonstration, but even as what you called a publicity stunt, our exhibit would have established a foothold. Yes, we expected the Fair to close it down until the lease was signed, but we did not expect to be arrested for trespassing!" Although the offense was only a misdemeanor, conviction carried a possible sentence of up to fifteen days in jail, and the District Attorney was sure to push for the maximum.

Fitz was enjoying this. Excluding Schultz had been a major mistake, as Kunze was now realizing. He had wanted to take credit for the scheme, and instead, he was going to take the blame for its failure and the resulting humiliation, not to mention criminal charges. No doubt he'd already had an earful from Kuhn, his overnight cellmate and courtroom companion at their bail hearing.

Kunze composed himself, and delivered the coup de grâce. "In light of your incompetence, you are of no further use to our organization. I am hereby rescinding your Bund membership. Your dues are forfeited. Goodbye, Mr. Fitzgerald."

With a sigh of relief, Fitz hung up the phone.

* * *

Why haven't I heard from Schultz? Fitz wondered. He'd been sure the guy who came up with the idea in the first place was as angry as Kunze that it had all gone wrong. And, like Kunze, wouldn't he want to unload on the trusted fixer?

At the opposite extreme, the entire Fitzgerald family was delighted that the operation had gone off so well. His father was proud, his mother was relieved, his brother was elated, and his sister immodestly took credit for suggesting it. He'd received a congratulatory call from Elaine, who said

Uncle Carl couldn't stop chuckling over the Bund leaders' arrest, though he had to keep quiet about knowing Fitz's role.

But why was Schultz keeping quiet?

It occurred to Fitz that he might be feeling guilty about not getting the lease in time. The outcome would have been very different if the Bund had been the building's legitimate tenant. *Maybe they're blaming him as much as me, if not more,* he reasoned. *If he did call and started taking it out on me, I'd just turn around and lay it on him, and he's probably had enough of that.*

Chapter Thirty-Six

When Fitz reported for duty on Monday morning, there was an eerie atmosphere of anticipation on the fairgrounds. Completed pavilions stood silently as the sunshine highlighted the colorful murals and striking relief sculptures that festooned their exterior walls. But with less than a week to go until opening day, many interiors were still beehives of activity, with swarms of workers putting the finishing touches on the government, private, and Fair-sponsored exhibits designed to enrapture the public.

Notwithstanding the critics who denounced the Fair as an overblown advertising scheme, and the naysayers who scoffed at its concept of future peace and prosperity, no one could deny that it was going to be extraordinary. Even those who weren't buying its optimistic forecast conceded that it had brought much-needed employment to thousands of New Yorkers and promised to give the city an economic boost when the anticipated hordes of tourists descended.

Already, a number of advance parties were attending press previews, receptions for financial backers, and tours for elected officials. Greyhound buses and tractor trains were kept busy ferrying them around. Thankfully, the Fair's own police force was now fully manned and pressed into escort service, freeing the NYPD officers from all but the most high-level occasions, hosted by Grover Whalen himself, who insisted on the presence of New York's Finest.

The sky was cloudless, the temperature was headed into the low seventies, and Fitz was having trouble paying attention on patrol. Apart from a flurry of preparation for the opening ceremony in the Court of Peace, where President Roosevelt's address would be televised, it seemed nothing special was happening that day. No visiting dignitaries, no work stoppages, no last-minute disasters. The artists were gone, their murals finished, so there'd be no more lunch breaks with Stuart or check-ins with the others.

What's it like here after dark, now that there's no night work going on, he wondered. He'd done late shifts a few times, when construction was going full blast and the arc lights made it bright as day. He decided to sign up for night patrol, just to see how it looked. After he finished his rounds, he headed back to the City Building and asked Nancy what was available.

"I only have the one-to-nine slot," she told him, "the graveyard shift. And you'll have to take it for the rest of the week, not just one night. What do you say?"

"Sure, why not? Next week I'll be back at One Ten, pounding the pavement in Elmhurst. After the Fair opens, I won't be here at night unless I'm with a million other visitors, so this is my only chance to have the place pretty much to myself."

"The night-shift guys tell me it's creepy, especially now that the outdoor work is done. You'll only have the street lights and the moon."

"Sounds romantic. Too bad I can't bring my girlfriend." Was he thinking of Mary, or Elaine? He didn't say.

Nancy gave him an indulgent smile and shook her head. "I don't get it, Fitz. What is it about this place that has you so stuck on it? The other cops have rotated on and off, but you've been here steady for months. I'm bored, doing nothing but answering the phone and handling the roster, same routine day in and day out. At least at the station house, I had company, and I could walk to work instead of taking the el."

"I wish I could give you a simple answer," he told her. "At first, it was the idea that such a disgusting dump could be turned into something beautiful. You remember what it was like before, something to be ashamed of. Now look at it! My mother used to tease me when I'd tell her how miraculous it was, and I've never gotten over that feeling."

Nancy chuckled. "I keep forgetting how young you are. Okay, even middle-aged folks like me have never seen anything like it, but it's been going on for so long that it's not amazing anymore. You still have that youthful sense of wonder. Tell the truth, I'm kinda envious."

Fitz was touched, and a bit embarrassed. "C'mon, Nancy, you're not middle-aged, just mature, which I guess I'm not. But I'm glad I'm still thrilled when I look at what's been done here. It makes me believe there's hope for the future, in spite of what's going on in the world outside." He took a moment to let that sink in.

"Then there's all the business with the muralists. You don't know the whole story, but I've gotten friendly with some of them and learned a lot about what goes on in their world. The artists I've been dealing with really want their work to benefit the public, not just decorate rich people's living rooms. The fact that somebody went after good folks like that really gets my goat. I sure hope O'Toole can figure out who's behind it."

"O'Toole, my foot," she scoffed. "You're the one who wants to solve those crimes. You think lurking around at night will help with that?"

"No," he said, "the murals are all done, so there's no one around to sabotage. And the most serious attack, the one on Feininger, was done in broad daylight. We may never know who it was, but I think it had something to do with their style. All the targets were what they call modernists. That's the only link that makes sense."

* * *

When Fitz told his father he had to report for duty at 1:00 o'clock the next morning, Tim assumed it was punishment. "So O'Toole found out you're meddling in his investigation, huh?"

"No, Dad, I asked for the night shift. It's only for a few days, and I want to see the place when it's dark and quiet."

"That's when the rats come out. Don't think just because they put in all that drainage, they solved the rodent problem. Doesn't matter how pretty they make it, a garbage dump's still a garbage dump."

Fitz hit the hay right after dinner and set the alarm for 12:15 a.m. A quick shower and shave, then he grabbed the sandwiches and coffee Bridget had left for him and headed out. In daytime, the Fair was only a fifteen-minute el ride away, but in the wee hours, there were far fewer trains, so he gave himself some leeway. As it happened, he got to the Queensborough Plaza platform just as the Flushing-bound BMT pulled in.

At the el station entrance, he greeted the cop on duty at the gate and walked down the ramp into the darkened fairgrounds. The night was clear and still, with only a crescent moon and street lighting to show him the way to the City Building, where the night clerk admitted him. He clocked in and changed into his uniform. Strapping on his service revolver, he remembered what his father said about the rats and wondered if he'd get a chance to test his marksmanship. He hadn't fired his weapon since his last proficiency training session on the shooting range.

The duty roster had him on grounds patrol for two hours, then two at Corona Gate South, two more on the grounds, and his final two at the Flushing gate. He decided to take a scooter. As he made the rounds, he thought back to what it had been like when construction was in full swing and the place was crawling with workers all night, the same as in the daytime, only with artificial light, like he imagined a movie set would look. There was definitely something theatrical about the whole production, and there'd be plenty of real theater once it opened.

He motored by the Belgium pavilion and saw through its glass façade that the interior was dimly lighted. An NYPD officer, equipped with a shotgun as well as his sidearm, could be seen guarding the gemstone exhibit. Evidently, the dispute with the electrical workers had not yet been settled, and Whalen had fulfilled his pledge to the ambassador.

Fitz allowed himself a smile of satisfaction as he passed the nearby Hall of Nations, where the doors to the abortive German exhibit were firmly locked. He noticed a few vehicles parked near various buildings where installations were ongoing and assumed they had been checked through at the Flushing gate.

Crossing the Empire State Bridge to the dormant Amusement Zone, he passed over a couple of cars driving along Horace Harding Boulevard, now renamed World's Fair Boulevard, but at 2:00 a.m., there was hardly any traffic.

In contrast to the main Fair's formality, this area was eclectic and haphazard. All part of the fun, but without the animated displays and milling crowds, it seemed somehow forlorn, even a bit eerie. And he was sure his headlight picked up more than one scurrying creature, especially near the lakeshore.

He turned right off the plaza to check the gate west of Fountain Lake and found it closed, then circled back to the Boulevard gate, which was equally secure. The IND subway entrance was also shuttered. No night service until the Fair opened, after which the backers were hoping people would be flooding in by public transit to enjoy the after-hours attractions. Then he motored out to the remote South gate and checked that it, too, was closed.

His rounds completed, he drove to the Corona gate and relieved the cop on duty there. A chill was in the air, and he was glad to be in the cozy booth for what was bound to be a dull two-hour stint, only relieved if a late worker checked out or an overnight delivery happened to need admission. He pulled the *Daily News* from inside his tunic and settled in.

* * *

Half an hour into his posting, Fitz heard raised voices piercing the still night air. Then sounds of a scuffle, and a shout, "Hey, you, copper, get out here! I got one for ya!"

Across the courtyard in front of the Marine Transportation Building, a large man was hauling a smaller one toward the guard's booth. He had one of the prisoner's arms twisted behind his back and was gripping his coat collar as he propelled him along under protest.

"Let go of me, you idiot! I have every right to be here. I work for the Fair! Let me loose and I'll show you my I.D. card."

"Show it to the cop with your free hand, asshole. No way I'm letting you loose."

Fitz stepped out of the booth as they approached. Astonished, he recognized the man in custody as Gustav Schultz.

The muscleman pushed his catch forward. "Leary's the name," he growled, "United Scenic Artists Local 829. The boss sent me over to keep an eye on Marine. After one of the brothers bought it, and it wasn't no accident, Browne put us on alert. There's been a night man here ever since." He turned and gave his squirming captive a hard look. "Good thing, too. This worm was fixin' to torch the mural."

Equally startled, Schultz recognized Fitz, whom he considered at least partly to blame for the Bund rally debacle. He had begun to wonder if the new recruit was as useful as he'd led them to believe.

Now, however, Schultz hoped he would prove to be very useful indeed. "Officer Fitzgerald, what a relief to see you," he blurted. "Tell this thug who I am, and order him to release me."

Instead, Fitz turned to Leary, whose grip had not relaxed. "What do you mean, torch the mural?"

"I was sitting in my car over there," said Leary, nodding in the direction of a Ford coupé parked in a shadowed area of the courtyard, "and I seen this guy climbing the ladder with a can in his hand. The painting ain't quite done, so at first I thought it was somebody getting supplies up there, ready for morning.

"But then I realize, hey, that don't look like no paint can, it's got a spout on it. So I get out and go over, and I see a couple more cans on a hand truck by the ladder. They're heavy, so he's gotta take 'em up one at a time. I check the label, and sure enough, it's diesel oil, not paint. Probably got it from the fuel dump for the generators. Then I step back so's I can see him, and he's splashing diesel on the mural. I reckon he was gonna set it on fire. So when he come down for another load, I grabbed him, and his pockets are full of rags and matches."

Schultz had stopped squirming. His face was set in a defiant scowl, which he turned on Fitz. "Surely you don't believe this ridiculous nonsense. You know I'm a Fair employee. I was there on official business."

Fitz scowled back. "You work for Exhibits and Concessions, Mr. Schultz. Why would you have anything to do with a mural on the outside of a building, much less at half past three in the morning?"

Schultz was silent. Fitz turned to Leary. "I'll take it from here, Mr. Leary. Give me your full name and address, and telephone number if you have one. You'll be contacted if we need further information. Mr. Schultz and I will go to the City Building, and I can take his statement there. Please leave the fuel cans where you found them."

"There's two on the ground," said Leary, "and one up on the scaffold. He woulda done a lot of damage." He made a rumbling sound that passed for a chuckle. "Woulda made plenty of overtime for our boys, too, so maybe I shouldn't be sore." He gave his particulars to Fitz, released his grip on Schultz's arm, and let go of his collar. "I'm off, then. Glad to be of help." He turned and walked back to his car.

Looking relieved and rubbing his arm to restore the circulation, Schultz opted to confide in his fellow Bund member, not knowing that Fitz had been kicked out.

"Thank you, Fitzgerald. That gorilla could have broken my arm. Let's wait and see if he leaves, now that he has, as they say in the movies, nabbed his man. Yes, look, he's pulling out. I'm glad you told him to leave the fuel. Now I can get on with the job."

Chapter Thirty-Seven

Fitz couldn't believe his ears. "Are you telling me you really *do* want to set fire to the mural?"

Schultz returned Fitz's stare. "That piece of degenerate filth has no place on a Fair building! I was appalled when I learned they had given such a prominent job—or any job at all, for that matter—to a disgraceful traitor to the Fatherland.

"Don't look so shocked. Feininger may have been a native New Yorker like me, but, just like me, his roots were pure German. He even went back to his roots, but instead of celebrating our glorious culture, he chose to foul it with his distorted, perverted version of so-called art. Hitler knows what to do with people like that. And so do I."

Suddenly, it all fell into place.

Schultz had access to every building on the fairgrounds. His job involved checking on exhibits in areas where muralists were working. He would know who and where the modernists were. He could look them up in the Board of Design files. And he was such a nonentity that no one was likely to notice if he hung around and watched them for a while, silently planning how to sabotage them.

Brimming with indignation, Schultz continued his rant. "His own work was disgusting enough, but he spread his ideas like cancer to students at the Bauhaus, that Communist sinkhole, until the Gestapo closed it. What if he had tried to do it here, like that other traitor, Hofmann, who got kicked out of Munich and transplanted his deviant concepts to New York? Both of them had to be stopped."

So that was Schultz's doing, too, thought Fitz. *He must have been the guy who failed to persuade Hofmann to change his ways. I wonder if Kuhn and company know what he's been up to. Probably not. My guess is he's a lone wolf, on his own private crusade against modern art.*

Realizing he wasn't getting the expected favorable reaction, Schultz paused and took stock. He had misjudged his audience.

"In light of what you've told me, as well as Leary's eye-witness account and the evidence at hand," said Fitz, keeping his voice level, "I'm going to have to charge you with attempted arson." This was going to be his first arrest. He stepped toward Schultz, ready to take him into custody.

Then he made a rookie mistake. As he reached for the handcuffs hanging on his belt, he took his eyes off Schultz, who slammed his knee into Fitz's groin with surprising speed and accuracy. The white-hot shooting pain and nausea doubled him over, and he sank to his knees on the pavement, while Schultz sprinted to the Motor Glide parked beside the guard booth, hit the ignition, and sped down the Avenue of Transportation toward the Bridge of Wheels. From there, it was only a few yards to the Administration Building. Maybe Schultz had a car parked there. Or maybe he was headed to the el station, in the hope that a train would come in before he was caught.

Humiliated and furious with himself, Fitz struggled to his feet and tried to follow on foot, but he wasn't up to running just yet. He watched in frustration as Schultz reached the bridge, where, unfortunately for him, another officer on scooter patrol headed toward him. Fitz saw the headlight shine on the hijacker and shouted, "Stop that man!" but Schultz had already made a U-turn and driven back across the courtyard. Fitz tried to sprint to intercept him, but the best he could manage was a staggering lope.

He flagged down the scooter cop. "Let me borrow your ride. That guy stole mine. He's the one who's been attacking the artists. Call the station for a car to come pick him up."

"Sure thing, buddy," said his fellow patrolman, who turned over his scooter and headed back to the City Building on foot. Trying to ignore the throbbing pain in his crotch, Fitz jumped on the scooter and followed Schultz toward the Bridge of Wings.

The two vehicles were evenly matched, and Schultz had a head start. Fitz struggled to keep him in sight as he rounded the turn onto the bridge. When he reached the crest, he saw that Schultz had swerved to avoid colliding with a couple of parked trucks, loaded with shrubs waiting to be planted around the Hall of Pharmacy, that were blocking access to the Court of Power. He had turned right and raced off toward the Empire State Bridge.

* * *

Plunging into the darkened Amusement Zone, Fitz lost sight of his quarry. He was aware that Schultz would be even more familiar with its ins and outs than he was. Apart from his adventure in Salvador Dalí's Dream of Venus, he had never been inside any of the buildings. Schultz, on the other hand, would have plenty of ideas about good hiding places. No doubt he'd spent many hours checking on the concessionaires and their displays. They might have to play cat and mouse all night, but Fitz assured himself there was no way he could escape. The only way out was where he went in.

There was a bank of phone booths just outside the IND station, so Fitz used one to report to the precinct. The desk sergeant told him reinforcements were on the way.

"Send a man to Corona Gate South," he told the sergeant. "I had to leave my post to pursue the suspect. He's somewhere in the Amusement Zone. Can you get a car to the Empire State Bridge? If he gives me the slip, that's his escape hatch."

Turning back into Times Square plaza, Fitz considered which was Schultz's most likely route. He decided to head along the East Loop.

With all the subtlety of the Coney Island midway, the buildings in this zone dropped any pretense of high-minded social progress and cultural uplift. Entertainment, pure and simple, was their purpose. But, as in all closed amusement parks, there was something desolate, bordering on spooky, about them. It was not an especially cold night, but Fitz shivered a bit as he rode slowly past the shuttered attractions, listening for the scooter's telltale hum.

When he got abreast of the Parachute Jump, he heard it coming toward him from the direction of the South gate. Seems Schultz had tried and failed to get out that way, so he was doubling back. Fitz swung in behind the Crystal Lassies exhibit, turned off his headlight, and idled the motor. Schultz's headlight was also off, but Fitz could see his silhouette against the backdrop of Fountain Lake as he drove past toward the West Loop. Fitz gunned his motor and shot forward to intercept him. Cursing, Schultz tried to evade him, lost his balance, and toppled off as the scooter skidded out from under him. Fitz pulled up and dismounted, but when he reached the fallen Motor Glide, Schultz had disappeared in the dark.

Wishing he had a flashlight, Fitz scanned the deserted area with his headlight for likely hiding places. He turned off the motors of both vehicles and listened for sounds of movement. Nothing. Then his sharp young ears picked up the creak of a door opening on the far side of the Parachute Jump base pavilion that housed the ticket booth and hoisting machinery. He reached the door just as he heard the bolt being thrown on the inside.

Maybe there was another entrance. How about the ticket booth? He ran around to it, smashed the glass with his nightstick, and jumped in. The door at the back was unlocked. He propped it open and turned on the lights in the booth, which revealed Schultz climbing the access ladder to the machinery room above. He was slowed by a knee injury from his tumble off the scooter, so Fitz had no trouble catching up to him before he reached the second floor. Grabbing him by the belt, he dragged him down to ground level, where he landed in a heap.

Fitz rolled him over and cuffed him. "Where the hell were you going, Schultz? Think you were gonna fly away on a parachute? Or maybe hide up there until morning and hope to blend in with the workers? No, buster, you're coming with me. There's a patrol car on the way to take you in for booking." He was looking forward to telling his father he had found a rat, a big one, and caught him.

"You've got nothing on me, you fucking turncoat!" blurted Schultz. "I know my rights. You can't use anything I said. Wait until Kuhn hears about this. He'll have a Bund lawyer spring me in no time. And he'll find a way to make you pay for your disloyalty. Don't think you're safe just because you're a cop." He smirked. "As you know, accidents happen."

"I'm shaking in my shoes," said Fitz as he hauled Schultz out of the Parachute Jump and marched him, limping, toward the Empire State Bridge. "You know all about accidents, and how to stage them, don't you? You're behind what happened to the muralists. But you'll be safely locked up on Rikers, so I won't have anything to fear from you."

"Those Commies got what they deserved. That union of theirs is nothing but a den of Reds, polluting the Fair with their ugly, meaningless abstractions. I know all about them, I've seen the files. A couple of them are actually Russians, and at least one is a rotten kike, calls himself Guston, real name Goldstein."

Without directly incriminating himself, Schultz had convinced Fitz that he was indeed the saboteur, as well as Feininger's killer. Unfortunately, the only evidence against him was the apparent arson attempt on the Marine mural, but even that wasn't conclusive. After all, he hadn't been caught in the act of setting the fire, just seemingly preparing to, which he could deny.

Reluctantly, Fitz admitted to himself that the only hope of establishing Schultz's guilt would be a confession, and that was O'Toole's department. He had no choice but to hand over his prize to the detective for questioning. If anyone could beat him down, it was Hammer. And if he did, how ironic would it be that he'd get the credit for solving a string of assaults, not to mention a homicide, that he believed were nothing but a series of mishaps?

How ironic, too, that Schultz's censorship efforts had failed. Injuring the artists hadn't prevented their murals from being finished, it only punished them personally. In Feininger's case, of course, the hatred had been doubly strong, for his abstract imagery and his perceived betrayal of their common German heritage. The heavy security at Masterpieces of Art probably deterred Schultz from attacking the courtyard murals, which, no doubt, was especially galling, considering the wealth of traditional art on display inside the building—just the sort of stuff Hitler and his cronies prized. And the Marine Transportation mural, exposed and vulnerable on the façade, had been saved thanks to Browne's wise decision to post a guard.

Chapter Thirty-Eight

The monthly United American Artists social, held at Stuart Davis' studio at 43 Seventh Avenue on May 6th, was a bittersweet occasion—both a celebration of the New York World's Fair's opening the previous Saturday, and a wake for the departed mural jobs. The Local 60 members who had worked there were elated by the positive reception the decorative program had received from the public and the press, but they were now unemployed and not guaranteed to be rehired by the WPA. Determined to face an uncertain future the way artists always have, they threw a party.

There would be no dancing for Arshile Gorky, still limping and now sporting a cane, or Ilya Bolotowsky, using a wheelchair during his recovery, but they both relished the opportunity to catch up on developments in the case against Gustav Schultz. Fitz was to be the guest of honor.

Knowing that Elaine would be there with Bill, he took Mary as his date. He had resigned himself to the hopelessness of both relationships, though for very different reasons, and made up his mind to act casual with Elaine, stay close to Mary, and enjoy being the center of attention.

As soon as he arrived, the music stopped, and everyone crowded around him. A drink was pressed into his left hand, and the other one was shaken by numerous admirers, who urged him to tell all.

Honesty compelled him to give credit where it was due. "You really need to thank Detective O'Toole for breaking the case," he said, to which groans, snorts, and cat-calls were the response. "No, really, he's the one who got Schultz to confess. They don't call him Hammer for nothing."

Davis spoke up. "But you're the one who wouldn't let it drop when O'Toole came up empty," he insisted. "You did believe it was sabotage, though you weren't sure I was right about Local 829 being responsible. While I hate to admit it, we also have to thank Browne for taking it seriously. I steered you in the wrong direction by blaming him, and you followed a few other false leads, but in the end, you fingered the guilty party."

"When I heard his fanatical tirade, I knew it was him," Fitz acknowledged, "but I had no real evidence. Luckily, I could charge him with assaulting a police officer and resisting arrest, on top of attempted arson. Once we had him in custody and I reported what he'd told me, O'Toole retraced all his interviews and found people who'd seen him lurking around. No one paid attention to him then, but in hindsight, they realized he'd spent far too much time in those areas just before the so-called accidents occurred. Showing them Schultz's photo helped jog their memories. The night watchman in the Medicine building remembered seeing him in there during the wee hours, but didn't think anything of it at the time.

"He also managed to track down a disaffected Bund member who recalled Schultz sounding off at meetings about degenerate artists and how they were invading the Fair, but no one was all that interested. They had more important fish to fry. So he decided to act on his own. Working for Exhibits and Concessions, he had access to every building. He could also check the Board of Design files to identify offensive artworks."

Fitz turned to Davis. "In your case, Stuart, he simply stayed in the building overnight, waited for a time when the night watchman wasn't around, then gave you the old heave-ho. Damaging the staircase in Aviation, removing the brackets from Ilya's scaffold, and splashing paint on Ref's murals also required him to stay after hours, but lots of people were doing that. He just let himself out after he did the deeds. Untying Philip's ladder rope was simple, he didn't even have to hide. There was so much activity that no one noticed a man on the ladder at night. And it wasn't just vandalism. Any of the mishaps could have killed his target. In Ilya's case," he said, laying a hand gently on Bolotowsky's shoulder, "it nearly did. And it was fatal for Feininger." There were murmurs of sympathy from the crowd.

"He took the biggest risk with him, attacking him face-to-face in broad daylight. According to the foreman, Olsen, he'd been hanging around the building, supposedly checking on the installation of nautical displays, so he knew when the mural crew broke for lunch. He only stood out because he wore a suit. Olsen pegged him right away when O'Toole showed him his picture."

"Isn't all that what they call circumstantial evidence?" asked Krasner. "No one saw him in the act, and from what you told me, there's nothing like fingerprints or something personal he left behind. It just doesn't seem like you had enough on him to make him confess."

"I don't get along with O'Toole," said Fitz, "but he's a brilliant interrogator. He has a way of confronting people that breaks them down. I wasn't in the room, but the cop guarding the door said he made the evidence seem iron-clad. The statement from the Local 829 guard was especially useful, since he caught Schultz with the fuel and the matches. And O'Toole said there were other eyewitnesses who identified him and placed him at the scenes, which is sorta true. But all that was to do with the sabotage cases, not the murder.

"To nail him for that, O'Toole made up a story about finding footprints in the dirt near Feininger's body that he'd be able to match with Schultz's shoes, which isn't true, but how was Schultz to know? O'Toole certainly earned his nickname, hammering away at him until he spilled his guts, raving about morally corrupt Commies, Jews, and atheists foisting their hideous modern art on the public."

Krasner was shocked. "You mean to say he lied to Schultz, tricked him into confessing? That's outrageous. No wonder we don't trust the police."

"Don't be naïve, Lee," said Guston. "The days of the rubber hose may be gone, but planting evidence and falsifying testimony are standard procedure. And Schultz can always claim coercion when he goes to trial. O'Toole's case is pretty flimsy. If some sharp Bund lawyer defends him, he could get him off."

Elaine had a thought about that. "Since the rally was such a disaster, and it was his idea, I bet the Bund cuts him loose. Besides, their lawyers are going to have their hands full defending the top brass. There's more than the trespassing charges. Did you know that the D.A.'s office raided Bund headquarters a few days ago and seized a bunch of financial records? Uncle Carl says rumor has it they're going after them for tax evasion. That's how they got Al Capone," she said with a grin.

* * *

Only a week after the Fair's official opening, cracks were already appearing in its visionary foundation. Attendance was falling far short of expectations, several major pavilions had yet to open, and there were many unfinished attractions in the Amusement Zone. And with a 75-cent general admission price and more costs once inside, visitors complained that the Fair was just too expensive for the average family.

Fortunately, Grover Whalen had come through with complimentary tickets for his boys in blue, so the Fitzgerald family had a free pass. They arrived at the el station entrance at midday on Sunday, well prepared with comfortable walking shoes but unprepared for the unseasonable heat, as the temperature headed toward ninety. With the prospect of a long walk and little shade, they opted to ride the tractor train.

Fitz was in his element, describing how the buildings and exhibits expressed the Fair's futuristic theme and extolling the streamlined architecture. He took them to see the murals that figured in his adventures, and told them that Guston's mural, "Maintaining America's Skills," on the WPA Building façade, had been voted the public's favorite.

When he finished his customized guided tour, he asked the family what else they'd like to see. They admired the Theme Center's grandeur, but didn't especially want to go inside. They did want to take the General Motors Futurama ride, which had been given a big buildup in the press, but the long line was too daunting on such a hot day.

Little brother Andy proposed what everyone else was thinking.

"The Living Liquid Ladies!"

Acknowledgments

My fascination with the 1939 New York World's Fair began in childhood, with family stories, home movies, and a set of souvenir spoons, as well as trips from my home in nearby Richmond Hill to the ice rink in the New York City Building. That building is now the Queens Museum, where I organized "Dawn of a New Day," a major exhibition on the Fair. For my fictional tale set in the World of Tomorrow, I relied heavily on my extensive research files from that show, including publications, photographs, ephemera, and interviews with some of the artists who had worked at the Fair.

As in my previous Art of Murder mysteries, all the artists mentioned are real people. The descriptions of their murals are accurate, but none of them were sabotaged. WPA muralists did receive special permission to work in the WPA and Medicine and Public Health buildings, but the others—including Arshile Gorky, who was not in fact a UAA member—were required to turn over their designs to members of United Scenic Artists of America, Local 829, A. F. of L., so the union rivalry is fictitious.

Nor was Lyonel Feininger murdered at the Fair. He died of natural causes in New York City in 1956, age 84. In 1939 he was living in California; his Masterpieces of Art murals were painted by Rambusch, a noted decorating firm still in business today.

The Fair's voluminous archives, deposited with the New York Public Library and digitized on the library's website, are the primary source for detailed examination of its history. There is also a wealth of Internet resources, including a Wikipedia entry with many reference links, historical photograph collections, and color film by Hildreth Meière, a former National Society of Mural Painters president, documenting many of the Fair's exterior murals and sculptures. Readers of this book will recognize some of them, and by searching online will find images of others I've described, as well as film of a Living Liquid Lady performing her underwater act. Sadly, the fictional Fitzgerald family wouldn't have been able to see her during their May 7th visit, since Dalí's Dream of Venus didn't open until the end of May.

I'm thankful to Nicholas Petraco, Sr., a retired NYPD detective who is currently a forensic art analyst teaching at John Jay College of Criminal Justice, for checking my characterization of the department. Though Nick wasn't around in 1939, he met some of the old-timers from that era who were retiring as he was coming up. His insights are sincerely appreciated, as are those of the composer and artist Edvard Lieber, Elaine de Kooning's personal assistant and the co-executor of her estate, whose forbearance with my casting her as Fitz's lover is gratefully acknowledged. By Elaine's own account, she and de Kooning were a faithful couple until well after their marriage in 1943. Thanks also to Michael C. Smith and Melissa Lawson of United Scenic Artists Local 829, who kindly supplied me with crucial information from the union's archives.

For background on the German-American Bund, of which Gustav Schultz is an invented member, I'm indebted to Arnie Bernstein's remarkable book, *Swastika Nation: Fritz Kuhn and the Rise and Fall of the German-American Bund.* As he reports, the Bund was done in by financial malfeasance; the original tax evasion investigation turned up much more. On May 18, 1939, Kuhn was subpoenaed by a Grand Jury. A week later, he was indicted on charges of grand larceny and forgery for embezzling Bund funds. He was found guilty, sentenced to 2 ½ - 5 years for each count, and sent to Sing-Sing.

James Mauro's engrossing *Twilight at the World of Tomorrow: Genius, Madness, Murder, and the 1939 World's Fair on the Brink of War* tells the story of Joseph Shadgen's role in the Fair's inception and his shabby treatment by the administration. (The titular murder is the killing of two New York City police officers by a bomb planted in the British pavilion, a crime that was never solved.) An NYU doctoral dissertation by Gerald Monroe, *The Artists Union of New York,* is a unique resource for the history of that New Deal-era organization and includes first-person testimony from many former members. Grover Whalen's memoir, *Mr. New York,* is an essential source for his role in bringing the Fair to fruition.

Before the first season ended on October 31, 1939, Europe was at war and the future was looking grim. The Fair reopened on May 11, 1940, with a reduced admission price, fewer exhibitors, and a new theme, "For Peace and Freedom."

Map of the World's Fair major attractions and exhibits reprinted from *The Highway Traveler*, vol. XI, no. 2, April-May 1939.

Map of the Amusement Zone reprinted from the *Official Guide Book 1939,* p. 32.

Photograph of the Theme Center by Underwood & Underwood, courtesy of the New York World's Fair 1939-1940 records, Manuscripts and Archives Division, New York Public Library.

About the Author

During her career as director of the Pollock-Krasner House and Study Center in East Hampton, New York, Helen began writing mystery novels set in the art world. A widely published author of books and articles on art, she enjoys making up stories in which fictional characters interact with real people from her own background and experience as a *New York Times* art critic, NPR arts commentator, museum curator, and practicing artist. Her second novel, *An Accidental Corpse,* won the 2019 Benjamin Franklin Gold Award for Mystery & Suspense. An active member of Mystery Writers of America, she and her husband, the artist Roy Nicholson, live in Sag Harbor, NY, with the ghost of Roy's beloved studio cat, Mittens.

AUTHOR WEBSITE:

https://helenharrison.net/

SOCIAL MEDIA HANDLES:

https://www.facebook.com/artworldmysteries/
https://www.facebook.com/helen.harrison.58152

Also by Helen A. Harrison

Fiction: Art of Murder Mysteries

An Exquisite Corpse, Poisoned Pen Press, 2020

An Accidental Corpse, Dunemere Books, 2018 / Poisoned Pen Press, 2020

An Artful Corpse, Poisoned Pen Press, 2021

An Elegant Corpse, Amazon KDP, 2023

A Willful Corpse, Level Best Books, 2024

Non-fiction:

Where the Bodies Are Buried: An Anecdotal Memoir, GCG Publishing, 2024

Guild Hall for All. Delmonico Books, 2021

Jackson Pollock. Phaidon Press, 2014

Subject Matter of the Artist: Writings by Robert Goodnough, 1950-1965. Soberscove Press, 2013

The Jackson Pollock Box. Cider Mill Press / Simon & Schuster, 2010

Hamptons Bohemia: Two Centuries of Artists and Writers on the Beach (with Constance Ayers Denne). Chronicle Books, 2002

Such Desperate Joy: Imagining Jackson Pollock. Thunder's Mouth Press, 2000

The American Art Book. Phaidon Press, 1999

Larry Rivers. Harper & Row, 1984

Dawn of a New Day: The New York World's Fair, 1939/40. New York University Press/The Queens Museum, 1980